The Dark Glamour

Also by Gabriella Pierce

666 Park Avenue

The Dark Glamour

A 666 Park Avenue Novel

GABRIELLA PIERCE

wm

WILLIAM MORROW
An Imprint of HarperCollinsPublishers

THE DARK GLAMOUR. Copyright © 2011 by Alloy Entertainment. All rights reserved. Printed in the United States of America. No part of this book may be used or reproduced in any manner whatsoever without written permission except in the case of brief quotations embodied in critical articles and reviews. For information address HarperCollins Publishers, 10 East 53rd Street, New York, NY 10022.

HarperCollins books may be purchased for educational, business, or sales promotional use. For information please write: Special Markets Department, HarperCollins Publishers, 10 East 53rd Street, New York, NY 10022.

FIRST EDITION

alloy**entertainment**

Produced by Alloy Entertainment
151 West 26th Street, New York, NY 10001

Library of Congress Cataloging-in-Publication Data has been applied for.

ISBN 978-0-06-143490-7

11 12 13 14 15   OV/RRD   10 9 8 7 6 5 4 3 2 1

The Dark Glamour

Chapter One

"THANKS." JANE BOYLE AIMED A FRIENDLY SMILE AT THE TIRED-looking barista, a sallow-skinned girl with a barbell through her septum. In spite of the fact that the macchiato in Jane's hands was approximately the eight hundredth she'd bought from the girl in the last three weeks, the barista didn't show the faintest glimmer of recognition.

Probably for the best, Jane reminded herself as she settled into the cozy-looking corduroy armchair that had quickly become her favorite. After all, she was in hiding.

Unfortunately, "hiding" was not turning out to be enjoyable or even particularly interesting. Jane could remember vividly the way her heart had pounded as she stood in Grand Central, making the life-or-death choice between leaving New York and staying. Clutching Malcolm's stock of money and fake passports, she had imagined a wild montage of magical discovery with her fierce and loyal band of friends, culminating in a pitched battle with Lynne Doran and her creepy twin cousins that left their massive stone mansion as a heap of ugly rubble beneath Jane's victorious feet.

Must. Stop. Thinking. In. Montages.

Jane hadn't gone more than two blocks when she caught a glimpse of herself on the news. Then the elegant face of her homicidal mother-in-law had filled the screen, and Jane instinctively backed away, afraid that Lynne would somehow see her. *Maybe she can,* Jane had thought wildly; she really couldn't fathom the limits of Lynne's powers. But after a tense few moments of listening to her own shallow breath rasping in the night air, the lure of Lynne's perfectly peach-lipsticked mouth was too much to resist.

The story the garbled closed-captioned ticker spelled out made it clear that Lynne was as much a mistress of PR as she was of black magic . . . and that Jane wasn't going to be able to so much as poke her nose out of hiding for a good long time.

Too afraid to contact her friends and with no idea how long the stockpile of cash would have to last her, Jane had to think quickly. A twenty-four-hour Duane Reade and twenty-seven minutes in the bathrooms of Grand Central had turned her from the blond newlywed Jane Boyle into the Ebony Mocha–tressed Caroline Chase, an anonymous New Yorker with a penchant for heavy eyeliner, whose passport Jane just happened to have. *Good thing I didn't choose Amber Kowalsky,* Jane thought, recalling the heavy Photoshopping of her picture in one of the other pseudonym-ed passports. *All those piercings would have* hurt.

Three weeks later, Caroline Chase was stuck in a depressing single-room-occupancy hotel near Port Authority with a shrinking pile of money and no idea what to do next . . . and Jane Boyle was still above the fold.

"Distraught Mother 'Won't Give Up Hope,'" the latest headline proclaimed. Jane reached for the newspaper.

Although today marks three weeks since the mysterious disappearance of her son and his new bride, sources close to socialite Lynne Doran say she is as determined as ever to find them. The tenacious Mrs. Doran is currently offering just over $3 million for information leading to the safe return of Malcolm and Jane Doran, who were married on March 3 in what many were calling the wedding of the century. Just hours later, however, their automobile was involved in a bizarre multicar accident on Park Avenue. Although most injuries were minor, Yuri Renard, the Dorans' family driver, was pronounced dead at the scene. Malcolm and Jane, however, seem to have simply vanished from the car, and the notorious playboy and his new wife have not been seen or heard from since.

"There is nothing on Earth that would stop my son from letting me know if he were all right," Mrs. Doran insisted on the morning after the accident. Looking more disheveled than we have seen her since the tragic death of her daughter twenty-two years before, the Upper East Side maven went on to speculate that Malcolm and Jane must both be suffering amnesia following the trauma of the crash.

The investigators of the NYPD have been looking into some much more disturbing scenarios, although so far they are reluctant to go on record with them. "Yuri Renard's head wound was weird," a source close to the investigation swore on the condition of anonymity. "And they found the Doran couple's fingerprints in a taxi that was in the accident, too, but no one can find its driver. If Malcolm was high, he could have freaked out and attacked Yuri and then tried to get away—maybe that's what caused the pileup, even."

The NYPD officially denies that this possibility is being pursued, but reiterates that Malcolm and Jane Doran are "persons of interest" in the puzzling crash. Anyone with information is asked to call the tip line at the bottom of the page.

Jane sighed and sipped her coffee. It was hard reading that Malcolm was a drugged-out criminal after everything he had given up to help her. Jane was the one who had killed Yuri, the Dorans' creepy driver and sometime hit man, the day before her wedding, and she had been completely sober when she had done it.

"Not to mention that I never actually changed my last name," she muttered, stabbing at a printed "Jane Doran" with one rather ragged fingernail. The Goa Sand polish from her wedding day was so chipped it looked more like camo.

How did she get Yuri's corpse onto the scene so fast? Jane wondered. *Had they stashed the thing in a closet somewhere, just in case? And what the hell did they do with my tree?* The cause of the pileup wouldn't have been nearly so "mysterious" if the tree that Jane magically uprooted from the median had still been lying across the downtown-bound lanes of Park Avenue when the police had arrived. Lynne must have gone into overdrive to manufacture her cover-up . . . or maybe witches had some way of altering people's memories.

Jane set the newspaper down, unable to read one more sentence about Lynne's "grief." This was, after all, the same woman who had ordered her son to murder Jane's grandmother, seduce Jane, and impregnate her with a witch daughter so that Lynne could kill Jane off and raise the baby as her own. Witches' power could only be passed through the female line, and Lynne's only daughter, Annette, had died tragically when she was just six years old, swept off to sea one day on the beach. Jane, a full-blooded witch who only recently learned of her powers, had become their very sickening plan B. To read about how Lynne "already considered Jane a daughter" and "hoped the girl's dear, departed family members" were watching from above so they could see how hard Lynne was working to bring her back "home" made Jane feel nauseated.

Distant thunder rolled overhead, and Jane wondered if her grandmother really was watching from above. Like Jane and all the women in her bloodline, Celine Boyle had been a witch. Jane's powers disrupted nearby electronics whenever she was upset or emotional; Gran's excess emotions had boiled over as thunderstorms. If she really was still watching in some way, then clearly she saw eye-to-eye with Jane when it came to Lynne's crocodile tears.

Jane picked at the cardboard heat guard on her coffee cup. There was still so much she didn't know about her own power, and it didn't look as though she'd be learning any more at her present rate. *I'm doing this all wrong,* she fretted miserably, *but what choice do I have?* The whole city—the whole country, probably—

was looking for her now, and any tiny mistake could give her away. It felt as though she were suffocating under a giant pillow stuffed with potentially fatal choices. Any movement could mean the end of the line, and so she was stuck sitting still. The fine blond hairs on her arms began to prickle and stand on end.

Jane glanced warily around. The shop's radio played inoffensive Muzak. Three giggling teenage girls on the center couch were watching Katy Perry on YouTube. The regular in a suit, who clearly had not yet told his wife he'd been laid off, was right where he always was, looking typically miserable. And in the far corner, practically tucked under the counter, a woman sat doing nothing at all.

She was perhaps in her late thirties, with close-cropped black hair and a deep, Mediterranean tan. Her skin was stretched tautly over high cheekbones and a chin like the point of a dagger. And, like Jane's, her eyes were hidden from view behind a stylish pair of completely unnecessary sunglasses. The hairs on the back of Jane's neck began to join the ones on her arms. The woman wasn't looking at Jane, but just moments earlier she had been. Jane was absolutely certain of it.

Anyone in the city, of course, might look at Caroline Chase. And if they had been primed by the media coverage and looked hard enough, they might even eventually recognize Jane Boyle in her features. But the people who might think they had found the desperately searched-for Jane and not approached her—who would hide the fact they'd been looking, even . . . those were the most dangerous of the people on her trail by far.

Jane froze in a painful moment of indecision. Should she try to read the woman's mind? Maybe the mystery woman really was just there for coffee. Or maybe she was some spy of Lynne's, and Jane could find out how close behind her mother-in-law really was.

Or, worse still, Jane's mind would run up against the blank wall that signaled the mind of a fellow witch.

But what if using her magic gave her away somehow? Of all the things she didn't know about her new powers, that one was by far the most frustrating. If magic left behind some kind of detectable trace, then Jane couldn't afford to use any at all.

The two possibilities fought in Jane's mind for seconds that felt like days. The pressure built in her head and she closed her eyes, trying to fight down her panic and think. The gleaming bulk of the espresso machine behind the counter let out an ominous "pop," and every pair of eyes in the shop turned toward it. The machine spurted scalding jets of espresso in one direction and steam in another. Jane had just enough time to see Mystery Woman ducking beneath the counter for shelter before her body caught up with her brain.

She hurled herself through the door and out into the rainy evening as fast as her feet could carry her.

Jane arrived at the Rivington Hotel sweating and out of breath.

"Mizz Chase," the red-faced, permanently greasy day-manager drawled sarcastically as she ran by, but her skin didn't even have time to crawl as she bounded up the stairs. She took them three at a time, careful to breathe exclusively through her mouth, and didn't stop until she'd slammed the flimsy door of her room behind her. She flipped the lock, but the temperamental latch refused to slide into place.

"Oh my God," Jane whispered, feeling the hysteria close around her throat like a hand. The familiar thrum of the magic in her veins could have been a lullaby or a battle cry, and she was sick of fighting it. She pushed away from the door with her fingertips, which left ten faint marks that looked suspiciously like blistered paint. She pushed her magic out like a third, invisible hand until it reached the unfinished chest of drawers in the corner. The dresser shivered, strained against the rusted bolts that tried to hold it to the floor, and then obediently slammed itself against the door. It was quickly followed by a moth-eaten armchair, an end table covered in the etched graffiti of previous residents, and finally by the squeaky twin bed, which tipped up against the rest of the pile with a dusty sigh.

When the entire contents of the tiny room were on her make-shift barricade, Jane's magic was spent. Her anger, fear, and frustration, on the other hand, didn't even feel as though they had quite peaked yet. *Enough is enough.*

"Who the hell do the Dorans think they are, anyway?" she demanded of the empty room, her voice echoing unfamiliarly off the newly bare floorboards. The new furniture arrangement allowed room to pace, and Jane took advantage of it. Sahara, the emaciated woman downstairs, protested the groaning floorboards by banging on her ceiling. "Seriously?" Jane yelled, prompting another emphatic thud.

Well, if she comes here to tell me off again, it's not like she could even get in, Jane realized with somewhat manic glee. But Sahara could decide to get the manager, and then Jane would have to explain her impulsive redecorating spree. *Well, it all started at an antiquities auction in Paris, with this too-perfect-to-be-true guy.*

As if by instinct, Jane's fingers rustled through the cheap straw carryall she had picked up at H&M a day after checking into the Rivington: her red alligator flight bag was a little too conspicuous for her new surroundings. She found the waxy edge of her passport and pulled it out, tracing the gold stamped letters briefly. She separated the thick pages with one fingernail and unfolded the scrap of paper that was taped to the inside cover, deftly catching the tiny plain key that fell out. FIRST TRUST NY, REC. & TRIN., 41811 was written carefully on the paper in Malcolm's blocky print.

Similar notes—and similar keys—had been attached to the other three passports as well, and Jane had quickly caught on that these were instructions to access four safety-deposit boxes around the world. She would have done so immediately, except that she was in New York, and Malcolm hadn't been in New York for more than a few hours between the night they had planned their escape and the day it had all gone to hell. In other words, First Trust Bank of New York, on the corner of Rector and Trinity, almost had to be a bank where Malcolm was known, where he had a reputation from even before it came time to plan his and Jane's escape. And that made it too risky for Jane to walk into.

Or it had, before the incident in the coffee shop.

The air went out of Jane's lungs in a rush, and she sat heavily on the floor. Malcolm's arrival had turned her life upside down and inside out and into some sort of diagonal twisting direction that didn't even have a name. "Too perfect to be true" had been a major understatement: in the space of a few short months, her Prince Charming had turned out to be a murderous mama's-boy who had been willing to ruin and then, eventually, end Jane's life to make up for his little sister's accidental drowning decades before. He had changed sides over time and tried to protect Jane, but in spite of his good intentions, she had had to rescue him from his vindictive mother in the end, which cost her valuable escape time and led to the now-infamous car crash on Park Avenue.

Nonetheless, he had ultimately tried his best to keep her safe, and whatever the little key was guarding was probably something she could use now. She knew that Malcolm had spent the month before their wedding setting up safe houses around the world for the two of them—in fact, he was probably in one of them at that very moment. She allowed her mind to wander longingly for a minute or two, wondering what kind of life he had imagined the two of them sharing. *Something beachy,* she guessed idly, *or maybe the desert.* After her eighteen years in bleak Alsace, six in rainy, dreary Paris, and a New York winter that involved multiple near-death experiences, Jane hoped that Malcolm would have thought "sunny."

She took a long moment to picture him in an unbuttoned white linen shirt, his tan glowing and his golden waves of hair throwing off light like a second sun. In spite of her better instincts, she felt an almost physical ache to be with him, wherever he was. She would never be the naïve girl who had fallen head-over-heels for him again, but it was impossible to completely forget their powerful chemistry . . . and the amazing curl of his smile.

He wanted to take care of me, she reminded herself, running her fingers along the edges of the key. *Even if he's not here to know about it, I should let him try.*

"First thing tomorrow," she declared out loud, and the words sounded good in her ears. A restless sort of shifting noise filtered up from the room below hers, but apparently her voice wasn't loud enough to warrant more banging.

Just wait until I put the furniture back, Jane thought ruefully, eyeing the jumbled mass against the door. Sahara would thump and shout herself into a premature stroke. *It'll keep,* Jane decided. The bed wasn't especially comfortable anyway, and although it felt good to have a plan, it felt even better to have a plan *and* a barricaded door.

She replaced the key in her passport, slid the passport back into her bag, and then propped the bag under her head like a pillow and stretched out on the floor. She didn't really expect to sleep, but as soon as her eyes closed, she lost consciousness. For the first night since her escape from 665 Park Avenue, Jane didn't even dream.

Chapter Two

THE BANK FELT MORE LIKE THE LOBBY OF A POSH HOTEL THAN anything. The glass doors vaulted into high glass ceilings, and the teller lines wound discreetly among exotic trees in pots and tinkling fountains. It was actually rather intimidating, Jane admitted to herself, but she drew her spine perfectly straight when it was her turn at the window. She set the key on the gray marble counter that separated her from the teller, a woman with a slick black bun and aggressively rouged cheeks. Jane opened her mouth, but suddenly realized that she didn't remember how her hastily rehearsed cover story was supposed to begin. "H-hi," she stammered, and then stopped.

Fortunately, the teller took just one quick look at the key and seemed to know exactly what to do. "I'll call the manager, miss," she announced in a clipped tone, and pressed a button on the console in front of her.

Calling the manager, or hitting the panic button? Jane wondered wildly, but the man who popped out of a side door in response definitely looked more "manager" than "security." He was a sturdy but somehow fragile-looking man with a delicate nose and tiny wire-framed glasses, who seemed almost painfully delighted to meet Jane. She hesitated for a moment after he introduced himself as James McDeary, but his hazel eyes darted first to the little key, and then to the passport she held loosely open in one hand.

"Miss Chase, I presume," he announced, wringing his hands in a thoroughly depressing mixture of anxiety and delight. "This way, please." McDeary whisked her along a dizzying series of glass-and-marble hallways, his voice pattering nearly as quickly as his footsteps. He had been happy, he told her—terribly happy, in fact—to see Malcolm Chase again last month. Of course, he had been handling Mr. Chase's account personally for quite some time, but, to his sincere regret, hadn't seen him in years.

At that last bit of news, Jane had to fight her impulse to turn and run straight back out of the bank. *He's known this "Malcolm Chase" for years?* Jane had only known Malcolm for a few months. What had he been up to that he had needed an alias, apparently, before even meeting her? It couldn't have had anything to do with their escape plan, and she wondered if she had even been supposed to come here at all. But she held her ground and kept her face composed as they turned into the silent, airless-feeling safe room.

"It's this one in the corner," McDeary told her, pointing with a finger that trembled faintly with his obvious joy. Jane took in row upon row of stainless-steel doors lining every wall. A simple table made of matching metal stood in the center of the room; other than that, it was as bare as the surface of a star. "Box 41811. I was concerned that it might be too small when your . . . your . . ."

Jane squeezed the fingers of her left hand together surreptitiously: Gran's silver ring never left her second finger, but she had removed her incredibly conspicuous engagement ring weeks ago. Luckily, she had also left off her plainer wedding band. "My brother," she told the manager firmly.

"Brother, of course! I see the resemblance, naturally. Anyway, I thought you might need a larger safe when he came in with the new item, but luckily it all fit. Many customers are, you know, very particular about keeping the same box, especially when it's one they've had for a long time. And Mr. Chase is one of our very valued, long-term customers, of course, so I was pleased to be able to keep his location consistent, as I'm sure that he hopefully was as well . . ."

Jane's head was swimming, and she could barely read the tiny numbers on the stacked rows of boxes. She held up the key Malcolm had left inside her passport in one faintly trembling hand. He removed a matching one from his pocket, inserted it into one lock on box 41811, and nodded meaningfully toward the other one. They turned their keys in near-unison, and the box slid smoothly free of the wall. Jane carried it to a stainless-steel table in the middle of the room, while McDeary lowered his eyes discreetly to the floor.

The box was almost completely filled by a black leather case, and Jane could feel her heart pounding in her ears as she reached for it. She fumbled with the latches, snaps, and ties—*just how many ways do you need to keep a lid on*—until finally, unexpectedly, the case opened.

Money, she told herself. *Of course it's just money.* There was a lot of it, in fact: certainly more than she had left in her Grand Central stash. But she couldn't deny the shiver of excitement that ran down her spine when, looking past the neat green-and-gray stacks, she saw the corner of something . . . else. She dug eagerly through the pile of cash, carelessly moving more hundreds than she could count out of the way like empty candy wrappers. Money was welcome, but the real proof that Malcolm had been thinking of her was finally in her hands.

"It's a . . . checkbook," she said out loud, flipping the faux-crocodile cover open. The checks were drawn on an account at the First Trust Bank of New York, in the name of Caroline Chase. After a quick search, Jane found a second book, with a different account number, for Malcolm Chase. *He was careful,* she thought sadly. *He knew one of us might be caught, and kept our names separate even when we were supposed to be together.*

McDeary cleared his throat, and Jane jumped. "Sorry," he mumbled, offering what looked an awful lot like a bow of apology. He pushed his glasses higher on his nose. "Your brother had some instructions about that."

My who? Jane almost asked, but bit the question back. *Right. My name is Caroline. Malcolm's name is Malcolm. My husband is my brother, because he killed my grandmother and now his mother wants to steal my as-yet-unconceived baby. It's simple, Jane; keep up!*

McDeary was eagerly explaining a complicated-sounding system of linked accounts and automatic transfers from somewhere offshore, triggered by withdrawals from her checking account. The gist, Jane eventually understood, was that she had as much money as she wanted, replaced into her account as fast as she could spend it. *No more Rivington,* she thought gleefully. After a quick mental catalog, she decided that she wouldn't have to go back even once. Everything that mattered was in her purse; everything else could be left behind. She was rich again, and money equaled freedom.

"Thank you," she said randomly, hoping it had come out during an appropriate pause in McDeary's lengthy elaboration on the finer points of international banking treaties.

"My pleasure, certainly," he chirped, looking as though he was seriously considering another bow.

Jane ran her hands over the leather of the case, looking futilely for a handle. She finally settled for folding it awkwardly in her arms. It was an inconvenient way to walk, but it was only temporary, she reminded herself: everything was about to get a whole lot easier.

"But, Miss Chase!" McDeary nearly whimpered in sudden concern.

Busted! her brain shouted, and Jane stopped breathing. But McDeary wasn't chasing her, setting off the bank's alarm system, or even looking at her at all: his entire focus was on the dark interior of box 41811. *Not busted. Yet.*

"Did you not want the personal item?" McDeary frowned uncertainly, straightening back up and turning a small blue box between his smooth palms. He hesitated and then cleared his throat, his Adam's apple bobbing vulnerably. "Mr. Chase didn't leave instructions about this, specifically, but he clearly assigned you full ownership of the safe . . ."

Jane turned, softening. Knowing that Malcolm had left her something personal, meaningful, suddenly meant much more to her than all of the stacks of cash she could carry. She fought the urge to rip the box out of his hands, and instead reached for it as politely as she could bear. "Yes," she answered firmly. "I'll be taking that as well."

The manager's hazel eyes, made small and watery-looking by the lenses in front of them, followed the box as Jane took it. "That was the item that brought Mr. Chase to us to begin with. He said we had excellent references among his friends, and I do hope he has been happy with our services." His thin chest puffed out with pride. "He *has* been a client for nearly fifteen years, of course, so I like to think that we have met his needs."

"Of course," Jane assured him automatically. "He told me so." McDeary smiled deferentially, but Jane's mind was racing. *Nearly fifteen years, and it started with this.* She lifted the box's catch with numb fingers. This box wasn't for her. Whatever it was, it had predated her in Malcolm's life by more than a decade. She felt a blush mounting on her cheeks and wondered if there was a graceful way to back out of taking it now.

Just then the catch released, and the lid fell open so easily that Jane, startled, nearly dropped the whole thing. The inside of the box was lined with soft blue velvet, and tucked securely inside was a glass unicorn. It was pretty, with finely pulled legs and an elegantly arched neck, and little touches of gold on the hooves and horn. But "pretty" was the only word to describe the unicorn: there was nothing about it that gave any impression whatsoever of magic, or even of substantial monetary value. It looked, Jane decided, like the sort of thing you could buy in any mall in America. *Why this?* she wondered, touching a tiny hoof experimentally with one chipped fingernail. She half-expected a magical frisson but got nothing. As far as she could tell, the "personal item" Malcolm had been storing all this time was nothing more than a piece of glass.

It's not for me. It's none of my business what it is, she reproached herself sternly. She closed the box with a snap. "Thank you," she began, unsure what to say next. *"I had no idea what was in here, and now I don't think I should be taking it"* doesn't really have a great ring to it.

"Of course; I'm thrilled to be able to help Mr. Chase and his family. And I'm sure that item is sentimental for you as well, since he told me it belonged to—" McDeary stopped midsentence, his small eyes narrowing to slits. "Excuse me. You *did* say that you are Mr. Chase's younger sister, yes?"

I didn't say younger, Jane's mind hissed. Not that it was a huge leap: Malcolm was eight years older than her, and anyone as ingratiating as McDeary had to know that it was always good policy to assume women were young. But his eyes were riveted on her in a new and unpleasant way, and Jane's skin crawled a little. The still, dead air of the safe room prickled at her skin with a new sort of static charge.

Jane fought her panic: the secure room of a secure building was a terrible place to freak out and blow her cover for good. She bit the inside of her lip so hard that she tasted salt, forcing herself to meet McDeary's eyes and smile at him. It was the very same smile she had turned toward Lynne countless times during the horrible, dangerous month after she'd learned that Lynne was a totally evil witch; it fit like her favorite pair of jeans. "Yes. And I'll be sure to tell him how *thorough* you've been in explaining all of this to me."

She saw doubt flicker over McDeary's face, and knew he was wondering if he might have somehow been indiscreet. She felt bad for making him worry, but she had no choice but to press her advantage. She shoved the little blue box into her straw purse, bundled the larger black case back into her arms, and turned resolutely for the door. "It's to the left and then the third door, yes?"

"I'd be happy to escort you, of course," McDeary offered politely.

"That won't be necessary," she told him frostily, doing her very best impression of Lynne Doran's effortlessly commanding voice. McDeary snapped to attention, his right arm twitching in an almost-salute.

Thank God he's used to being bossed around, she sighed as her kitten-heeled feet clicked out of the safe room. *And that I've learned how to do it.* As she strode purposefully out of the building, not even the two armed guards hulked at either side of the front door could stop her from smiling at the irony of Lynne having taught her such a useful skill.

Chapter Three

"Now it's a *LITTLE* bigger than we'd discussed, but I simply can't not show it to you." Jane's new real-estate agent giggled, shoving her ample hip against the apartment door.

"Ooh." Jane breathed, taking in the wall of windows that made the living room glow like a piece of amber. The floor was lined with close-fitting hardwood planks, which had been polished to a uniformly pale-gold glow, and the room was pleasantly asymmetrical. The walls were a creamy white that made the high ceilings look even higher, and the scattering of furniture was made exclusively of glass, nubby white fabric, and pale, bonelike sticks of driftwood. Spare, minimalistic prints on the walls added unexpected touches of vivid purple ink to the room's palette, echoed by a cozy-looking blanket folded neatly on the couch.

Jane spied a kitchen, off to her left, full of gleaming appliances. It was a bit narrow to her eye, especially after the Dorans' huge green-marbled one, but there was room for a thin-legged table and more than enough room for a person to cook—especially one who cooked as infrequently as she did. A long, narrow hallway ran out from the angled right-hand wall, which, she assumed, led to the bedroom. Although she was sure that she should probably play it cool, she couldn't help returning the agent's broad, eager smile.

The perfectly frosted-and-set woman had been openly skeptical when Jane had arrived in her office in her thrift store–heavy ensemble asking about Manhattan properties. But when Jane, who had come straight from the bank with her helpful case of money, named what she felt would be a reasonable monthly sum for a living space that would drive every last vestige of the Rivington from her mind, the agent had gotten a *lot* friendlier. Apparently concluding that Jane was a trust-fund baby in the midst of a totally fake "rebellion," or possibly a minor celebrity who was committed to seeming "quirky," she had immediately come up with a long list of apartments that were "just a little" pricier than Jane's budget.

Jane, who loved open, airy spaces and whose budget had been well below her new, nearly unlimited, means, didn't mind a bit.

"Now, I know it looks like a lot of glass," the agent warned, "but the bedrooms have more privacy, of course. And you're on the top floor, so do come and see the view."

"Bedrooms," plural? Jane wondered wryly; she had definitely inquired about one-bedroom apartments only. But then she saw the view, and she stopped caring. The wide wall of windows looked out over block upon block of quaint brick and low roofs, eventually ending in a strange glimmer that Jane was pretty sure was the Hudson River. It looked almost European; nothing at all like the brittle, vertical city that had already cost her so much.

"And this room would be perfect for an office," the realtor prattled on, waving her arm into the second bedroom while Jane peered into the first. *Walk-in closet, skylight, king-size bed, en suite bathroom. Check, check, check . . .* "Or for guests—everyone I know with an extra room has guests nearly year-round if they want them! Or sometimes young women prefer to live with a friend, which, if the rent is more than you had planned on, could be a lovely alternative." She nodded sagely, curls bobbing in steely unison, and then vanished back down the hall, presumably to show Jane the "incredibly efficiently conceived kitchen."

Jane, whose main requirements for a kitchen were a phone and a place to stack takeout menus, didn't follow her. Instead she kicked off her scuffed kitten-heeled slides and sat gingerly on the nubby white couch. It was comfortable, and she curled her feet up underneath her, watching the roofs glow suddenly and sporadically in the rays of light that peeked tentatively out from the low-hanging clouds.

The agent clicked back into the living room, an alert and searching look on her face. She was clearly nonplussed by the sight of Jane barefoot on the couch, and hesitated long enough for Jane to speak first.

"I need to make a call," Jane told her calmly, relishing the way the careful angles of the room swallowed her voice. She had always intended to build spaces just like this, before she'd gone and let "true love" completely derail her budding architecture career. Just being inside of it made her feel more grounded, more like herself again. She remembered the version of herself that had made an Eiffel Tower out of matches; the bright-eyed student who had walked into her internship at Atelier Antoine for the first time. She felt as though it could actually be possible to get her world back, and after her three hopeless weeks of trying to disappear, she didn't intend to lose sight of the real goal ever again. *It's not just about safety. It's about freedom.* She turned her body toward the realtor, who stiffened slightly. "I've forgotten my phone."

"Please, use mine," the realtor murmured, pulling a sleek Prada phone out of her quilted-leather purse—Chanel, Jane noticed clinically. She was feeling stronger by the second. The other woman had clearly noticed the change as she backed hurriedly out of the room, never taking her eyes off Jane.

Jane slid the keyboard out from behind the screen. She hadn't "forgotten" her phone, exactly, but she had put it in "airplane mode" the night of the accident for fear that the Dorans could use its signal to find her somehow. She fished it out of her straw tote and scrolled through the contacts to the Ds, where she found the number she was looking for. She entered it into the agent's phone, and waited with mounting anxiety through the strange, fluttery American ringing noises.

"Diana Rivera," a familiar, throaty voice answered, and Jane's throat closed briefly with joy.

"Dee," she sighed, "you're safe." After Dee had helped Jane to kill the Dorans' driver, Yuri (in an alley in Brooklyn, *not* on Park Avenue the way Lynne had apparently made it look), the Wiccan with a gift for pastry had had to leave her job and her apartment. They had considered it too risky that the police might link Yuri's corpse to the address of one of the women who had made Jane's wedding cake, and much too risky that Lynne might do so. And although the magically transported body had probably removed any threat of legal suspicion, it did nothing to make Dee any safer from the witches' retaliation.

"Ja— Are you kidding me? Is that you?" There was a scuffling noise, and Jane guessed that Dee might be taking her phone to a more private place. *She's probably at that Misty woman's bookstore,* Jane reminded herself. *There might be customers.* Dee's oldest friend in New York owned an occult bookstore, and Jane had been fairly sure that Dee would go there to lie low. "Wait." Dee's voice came a little more clearly through the speaker now. "Actually, I think I need you to prove that it is you. I don't really know what's possible for . . . you know . . . people like you."

Jane felt a grin tug at the corners of her mouth. "'People like me'? Seriously? Fine: ask me something only I would know. Ask me about how I nearly set your living room on fire during that Wicca meeting, or about the cookies you gave to Mal—um, my husband—to give to me on my wedding day, like a total reckless idiot. Which were delicious, by the way."

"Damn right they were." Dee chuckled, and Jane could hear that she was smiling, too. "I'm at Book and Bell," she went on. "Misty's been putting me up on her couch, but I'm hoping I can sublet from one of the girls who was at that Wicca meeting when she goes to Peru next month. Everything's fine over here, but Jane, I've been reading the tabloids. Are *you* okay? The phone number you're calling from is . . ."

. . . *a 917 number,* Jane realized. *A Manhattan cell code.*

"Jane," Dee whispered, and Jane heard real fear in her voice. "You're still here. But they're looking for you, which means that they haven't found you, so . . . Jane, I don't get it. What the hell are you doing?"

"Renting an apartment," Jane quipped brightly. "Wanna be roommates?"

There was a long pause, during which she wasn't even sure that she could hear Dee breathing. "Yes," Dee answered finally, although Jane could hear a "but" coming, which she hurried to cut off.

"Cool. I don't remember the exact address, actually, but I'm about three blocks west of Washington Square Park. Meet you under the arch at six? I'll need a little time to get the paperwork taken care of, and you'll probably need to pack everything up from your . . . couch."

"Washington Square at six," Dee repeated dutifully, and then lowered her voice to a husky whisper. "Jane, are you sure this is safe for you?"

"I'm done with the cringing-in-a-dark-corner thing," Jane announced firmly. "I've got some unexpected resources—courtesy of the people who cost us our old jobs and apartments, in an indirect sort of way—and I'm ready to get back into the game here. Oh! And before I forget: my name is Caroline Chase now."

Dee giggled throatily. "Do I get a code name, too? Can I be Anna Chapman? I think I have time to pick up a red wig."

Jane rolled her eyes at the phone. "Absolutely not. Although, now that you mention it, I'm a brunette these days, too."

A heavy sigh came from the receiver. "You couldn't have picked a disguise that flattered your complexion?"

"You sound like my mother-in-law," Jane growled playfully, and Dee laughed.

Jane ended the call and looked around. She was pretty sure that she hadn't said anything that would tie her to her old life or the tabloid stories about her, but the real-estate agent might understandably be a little curious about why her newest renter had recently changed her name and appearance. *Must find out if there's a way to erase memories,* Jane noted to herself. It wouldn't be the nicest, most ethical use of her magic, but it would certainly

come in handy now and then. *And now.* She had had some suc-
cess in tampering with someone's mind, she realized: just before
her escape from the Dorans' mansion, she had been locked in the
attic with Malcolm's crazy brother, Charles, whom their mother
had hidden from the world due to the severe damage her magic
had done to him during her last dangerous pregnancy. It had been
a desperate attempt to have a daughter who could inherit Lynne's
power, but poor Charles had turned out less than satisfactory in
absolutely every regard. When she had been imprisoned in the
attic, Jane had persuaded him to help her by reorganizing the
thoughts in his head, moving them around like squares on a Ru-
bik's Cube to convince him that they were friends. But she hadn't
tried to change anything in his memory; she had just used what
was already there. *Could I make things up? Take things out? Can Lynne?
Shit.*

Fortunately, the question was moot for the moment: a few
seconds of searching turned up the realtor on the bedroom's bal-
cony, puffing away at a Virginia Slim as though her life depended
on it. Jane slid the door open, causing the woman to jump a little.

"I'll take it," Jane announced firmly, and the realtor beamed
so broadly that even her hair looked as though it got a shade
brighter. "I'll want to move in today," Jane went on, tipping the
black leather case from the bank open to show the stacks of cash
inside. "I've already got the security deposit and your commission, so let's get right to signing the lease."

The agent blinked twice rapidly, and then crushed her cigarette
out under the heel of her fringed white boot. "I'll just get my brief-
case from the kitchen," she agreed levelly, and followed Jane back
into her new apartment.

Chapter Four

"HAVE YOU SEEN THIS OVEN?" DEE CHEERED FROM THE KITCHEN. Her voice sounded strangely muffled, and Jane wondered idly whether her new roommate had, in fact, stuck her head all the way into that appliance, too, as she already had done with the refrigerator.

"I heard there was one," she called back. "But this is like me asking you if you've seen the closet space."

"Gotcha," Dee acknowledged, wandering back into the living room. Her long black hair was tied up in a messy knot, and she had taken advantage of her new bedroom by changing into fuzzy purple pajamas within moments of crossing the threshold. "And I didn't have time to pick up groceries, anyway, but this is the last night I'm going to let you get away with ordering takeout." The takeout in question (spinach pie, tabouleh, lamb gyros, stuffed grape leaves, cucumber yogurt, and four kinds of rice) was spread over the polished-driftwood coffee table, and Dee waved a pair of forks in the air triumphantly. "The equipment in that kitchen is better than Hattie's."

Jane froze with a forkful of spinach and feta halfway to her lips. Because of all of the Doran drama, Dee had been forced to quit her job at Hattie's SoHo bakery with no notice. She had also had to leave her cozy little apartment in Brooklyn, and had wound up living on a couch for three weeks. Jane felt a twist of guilt: she had been so busy feeling sorry for herself that she hadn't even thought about how Dee had been coping in the meantime. *I had a plan,* she reminded herself. *I was going to send her money and a new ID once Malcolm and I were away.* But she hadn't gone with Malcolm, and Dee had been left to fend for herself. It almost made it worse that Dee acted fine with the wreckage of Jane's plan: a few professional-quality pots and pans and she seemed to be completely back on her feet.

"I'm so sorry about that," Jane told her honestly. "You helped me so much, and I thought that me and Malcolm getting out of town would be the best thing for everyone. And then everything went to hell, and now . . ." She waved her fork, too upset to go on.

"Oh, eat your damned pie," Dee snapped, wrinkling her nose comically. "You can't make speeches flinging feta all over the room. But what did go wrong at the wedding, anyway? I certainly didn't get the real story from Page Six."

Jane swallowed thickly. "We got through the ceremony, and then I read Malcolm's mind."

It hadn't been easy, since he had so much magical blood in his veins, but she had been so worried about Lynne retaliating against Jane's friends after they fled the city that she had forced her way through the magic's natural barrier anyway . . . and had seen Malcolm's memory of killing Gran. In her shock and revulsion at this incredible betrayal, she had tried to run away from him, but that had tipped off Lynne and her creepy twin cousins that something was wrong. They had used their combined magic to knock Jane unconscious and then, she had eventually guessed, read Malcolm's mind themselves. He had learned over the years to keep some secrets from his mother, but three powerful witches who knew what they were looking for were far too strong for his defenses. So Malcolm had been locked in the basement, and Jane had been taken to the attic to be impregnated by Charles.

"Ew!" Dee squealed. "And here I thought Lynne's fondant doves were the height of her creepiness."

Jane took a hearty swig of the champagne the realtor had messengered over. "The doves were just a warm-up. But I got out, of course, before . . . My magic came back in time, and I knocked him out and got away." Although she knew that Dee was a trustworthy friend who was deeply interested in all things magical, Jane found herself reluctant to talk about the thought-moving power she had discovered during her desperate minutes of captivity in the attic. Even more than her ability to read thoughts, the ability to shift them around in someone else's head made Jane feel freakish, and she didn't think she could deal with Dee getting nervous around her. *I'll tell her, of course*, Jane promised herself. *Just not tonight.*

She told Dee the real story of the "accident" on Park Avenue: how Lynne had held their taxi in place while stalking down the middle of the street in a protective bubble of her own magic, and how Jane had pulled a tree out of the median to cause a five-car pileup so that Lynne would have to focus more on her shield and less on the taxi. She glossed over the sad scene in Grand Central

Station, where Malcolm had tried to convince her to go with him, obviously hoping they could somehow carry on with their relationship even after everything Jane had learned. But no matter how frightened she was or how dangerous her enemies were, Jane had no intention of hiding behind anyone . . . and especially not anyone who had already betrayed her so completely.

When she got to the part about Mystery Woman in the coffee shop, Dee sat straighter on the couch, her amber eyes fixed intently on Jane's. Jane understood her worry, but the contrast between her sudden vigilance and cozy flannel made it hard not to laugh. "I totally freaked out," Jane admitted, "and I was too scared to even read her mind in case she could tell somehow, which pretty much sums up how depressingly pathetic I've been these last few weeks."

"So you don't even know for sure if she was really there for you?" Dee gasped.

Jane refilled her glass, hoping the action would hide her sudden blush. "No. I just . . . um . . . blew up the espresso machine and left."

Dee choked on a piece of lettuce. "Subtle," she declared when she was able to talk again. "This life of stealth is clearly for you."

Jane stuck her tongue out, then popped a cucumber slice onto it for good measure. It was certainly true that she wasn't shaping up to be spy material: after three weeks of zero progress on her mission, it had taken a never-ending bank account to pull her out of a total nervous breakdown. *But I happen to have a never-ending bank account, so there's no use beating myself up about that.* "You're one to talk," she retorted. "I knew exactly where to call to find you."

Dee sighed and slumped cozily against the back of the couch. "Book and Bell seemed like the thing to do at the time, but then

Misty was so nice I was ready to sink into the ground. She had me working shifts when the store wasn't even supposed to be open. No one would come in for six hours, and she'd swear I was earning room and board. It was really sweet, but there came a point where I was, like, desperate for a fairy godmother. Speaking of which . . ." She glanced around the apartment curiously before fixing her questioning amber stare on Jane.

"Malcolm hid money for me," Jane explained succinctly, and then remembered the mystery that he had hidden along with it. "And this," she added, hopping off of the couch and padding over to the closet that contained her purse.

She fished out the little blue box and tossed it to Dee, who opened it curiously. After a long moment, she tapped at it with a cautious fingernail, then shrugged at Jane. "I've honestly got nothing."

"Malcolm never struck me as the collector type," Jane mused, "and even if he were, I don't think glass figurines would be his thing. Or unicorns."

"Plus, he'd probably have more than one," Dee pointed out, and Jane nodded seriously.

"One of anything is a pretty crappy collection. But it obviously was important to him, so now I have it and I have no idea what to do with it. I don't even know when I'll see him again." Jane frowned and twisted a paper napkin around her fingers. "I couldn't even worry about him, really, when I was so worried about everyone here. At least I know you're okay, but I'm still worried about Harris, and especially Maeve." Jane had last seen Maeve Montague, her first friend in New York, looking bruised and broken in a hospital bed. Maeve, who came from a family of witches herself (although the magic was on her father's side, so she hadn't inherited any), had been just about to tell Jane the truth about the family she was marrying into when Lynne had magically steered the tiny redhead out in front of a hurtling taxicab. Later that night, Malcolm, suffering from a crisis of conscience, had leveled with Jane about his mother's power . . . but the near-fatal crash had already made things pretty clear.

"Mae's doing really well," Dee told her comfortingly, setting the open blue box carefully on the coffee table. "She had some trouble walking at first, but they got her a physical therapist. And, go figure, he's this hunky twenty-six-year-old guy with a degree in music composition, or something, who also cooks. He got her 'walking' in no time." Dee winked saucily, and Jane wrinkled her nose. "No, they're really cute!" Dee insisted. "Harris even likes him, and you know how protective he is."

Dee rolled her eyes conspiratorially, and Jane forced hers to follow the same track. *Harris.* His dancing green eyes, his long, lean body, the touch of his hand on her shoulder, her arm, the small of her back . . . She and Maeve's older brother had never crossed any kind of line together, but her body could still remember every place that his skin had touched hers. *It's just the magic,* Jane reminded herself: magical blood sparked and enhanced attraction. It had made her an easy target for Malcolm, and then had sent her into a near-swoon every time Harris brushed past her. *Plus I was lonely and scared,* Jane reminded herself, *and he's handsome and flirtatious.* It had been a volatile situation to begin with, and Jane had done her best to keep her head, eventually even pushing Harris and Dee together. They would make a much more appropriate couple, not to mention a safer one, but Jane found that there was a sour taste in her mouth at the thought that Dee seemed to know so much about what was going on with the Montagues.

"So you've been in touch with Harris?" she asked awkwardly, the fork handle digging into her thigh.

Dee, busy chewing a chunk of eggplant the size of a golf ball, didn't seem to notice any strain in Jane's voice. "Well, he was convinced that the tabloid stuff was complete fiction," she confirmed breezily. "He kept trying to tell me that you were off with Malcolm in Thailand or whatever, and that Lynne was just trying to smoke you out. He'll be glad you're safe, but pissed that I was right," she concluded with a smirk.

"Don't tell him," Jane blurted out, surprising them both. Her brain tried to catch up with her mouth, but there were just too many pieces of the puzzle to see the whole picture. "He thinks I'm safe," she finally said, and it rang true in her ears. "He'd just worry, and I *am* safe, so there's no point in that. Plus, now that I know they're both okay, I can stop worrying, and that's all I really need. I mean, Maeve almost died." Jane's eyes felt hot, and she realized that she was near tears. She flipped her fork over and stabbed it into a slice of lamb. "I'm sorry I ever involved them in my drama, and I'm sorry to you, too, and I probably shouldn't have even called you today, but the least I can do to make up for that is not drag them back into this craziness."

She sighed, feeling almost cleansed, and waited for Dee's inevitable sensible argument. It didn't come, though; instead, Dee bit her lower lip and looked thoughtful. Finally she spoke, her voice even throatier than usual. "I won't tell him for now. The thing with Mae was so hard on him . . . I know he would want to help you, Jane, but I think I have to agree that your way is best. For now," she repeated, her black eyebrows arching meaningfully. "If you plan to get into trouble again, I don't make any promises."

Jane smiled weakly. She knew she was doing the right thing,

but she had half-hoped to be talked out of it. "It's okay," she declared, to both Dee and herself. "I don't have a plan yet, but I'm set up to wait it out here until I come up with a really good one. No crises, no panics. Thanks to Malcolm, I've got as long as I need to figure out my next step." A stab of jealousy twisted in her abdomen, and she deliberately misinterpreted it as concern. "I just wish I knew where *he* was," she added pointedly. She did wish that, even if it wasn't the main thing on her mind.

"He didn't leave you any clues?" Dee asked sympathetically.

"Not one." Jane shook her head. "I told him to set up an e-mail address to get in touch, but if he ever did, it was too realistically junk mail–like for me to even notice." She certainly had been getting plenty of junk mail since she'd become associated with the Dorans. Vendors were still fighting to work on her wedding, which had gone off in such spectacular fashion three weeks before. She twisted her lips wryly. "I think I got caught up in the *Mr. and Mrs. Smith*–ness of the situation, but I really probably should have been a little more specific. I really wish that I at least knew . . ." Jane waved her hands vaguely; there was so much she didn't know about Malcolm's current situation that pretty much any information would be an improvement.

A beach somewhere. Maybe some palm trees, she reminded herself firmly, returning to the vision of Malcolm she had imagined earlier that day in the bank. His full lips curled up in the warm, tropical sunlight. Jane felt some of the tension in her body relax.

Dee frowned, turning her champagne glass so the glow of the street twelve floors below them made gentle gold sparks in the liquid. "You read minds, though," she pointed out, although it sounded as though her mind was on something else.

"I do," Jane admitted, "but I think I need to see the person.

Or . . . not, because I did hear Malcolm's mind when he was locked in the basement. So maybe I need to be nearby, or be able to see them, and I get a little more distance if I know the person . . ." She trailed off and spread her hands helplessly. "I have no idea how this stuff works."

"I do," Dee said, still thoughtfully. "I've been putting all of those pity shifts at Book and Bell to good use, research-wise. I just have to sift out the nonsense from the rumors from the true stuff, which is much harder to do without a real, live witch to experiment with." She grinned, and Jane smiled back, but the amber eyes were still somewhere far away. "I think it's time for bed," Dee announced, standing and stretching to her full, purple-pajama'ed height. "I've got a little reading to do, now that . . ." she waved her long-fingered hands to encompass Jane, the apartment, and possibly the leftover pitas.

"Sure," Jane agreed uncertainly. "I'm sleepy myself. Big day." But Dee was already vanishing down the high-ceilinged hallway that led to her room, and Jane sighed. No matter how dire things had been lately, she had a wonderful new roof over her head and a good friend underneath it with her. She felt a silly smile creeping back onto her face at the thought of the progress she had made toward fixing her life in just one day.

Chapter Five

"WAKE UP!" DEE'S MUFFLED VOICE CAME FROM THE OTHER SIDE of the door. "Jane, it's, like, nine."

"G'way," Jane called back before burying her face in her squishy white pillow. The bars of sunlight creeping closer to the white rug under her bed made it clear that Dee was right about the hour, but Jane didn't intend to care until the sun was directly in her eyes. *Which could take hours, with any luck.* Between strange nocturnal noises and her own nightmares, Jane hadn't gotten a single full night of sleep in three weeks at the Rivington.

Dee went quiet for a moment, and Jane could hear her shifting awkwardly behind the door. "Um . . . Misty's kind of on her way, and mostly to see you. I hope that's okay. She was all worked up, and I didn't know you were this anti-morning."

Jane threw her pillow at the door. It hit the wood with a completely unsatisfying lack of thud. Then there was really nothing to do but swing her legs out from under the cream-on-white quilt and shuffle off to her en suite bathroom. It was tiny, but closing her eyes and standing under the waterfall showerhead, she could almost convince herself that the last month had just been a bad dream, and she was really on her honeymoon in Belize. *With Malcolm.* She sighed and groped blindly for a towel. The romantic part of their relationship was done; she was sure about that. Too many secrets; too many belated confessions. There was no amount of charisma, attentiveness, money, good looks, or even phenomenal sex that could make up for what had already passed between them. Still, she could imagine worse company to be stuck in a jungle paradise with . . . and after seeing how thoughtfully he had prepared for their post-Lynne life, she was more concerned than ever about his well-being. *He should have someone looking out for him as well as he's looked out for me,* she thought sadly, shrugging into a terrycloth robe the apartment's owner had clearly stolen from a very nice hotel at some point. *Which reminds me: once I find out what Misty wants, the rest of the day will just have to be a shop-a-thon.*

She followed the scent of coffee and something richer into the kitchen, and pulled a chair up to the small, spindly table. The ivory granite counters were covered in reusable shopping bags with food practically exploding over their tops. Dee, looking annoyingly efficient and wide awake, plunked down a smooth white espresso cup and a matching porcelain ramekin in front of Jane.

"I was going to just do scrambled eggs," Dee explained, ignoring Jane's death glare, "but I don't know if French people even eat them that way, or if scrambling them is all vulgar and American. So I did them *en cocotte*"—Jane winced at her friend's appalling version of a French accent—"and there'll be toast." Something popped in a corner behind Jane, and she jumped awkwardly in her chair. "Toast!" Dee cheered, leaning across the table to flip a couple of perfectly browned slices onto Jane's plate.

Jane carved a creamy wedge of egg out of her ramekin, dropped it on a corner of toast, and bit. The crispy, creamy, salty, and rich combined into a perfectly extraordinary bite, and Jane sat up a little straighter in her chair. "Okay. So Misty's coming?"

"Um." Dee plunked down in the other chair, then reached out automatically to stir something on the stove. Steam rose from the pot, and Jane's stomach growled. She stuffed some more egg into her mouth to keep it calm, and waited. "Remember how, last night, you said you were worried about Malcolm and wanted to know if he was okay?"

Jane tried to wash her bite of egg down with some espresso, but the combination was even tastier than its individual parts, and she decided to savor the food and nod instead of speaking.

"Well, I kind of remembered this thing in Browning's—like a spell—except I couldn't find the exact one I wanted. But then there was something similar in this manuscript from—oh, well I don't have the manuscript, anyway, but they refer to it in *The History of Ritual*, which refers *back* to Browning's, which makes no sense. So I called Misty, and she actually has the manuscript, or at least a copy in some *other* book, which Rosalie Goddard—you remember her?—referred to as source material for—"

Jane waved her toast in an impatient "get on with it" motion before taking another chunk out of it with her teeth.

"We think you can find Malcolm. Or see him, or see *with* him, or something we don't really get, but it should put your mind at ease either way, don't you think?"

Jane considered rushing to swallow again, but couldn't quite bring herself to do it. Instead, she leaned across the table, holding her toast safely out to one side, and hugged Dee loosely around the shoulders. She sat back and decided to give her resourceful friend a thumbs-up for good measure.

"Cool. All you need is something of Malcolm's, to focus the magic on, and Misty's bringing the rest."

Jane wiggled her left hand pointedly. She still hadn't put her wedding ring back on, but in the safety of the apartment, she had given in to the temptation to put the five-carat, emerald-cut diamond back on her ring finger. It was a lot of ring, after all, and she had had a relatively short amount of time to enjoy it during her whirlwind engagement.

But Dee shook her head. "That's not Malcolm's; it's yours. This is the tricky part: it has to be something that really belongs to the person you're looking for, present tense. Something meaningful to them, that they would consider their property." Jane's face fell, but Dee waved her concern away. "I know it's a pain, but it's a good thing if you think about it. Otherwise witches would be able to find you from, like, a napkin you used and left on the table. Or a closetful of designer clothes that you abandoned in someone else's Park Avenue townhouse in a bit of a hurry," she reminded Jane, and Jane had to admit that she made a good point. She wanted to find Malcolm, but she'd rather stay in the dark about his whereabouts than know that Lynne had a whole suite's-worth of ways to find her.

Jane swiveled in her chair and gazed doubtfully toward the hallway that led to her bedroom. She had brought so little with her from the mansion, and then even less from the Rivington. As she turned back to point that out to Dee, a flash of blue on the driftwood coffee table in the living room caught her eye. She swallowed her last bite hurriedly, hoping that at least one of the two extra ramekins on the edge of the sink might contain more of the heavenly eggs, but so excited that she was willing to wait another minute or two to find out. "Unicorn," she blurted out as soon as her mouth was mostly empty. "The glass unicorn thingy I showed you last night. The 'personal item'! It obviously wasn't for me, which means Malcolm never gave it away, and he hid it in the safe, so it must be personal and meaningful, right?"

Dee quirked her mouth sideways thoughtfully. "That should do it," she announced after a moment. "It's actually way better than the possibilities I was going to suggest. This is good!" Her eyes flickered briefly toward the oven's digital clock. "Misty should get here anytime now, but it'll take us a while to set up. You've got time to get a little meditation in, and I think you should. The more power you have ready, the more you can see. Raid my closet for something you haven't been wearing for days, and then meet us in the living room in about half an hour, okay?"

Jane nodded and rose obediently. From her standing position, she could see over the lip of the ramekins. A perfectly smooth yolk glistened invitingly in the center of the smooth custard inside each one, with a delicate dusting of cracked black pepper providing inviting contrast. Jane stretched out her fingers, snagged the lip of one of them, and then shrugged at Dee. "Magic is hard," she explained innocently. "I need the calories." She tucked her spoon between her palm and the ramekin, hesitated, and then picked up the second porcelain container in her other hand. "And lots of protein," she added over her shoulder, retreating hastily toward the bedrooms.

The first egg was gone by the time she reached Dee's closet. In the careless jumble of mostly black clothes, Jane found a dark green knit dress that looked like it would do for the day. The skirt would be pretty mini on Dee's tall body, but on Jane it fell just a couple of inches above the knee. Smiling and slurping at her other egg, Jane wandered back to her room, sprawled on her back on the bed, and tried to locate the diffuse tingling that would begin the process of calling her magic together.

It was a struggle to keep her mind from wandering after the events of the last two days, but she concentrated on her breathing the way Dee had taught her, and eventually was able to calm her swirling thoughts. Underneath the new stillness it was easy to pick out the peculiar, electric rush of magic humming along in her blood. It was peaceful and gentle now, nothing like the raging lightning it became when she was emotional. This kind of power could be harnessed and controlled, applied to whatever task she needed it to perform, instead of just lashing out wildly. She drew in three deep breaths, exhaling until her lungs burned, and began to collect her magic in her fingertips, coaxing it, pushing at it, and corralling stray currents that tried to escape.

By the time thirty minutes had passed, Jane had a respectable bundle of power resting invisibly inside each hand. She wasn't sure if it would be enough, and considered trying to make herself angry or something to add to it, but in her calm, clear-headed state she understood that this would be a silly risk. She might not be the most powerful witch in the world—she might not even be at *her* most powerful right then—but she was ready to get to work on the spell, and that mattered more. She swung her legs off the bed, enjoying first the velvety shag beneath her feet, and then the waxy hardwood beyond it. Her senses felt heightened; every touch was meaningful, every surface complex and compelling.

She found Dee in the living room with Misty, a thirtysomething woman whose super-processed blond waves and just-a-little-too-tanned skin made her look as though she'd spent her life on some windswept beach. In reality, Dee had told Jane, Misty Travers (née Lois Trapinski) had been born on the Lower East Side, just blocks from where her occult bookstore now stood. She had apparently brought about half of the shop's more private stock with her: crystals of all sizes and colors formed a large circle around the two women, a bundle of sage smoldered acrid smoke in a copper bowl off to one side, and Misty was carefully measuring out tiny vials of something clear and viscous.

The two of them looked up at Jane simultaneously, and she could see their mouths moving, but the gentle buzz of the magic in her ears muffled their voices. Jane waved as a response, and they seemed to understand, so she joined them inside the crystals and set the glass unicorn in the middle before tucking the dress around her thighs. Misty handed her and Dee a full vial of the clear goo, keeping one for herself. She mimed drinking it, arching a brown eyebrow at the other two to make sure that they understood.

When Misty and Dee tipped their vials into their mouths, she did the same. It tasted like nothing at all, but as it spread down her throat, she felt her mind detaching even further from her seated body. It felt like she might float away entirely, and she reached blindly for the hands of the women beside her. She found them so easily that they must have been doing the same, and she felt Dee's warm, calloused hand and Misty's thin, soft one in hers. She could see, out of the corner of her eye, Misty chanting fervently, and sent the magic she had been holding in her hands flowing through the other two, starting circles in both directions, which began and ended in her heart.

The crystals around them started to glow, and the buzzing in Jane's ears grew so loud she almost moved her hands to cover them. But the unicorn was starting to glow, too, and she held on. She kept sending the magic around their Circle until, with a tearing pain, everything around her was gone. She couldn't see or hear; she couldn't feel her own body anymore. All that she could feel was a nauseating burning in every inch of her, and although she tried to struggle, without her physical form there was nothing for her to move. When the pain finally, mercifully stopped, it was a long moment before she was able to ask herself why. But her vision slowly refocused itself, and she guessed that she must have arrived at her destination.

Instead of her airy, soothing new apartment, Jane was in a room with one grimy window. She tried to look around, but it was as if her head were stuck in one position, her eyes fixed on a sitcom on a small television with an old-fashioned curved screen. She tried to reach out magically to find Malcolm's mind, but her magic was as immobile as the rest of her. *Because I'm not really here,* she reminded herself. *I'm just seeing Malcolm—except I'm not. Where is he in this pit?*

Her view lurched and changed, and she was moving through the tiny room at an alarming rate. *I'm seeing* with *Malcolm,* she realized, remembering Dee's attempt to explain the spell. *I'm seeing what he sees.*

She scanned the room, searching her peripheral vision for any clue to where he might be. The apartment was shabby, with bare walls and an unappealing hodgepodge of furniture. Jane saw a twin bed in one corner and guessed that Malcolm's place was a studio, and a rather small one at that. Clothes were scattered around carelessly: a puddle of geometric black and white lay half-on, half-off the bed, a pair of slim loafers by the coffee table, something red and shiny draped on the back of a wooden chair.

I'm missing things, her brain complained, but it was impossible to really take anything in while Malcolm's body was sweeping her along. Just before she was certain that she would crash into a dingy, off-white wall, she turned sharply toward an opening that she hadn't even seen.

Malcolm was in a tiny bathroom now, pooling slightly reddish water in his hands before splashing it onto his face. His hands looked like she remembered, with the same golden tone under their skin, but they were slimmer and smoother. Jane felt a knot forming in her disembodied stomach. Something about this vision was wrong.

Jane felt her head being raised, and she found herself looking in a water-spotted mirror. She saw Malcolm's dark, liquid eyes first, then his square jaw and dark-gold waves of hair. But the similarities ended there, because the face in the mirror was, unmistakably, a woman's.

Jane shoved herself backward out of the mind she was in, scrambling on her absent knees and hands for her own body. Her hands came back first, nearly glowing with the spell's unspent magic. She wrenched them free of her two friends' startled grips and reached violently for the unicorn. At first, she wasn't even sure why she was holding it, and then she had no idea what to do next, but the magic in her veins was feeding on her fear and whispering secrets to her. She closed her eyes and opened her mind, forcing it into the curves and twists of the glass in her hands.

She saw things then: little fingers tearing at wrapping paper to reveal a blue box, a little girl with dark-gold hair dancing around a lavish parlor with the unicorn held up to her eyes, a chestnut-haired mother almost vanished down the hall while a nanny held the girl's hand, a sun-swept bedroom with a view of the ocean, and Malcolm, barely twelve but already growing tall, watching older boys playing soccer on the beach. *He tried to get her to stay and watch, but Annette wanted to play in the sand.*

The images swirled sickeningly and resolved, reordered themselves. There was a distant explosion, and someone must have screamed; it might have been her. Jane saw the face in the mirror again, and then she was completely back in her living room with Dee and Misty. They had backed outside of the crystal circle, and were brushing shards of glass from their clothes. Jane felt a stinging on her face and her now-empty hands, and realized slowly that the energy she had poured into the little unicorn must have shattered it.

"Annette," she whispered hoarsely, and Dee's head snapped toward her. She stepped closer, trying to help Jane wipe off the glass and blood. Jane held up her hands to ward her off. "Malcolm's little sister. I saw her. Annette Doran is alive."

Chapter Six

JANE SIPPED A BANANA-GUAVA SMOOTHIE AND WATCHED A PAIR of Taylor Momsen–wannabes struggle through Washington Square Park on perilously high, studded stilettos. *"Healthy" my ass*, she thought cheerfully as she swallowed the sugary drink. *Just crushing up a vitamin in it doesn't change the fact that it has as many calories as a three-course meal.* Dee had gone out to lunch, and Jane had burned farfalle in a halfhearted attempt to prove that she still kind of remembered how to cook. She didn't intend to try again. Dee was just too good at it for Jane to struggle through measuring and chopping and washing and all that just to be left with a weird, blackened mess in a dirty kitchen.

Besides, it was nice enough weather for sitting outside, and Jane had been driving herself almost stir-crazy since her misfired spell the morning before. She had paced and muttered and tried to put her thoughts down on paper, but instead had wound up drawing scrolls and vines and theatrical masks that had eventually spilled out of the margins and covered the entire page. Finally, Dee had snapped. "I'm going out," she'd announced, "with or without you."

Probably with *Harris, from the way she was checking her phone every two minutes,* Jane had realized after the fact, but she reminded herself that that was even more reason for her to stay away. Dee had promised to keep Jane's real situation to herself unless she decided to do something reckless, and Jane had been far too shell-shocked by the results of their spell to plan anything. But some dedicated shopping, a tuna sandwich, and now an intense session of people-watching felt like exactly what she needed to get to the bottom of what she had seen.

How is Annette Doran alive? To the best of Jane's knowledge, Annette had drowned at the age of six while her family was vacationing in the Hamptons. While Lynne and the other grown-ups had gotten an early cocktail hour under way on the veranda, Malcolm had been left in charge of his little sister. But preteen Malcolm's attention had wandered, and then Annette was just . . . gone. *I never asked if they found her body,* Jane realized. It would have seemed insensitive. Malcolm had said his sister had been swept away by the waves, but never mentioned a word about what had become of her then.

Jane shivered a little, although the spring day was mild. The sky was mostly blue, pregnant-looking clouds drifting slowly across it. Even in full sunlight, her mind kept returning to the dark coldness of being sucked underwater. Jane herself had nearly drowned once, although that had been in a murky pond rather than in a chaotic green ocean. Gran had saved her then, although it was only recently that Jane had realized that magic had probably played a part in her rescue. Having a witch for a guardian had been the difference between life and death . . . for her, at least. Might it not have been for Annette?

If she had survived, how could Lynne not know it? Could Annette's fake death have been some elaborate plot of Lynne's? But there was no way. Malcolm's entire life from the age of twelve on had been overshadowed by the loss of his sister, and it was Lynne who had made sure that that shadow stayed firmly in place. When he had balked at her nastier demands and more vicious plots, she had reminded him of how he owed her; how he must do whatever it took to make up for letting her precious little girl die.

And the girl *was* precious: since men could only carry magic passively in their genes, losing her only daughter had meant the end of Lynne Doran's remarkable family legacy. That legacy stretched back in an unbroken line to Ambika, the very first witch, who had bequeathed her magic on her deathbed to be shared among her seven daughters. Hasina, one of the seven, had gone on to begin a centuries'-long chain of mothers passing their magic to daughters, sisters concentrating their power under the same roof, working together to create one of the most notoriously powerful families—magically or otherwise—in the world. And now it would all end with Lynne, who was so fiercely proud of her position and name; Lynne, who had to face the family tree carved on the marble wall of her parlor every day.

Jane spun the straw in her smoothie, wondering whether her name had been added to that tree yet. She had, after all, married Malcolm. And Lynne had intended to make sure that everything about their union was legal and binding, because it was their eventual daughter who would infuse Malcolm's bloodline with Jane's magic, revitalizing the House of Hasina all over again. It was a desperate plan, and Jane knew Lynne never would have resorted to something so complicated and Gothic if she had thought there was any chance that her own daughter might be alive and well somewhere.

A super-thin woman in the fluid, knee-length pants that Jane identified as "over two years ago" surreptitiously tossed about half a pretzel to a pigeon before striding away out of the park. Within moments, the pigeon had been joined by about a hundred of its friends, flapping and jostling their fat gray bodies against one another for the best shot at food.

How could Lynne not *know?* Jane had found Annette by accident, after all. But the glass unicorn that Malcolm had saved as a memento couldn't be the only sentimental object of Annette's that had been lying around after her "death." In the absence of a body, surely Lynne would have exhausted every option, both mundane and magical, to find out for sure what had happened to her daughter. Even if she didn't know Dee's exact spell—which seemed unlikely, given how long Lynne had been practicing magic and how many generations of witches she had learned her craft from—she must have had ways of verifying that Annette was really gone before giving up on her.

Jane slurped at the remains of her drink, thinking hard. Whatever Lynne had done to find Annette obviously hadn't worked, because Annette was still alive and Lynne still didn't know it. Whatever had stopped Lynne from finding her daughter had *not* stopped Jane. *I could actually* find *her,* Jane realized in a flash.

She didn't know where the depressing little studio apartment had been, which was a problem. But she was pretty sure that the sitcom she had seen secondhand was on the BBC. That didn't narrow down Annette's location much, it was true, but still: if

Jane could redo the spell, she might see something that *did* lead her more specifically to the location of the flesh-and-blood heiress to the Doran magic. *And if I found her, Lynne would give me anything. She would give me more than anything: she would lose any reason for chasing me and Malcolm in the first place.* It was perfect: Lynne would be willing to let Jane go about her life, and she would be grateful enough to want to.

But the unicorn shattered, Jane remembered sadly. She was completely out of Doran-owned objects, and so had nothing to use to find Annette *or* Malcolm. Still, though, the mere fact of Annette's existence meant that there was hope. If Jane could find her *somehow*—maybe Dee could dig up another spell, or maybe Jane could somehow get another item of Annette's—then Jane would never even need to fight Lynne. She could just give Lynne her daughter and go on her merry way. The thought alone was intoxicating.

Two pudgy little boys ran full-tilt toward the pigeons, who flocked into the air in a heavy, thrashing mass. Jane watched them carefully, trying to decide if she should abandon her bench and move farther away from the central fountain. The outer branches of the park's paths were a little more peaceful, but still good for people-watching, and pigeons or no, she didn't feel ready to leave the park entirely. In the meantime, she settled for glaring at the giggling boys, only realizing after the fact that her habitual sunglasses made that compromise basically invisible. The boys took off, careening around the lip of the fountain pool toward the wide white arch that reminded Jane so achingly of home. The pigeons, emboldened by the remnants of the pretzel and their natural New Yorker cockiness, were already settling back down.

Jane watched them idly, waiting for the disparate threads of thought to come together in her head. *Just like the pigeons,* she re-

flected smilingly: they seemed chaotic but could resolve into a coherent pattern at any time.

One pigeon broke away from the flock, hopping and pecking
until it was completely clear of its cohorts. *Vulnerable,* Jane's brain
supplied automatically, and she realized that she was probably
reading a little too much into the birds. *It's just me,* she told herself
sadly. *I'm vulnerable and cut off from the people who love me—most of the
ones who are still alive, anyway. But how can I put them in danger just to
make myself feel safer?*

A red leather boot kicked at the lone pigeon, scaring it back to
the safety of its flock. Jane's gaze followed the boot up a camel-
hair-sheathed leg, the riding pants clinging so obediently that
Jane could see every contour of the kicker's lean calf and thigh.
Her eyes traveled onward, over a red leather jacket that matched
the boots, and then on to the sharp point of a chin and violently
high cheekbones with tanned skin stretched over them like Saran
Wrap.

I know that skin, Jane's mind shouted at her as her gaze reached
the woman's oversize sunglasses. She didn't even have to register the short black hair to realize that she was looking right at
the mystery woman who had frightened her out of her old coffee
shop.

It was true that the two places in which she had spotted Mystery Woman were connected by the A, C, and E trains. It wasn't
exactly impossible that the same person might be in both. But she
could feel in her bones that this was no coincidence: this woman
had been in the coffee shop to watch Jane, and she was watching
Jane from behind those huge reflective lenses right now.

"I want to know who you are," she whispered, her lips barely
moving, as she focused on the mystery woman a few benches

away. She pushed the sensitive tendrils of her magic toward the woman's mind. "A fan? A reporter? A henchwoman? What do you know about me?" But her magic ran up against a smooth, blank wall, and Jane grimaced. She searched for a few more seconds, looking for any kind of opening, but she knew that it would be futile. Mystery Woman was a witch.

Jane slid off her bench and headed for one of the paths out of the park. She could feel Mystery Woman's eyes following her, and in a burst of inspiration, Jane turned back and tossed her empty smoothie cup toward the trash can behind the swarm of pigeons. The cup missed, falling instead into the middle of the flock and sending it wildly skyward again. A shower of feathers littered the ground, and the air around the flock grew thick with dust.

Jane hurried away down a paved path, trusting the beating gray wings and angry shoving of beaks to hide her from view. She didn't turn around again, even once she had reached Washington Square West safely and alone.

Chapter Seven

"It's sort of greenish," Jane observed doubtfully, poking at the inside of her falafel with a fork.

"That means it's fresh," Dee explained, rolling her eyes. "Try it with the tomato and some of that sauce—not that much, it's spicy. You're going to learn about food that isn't French if it kills me, Jane."

Jane stuck her tongue out and then pushed it back in with a bite of falafel. Just as advertised, it tasted fresh, spicy, and good with the tomato. She liked to grumble at Dee, but considering that most "foreign" foods readily available in Paris were tone-deaf, preservative-laden shells of the real thing, Jane was more than happy to branch out. And although she had been skeptical of this place—brightly lit and a little grimy with a long, fast-moving line of takeout customers filing by their cramped little wooden table—it had turned out to be just as good as Dee had promised.

Jane couldn't help but compare it to some of the stuffy, elegant Doran family dinners she had endured during her time on Park Avenue. The food had been good, certainly, in a refined sort of way, but this cheap-eats hole in the wall had a pulse and character that felt much more honest and appealing to Jane than the Dorans' celebrity-filled haunts ever had. It reminded her of her student days, and then the low-key places she and her BFF (Best French Friend) Elodie had frequented. Although she had believed that Malcolm Doran was the love of her life, in a way she felt lighter, safer, and more at ease than she had since meeting him.

But I'm not quite out of that relationship yet, she reminded herself conscientiously, and mentally settled in to get down to business. She had already told Dee about Mystery Witch in the park that afternoon, but so far she had avoided bringing up her plan to find Annette. She knew that Dee would worry and would probably be right to: it was dangerous. But she also knew that Dee might be able to help, and if the last three weeks proved anything it was that Jane couldn't afford to cut herself off from help.

"So," she announced as casually as possible around a mouthful of lentils, "I want to do that . . . thing again." She avoided saying "spell" at the last possible second with a pointed glance at the customers currently filing by them: a skinny, impossibly pretty boy in eyeliner and two women in short, floaty dresses. "From yesterday," she clarified when Dee didn't immediately react. "I still want to find *him*, of course, but what I want to focus on first is finding *her* again. The sister."

Dee started to shake her head, but Jane waved her protest away and leaned closer across the wooden table.

"She's my way out of this," she explained in a hiss. "My *mother-in-law* wouldn't need me anymore if she was back. Hell, she'd probably throw me a parade. All I have to do is find the sister, and I'm safe. *We're* safe; all of us."

"I know," Dee whispered, "but there are some pretty major obstacles." Her throaty voice rose a little as she got more strident. "For one thing, the unicorn is gone. There's not a single piece big enough to pick up without tweezers, and you don't have anything else to use in its place. For another, even if you found An— the sister, how do you think the negotiation would go? Your psycho mother-in-law would attack on sight."

" . . . *Bullshit like that is why I'm glad I'm not married, seriously, no matter what my mother says* . . ." The stray thought drifted over to their table from a faux-redhead in black patent ankle boots. Jane suppressed a smile, but pressed her index finger over her lips anyway to remind Dee to keep her voice down.

"I know there are problems," Jane whispered, and Dee snorted a laugh. "Okay, there are some huge, apparently insurmountable problems. But that doesn't mean we should just totally ignore this massive opportunity that just landed in our laps, either. Obviously there's no easy way to bring about this little family reunion, but if there's any way at all I think we need to try."

Dee ran long fingers through her tangle of black hair, looking pensive. "That makes sense," she agreed finally. "So I guess we just have to start at the beginning and worry about the next problem when it comes up. Which means, first things first, we have to replace the unicorn."

"I was thinking about that," Jane admitted excitedly, feeling a bit of a flush rise on her cheeks. She had barely been able to think about anything else all afternoon. "Look, losing a child is a big deal for anyone, even if they're pretty thoroughly evil, right? I mean . . . my mother-in-law is soulless, but I bet she's still a little sentimental, too. She still lives in the same house as when An—I mean, her daughter, died. Her daughter had her own room there, and all of her clothes and toys and things. And it's not like they would have ever needed the space for anything else in a mansion that size, so maybe her room is still her room."

Dee chewed slowly, her amber eyes far away. "It's possible," she said carefully. "I still have my access code for the staff entrance from when I was working on your wedding, and I bet they haven't bothered to change it. No one ever thinks about the help." She winked saucily, but Jane could see strain in her jaw. Her friend wasn't nearly as confident as she was letting on.

"Absolutely not," Jane told her firmly. She appreciated Dee's willingness to help, but she had already considered and rejected that option as a million times too dangerous. "The moment my mother-in-law or her cousins got near you, they'd know every-thing that you know." Jane tapped her temple meaningfully. Dee would never intentionally give up Jane's secrets, she knew, but that didn't mean a whole lot around a family full of mind-readers. "And don't forget who was with me when we first met," she reminded Dee. Lynne had spent the entire meeting barking orders at Dee's boss and completely ignoring the bride-to-be and the baker's assis-tant, but when Dee had asked Jane about Gran's ring, Lynne's full attention had turned toward them. "She would probably recognize you if she saw you; her mind is like one giant 'Contacts' file." Dee's face fell. Jane pressed her fingertips together on the table. She knew she had covered all the angles, but the next part was still going to be a tough sell. "I'm going. I know the house, they can't 'hear' me coming, and I've got some . . . special skills, just in case."

"You can't be serious," Dee snapped, leaning away from their table. She glanced around and then leaned back in, clearly wishing that they were somewhere private enough to yell. "You think that the solution to your little dilemma is to shove your head into the lion's mouth?"

"It's my head I'm trying to save," Jane pointed out reasonably. "It should absolutely be mine that I risk. And if it works—"

"No," Dee told her flatly, reaching into her studded denim purse. "I'm calling Harris. If he can't talk sense into you, at least maybe he can help me lock you in your room or something. Oh!" Her eyes lit up. "He would go. Jane, he would absolutely go into the house and look around for you if we ask. And he's been there before, he's part of their social—"

Jane glared at the cell phone that Dee was beginning to dial, and it jumped out of her kitchen-calloused hands. It lay on the table between them like an accusation, a tiny curl of smoke rising from the battery compartment.

"Jane," Dee whispered, "did you just blow up my phone?"

Jane opened her mouth, but no sound came out. Dee covered her mouth with a long-fingered hand, and after a moment, Jane saw that her shoulders were shaking slightly. A smile tugged at the corner of Jane's lips, and within moments, the two women were laughing so hard that nearly the entire line of patrons had turned to stare.

"I didn't mean to," Jane admitted when she had her giggling more or less under control. "I was just trying to move it—I guess I need more practice."

Dee nodded faux-seriously. "Just don't go trying to 'move' any people until we do a little more work, okay?" She tapped at her dead cell phone with one unpolished fingernail, the half-moon at its base glowing against her tawny skin. "So that was a 'no' to the calling-Harris idea."

"It's not like I'm about to go running headlong into the mansion," Jane explained lamely. "You don't need to be that worried yet. And he does know that house a little, I guess, and he's harder to 'read' than you, but not by that much. Not by enough." Harris's mind was more protected than most because of his magical blood, but he didn't even have as much of that protection as Malcolm or Charles, and Jane had managed to read both of their thoughts at one point or another. Surely Lynne and the twins would make short work of Harris if he were caught, and Jane couldn't stomach the thought of what they would do next. She spun the salt shaker around on the wooden tabletop, trying to put her thoughts into words. "Obviously we need a plan. But Harris isn't the answer here, so we shouldn't drag him into it."

Dee nodded briskly, removing the salt shaker from Jane's reach. After a brief hesitation, she moved the pepper, as well, and then the sad, still-smoking cell phone. Jane, left with nothing handy to fidget with, rested her hands awkwardly on her thighs. Dee cleared her throat, and Jane looked up expectantly. "So. We need someone who Ly— Who no one in the house will recognize. We need someone who either doesn't know why they're really there, or whose mind is protected. It would also be nice if they'd been in the house before, so they don't waste all their time on places that obviously aren't the room they're looking for. Or, if not, then they should be someone that the people in the house expect to see there, so they don't have to hurry back out again."

"Umm . . . are you guys, like, done?"

Jane jumped, clutching her plastic fork like a weapon. She turned to see a tween in a green vinyl raincoat, with expertly moussed hair, holding an overflowing paper plate and tapping her Mary Jane–shod foot impatiently. Dee bristled, but they'd finished eating a while ago, and the restaurant was packed.

"We're going," Jane assured the girl, who turned to wave over a cluster of similarly trendy friends. Jane and Dee tossed away their plates and napkins and stepped out into the cool night air. When they were safely away from the small crowd on the restaurant's steps, Jane lit a cigarette—one of three she allowed herself each week—and returned to their previous conversation. "We don't know anyone who meets all of those criteria, but we can't just toss out the whole idea because of that."

Dee nodded. "Technically your Mystery Witch is the closest person we know who fits the bill, but you probably shouldn't ask her."

"Agreed." Jane tried to imagine recruiting Mystery Witch. It was the sort of thing Lynne might do, she decided, and maybe even the kind of thing she herself might do after a few more decades of being the most powerful person she knew. Right now, though, it felt like suicide.

"Jane," Dee said hesitantly, and Jane turned toward her. "I've been practicing some stuff on my own while I was at the bookstore. Not magic," she rushed on when Jane cocked a bewildered eyebrow, "but not just research, either. I've been trying to learn that thing you said Malcolm could do, to hide his thoughts from his mother. Locking secrets in his mind somewhere that she couldn't see them. I thought I might need it someday, so I've been practicing for three weeks. I think I'm getting the hang of it."

"Malcolm had been practicing that, too, for more than thirty years," Jane reminded her, "and he still had the good sense to stay the hell away from Lynne during the month when he really had something to hide." Dee looked disappointed, and Jane felt a pang of guilt for her flippant dismissal. "I'll practice it with you if you want," she added more gently. "It would be a really good thing for you to be able to do—it was smart of you to think of it. I wish that I had suggested it myself. But it won't be enough to keep all three of those bitches out of your head indefinitely, and that's what you'd have to do if they caught you. Not to mention the fact that I can't cope with the possibility that they might catch you running this kind of risk for me, period."

Dee sighed. "I know. It was worth a shot, but I knew you'd say that. What we really need is your insides with someone else's outsides. Like one of the staff's, or some high-society friend of the Dorans' that they'd *invite* into their house."

"Could I be royalty?" Jane asked cheerfully, hopping agilely out of the way of a fortysomething man with a mohawk. Although it was fully dark, she could still feel the damp springiness from her morning in the park, and she inhaled the night air deeply. "I always used to pretend that I was really some missing princess, like Anastasia, being raised by my grandmother the exiled queen. Except in some versions she was the crazy maid who'd kidnapped me, but that was just when she was being extra-overprotective, which makes a lot more sense to me these days than it did when I was a kid."

Dee stopped walking, and for a moment Jane was afraid she had tripped. But her friend was just standing stock-still on the concrete, her amber eyes far away. The neon sign of a nearby bar changed her black hair into a collage of red, blue, and gold. "Like a glamour," she whispered. Jane waved a hand in front of her face, and her eyes finally began to track the world around her again. "We just need you," Dee explained slowly, beginning to walk again. "We need you not to look like you. And that's something pretty much everyone agrees witches can do."

"A magical disguise." Jane breathed. Across the street, a white stick figure turned into a glowing orange hand, and she stopped obediently for a stream of cars and taxis. "It would have to be complete; I'd have to look like a whole other person. And it couldn't take too much power to maintain, or else I might burn out. And it would be better if it were something that didn't leave any kind of signature Lynne might sense. And do you think I could choose a specific face?"

"Holy hell, Jane!" Dee laughed heartily. "Look, it's the best plan so far. I'll call Misty in the morning, and we'll start up the research engine, but in the meantime you can't sweat the details. Haven't you figured out yet that magic has a mind of its own?"

Jane stuck her tongue out at Dee and was nearly run down by a speeding bicycle that left the faint aroma of scallions and toasted sesame oil in its wake. "Karma," she observed. "Okay. I'll do the meditating stuff and let you ladies be the brains of the operation. Just let me know when you've got something, because if we could wrap this up by the weekend, I'd love to check out this Coney Island thing everyone talks about."

Dee rolled her eyes. "Nobody talks about Coney Island anymore, but duly noted. Jane, stop. We're home." She pointed to the discreet, steel-edged glass door that Jane had been about to walk right past.

"Almost," Jane murmured under her breath, and followed her friend into the lobby.

Chapter Eight

"HERE IT IS."

Jane leaned forward over the driftwood coffee table, eager for her first glimpse of the indispensable charm that would give her a new face. Misty hadn't even been sure that there were any left in the world, but had tracked down the rumors tirelessly for two days until she'd found a person who, for tens of thousands of Jane's dollars, was willing to produce the genuine article.

"A Forvrangdan orb," Misty declared proudly, setting it on the table and pulling aside the cloth that shrouded it. It was a smooth, clear-glass sphere. It looked heavy, and seemed solid except for a few tiny bubbles caught motionless in its center.

"It's beautiful," Dee said breathlessly, tilting her head to take it in from more angles.

"It really is," Jane agreed. "And nothing at all like an incredibly expensive paperweight."

Dee looked alarmed, but Misty laughed. Even her laughter sounded beachy. "It's the real thing," she assured Jane confidently. "Paperweights don't do this." She slid a gray-and-white, pigeon-esque feather out of her supply bag. Careful not to touch the surface of the orb with her skin, she set the feather down gently on top of it.

At first, nothing happened, but after a short while, Jane was almost positive the feather was darker. A few seconds later, it was definite: the feather was almost as black and shiny as a raven's. It elongated and became even glossier and uneven on one long edge, and Jane abruptly realized that now she was looking at a plastic comb. The comb began to lighten until it was distinctly purple, and then transparent. Moments later, it was a cheap-looking red pen, and briefly a salamander, then a chameleon, then a candle, then a white leather bookmark. And then, as Jane watched in growing horror, the bookmark's edges began to curl and peel as if it were being consumed in an invisible fire, which ate its way through the leather with increasing speed. The bookmark looked like a pigeon feather again, for the briefest of moments, before it was gone, without the slightest trace of it remaining on the perfect surface of the orb.

"Okay," Jane agreed, swallowing thickly. "Paperweights *don't* do that. But I . . . um . . . I don't want it to do *that* to me."

"It won't," Dee reassured her quickly, although her face was a few shades paler than normal.

"It won't," Misty echoed, far more convincingly. "The spell controls it; channels the power and sets limits on it. That's why the orb is destroyed at the end of the spell, instead of the object of the change. That means you," she added, glancing up at Jane. "And that's why there are so many rules, because you don't harness something this major without a lot of rules. It was this coven in Sweden—I guess they were the real thing, like your family and the Dorans. They made these as weapons; tools they could use that would destroy anyone else who tried without the proper rituals. But it wasn't enough, I guess, because rumor has it that they were wiped out centuries ago. We don't know how many orbs were left in their stockpile when that happened, but they're almost never heard of these days. We got this one because a friend of mine from fifteen years ago bragged about seeing one once after a little too much blessed wine, but I honestly wouldn't know where to even begin with finding another one. So I want to be very sure before we begin that you really, really understand the rules."

Jane opened her mouth to answer, but the words caught in her throat.

"We should review," Dee murmured softly, and Jane nodded gratefully.

"The spell lasts for twenty-eight days exactly," Misty began pedantically, "one full cycle of the moon. There's no way to know what you'll look like once it's done, so we can't really lay any groundwork for your new persona *before* we do the spell. But that means that you'll really need to hit the ground running once it's done, because once the twenty-eight days are up, that persona will be gone for good. But the good news is that the fuel for the spell comes from the orb that whole time, not from you, so you'll have all of your magic in case you need it."

"That's good." Jane nodded. She had tried what Dee had called a "glamour" the day before. After a few attempts, she had succeeded in making her hair look blond again, but it was exhausting work and slipped back to its dyed shade every time she thought about anything else whatsoever. It was an interesting parlor trick, but it wouldn't hold up.

"It really is," Dee reminded her encouragingly. "A month isn't very long for everything you'll have to do with your new face. As soon as you talk to Lynne, she'll know you're a witch no matter what you look like, so you can forget trying to pretend you're anything else. She'll expect you to be able to do magic. The more power you have at your disposal, the more interested in you she'll be."

Jane nodded again, trying to look a little more enthusiastic this time. But she couldn't keep one thought from fluttering around the corners of her mind like a bat: *Magic has a mind of its own . . .*

The spell might work, but it could certainly work in unexpected and wrong ways. *I could get stuck. The spell could end while I'm in the middle of a conversation with Lynne. I could turn into a toad for a month. My mind could change along with my face. This could all be for nothing, or it could be for worse than nothing.* She shivered, drawing the black hoodie that she had borrowed from Dee tighter around her shoulders. *But it's the best plan I've got.*

"The disguise might start to fade out toward the end of the month," Misty went on, echoing Jane's fears a little too closely for her comfort. "The stronger we manage to make the initial spell, though, the less likely that will happen, so if you want to take some more time to get ready—"

"I've been getting ready all day," Jane interrupted. She had felt the bars of sunlight move across her bed as she had sent ripples through her magic, listened to it murmur. Her awareness had spread to every corner of the apartment; she had known about but ignored the trays of food Dee had left by her door, and had heard every worried thought of Misty's since the wild-haired blonde had stepped across their threshold. She had even heard some thoughts of Dee's, although she had tried to avoid it, but to her pleasant surprise, Dee's mind-closing efforts seemed to be paying off. Her available thoughts were superficial, and while Jane was sure she could dig out the more substantial ones if she wanted to, it was a relief not to have them floating at her and distracting her from her calm.

Now the sun was setting in a riot of red and gold out her remarkable panoramic living-room windows. A heavy lid of star-flecked dark blue chased it to the horizon, and Jane was pretty sure she wasn't going to feel readier anytime soon.

"The spell takes time," Dee told her softly. "We're ready to start when you are, but it'll be a long night once we do. If you'd like to at least eat something . . ." She trailed off uncertainly.

Jane unfolded her legs from the nubby white couch and spread her toes over the cool, glossy finish of the bleached hardwood floor. "Now's good," she insisted gently, drifting over to the spot in front of the windows where hundreds of candles marked out a strange symbol on the floor. The view through the windows shifted slightly as she moved, and Jane felt an almost seasick light-headedness. *What's some archaic Swedish mark doing on the eleventh floor of a building in Manhattan?* Or was it even Swedish to start with? Ambika and her daughters had lived and died before there were maps.

Misty appeared beside her with the orb wrapped carefully back up in its shroud. *Magic-proof,* Jane realized. *The cloth saved my coffee table from whatever happened to that pigeon feather.*

Dee approached on her other side, the growing starlight washing her eyes and face out to the same dark silver. "It starts with blood," she told Jane softly, and there was something even more silver in her hands. She handed it to Jane, who recognized the two-edged blade that Dee had called an "athame." They had used it to help focus Jane's mind when she had first learned to use her power, but never used the edges for what Jane realized was probably their actual purpose. *Lynne did, though.* Jane suddenly saw her mother-in-law as vividly as if she were on the deck of the harbor-cruise boat with her again, watching the older witch slide something half-seen into her purse; watching her blood drip in the near darkness. Lynne did things with her power that Jane hadn't been able to even imagine, but now she was beginning to. Whatever they were about to do was major magic, and Jane could feel the Earth turning ever so slowly ten stories beneath her bare feet.

Of course it starts with blood.

She held out her hand to Dee, who held up the athame and began to whisper. The starlight flashed wildly as she spun the blade downward, and the spell began.

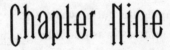

Chapter Nine

JANE WOKE UP IN HER BED. SHE STARED AT THE WHITE CEILING for a while, feeling powerless to even shift her eyes to the skylight a few feet away. Every muscle was sore and even her lungs felt ragged, as if she had been running. Or screaming. *Maybe I was doing both,* she thought curiously. *There was a spell . . . wasn't there?*

It had lasted for hours, or maybe she had dreamed the whole thing. Her muscles and joints protested loudly as she turned her entire body toward her window; the stars she remembered were still out there, although the sky behind them was fully, finally dark now. She slid carefully off the bed, wobbling a little on her bare feet. Her fingertips brushed the soft, powdery paint of the wall, and she followed it, coaxing her body to stay upright with each step. By the time she reached her little bathroom, she felt fairly confident that her legs would cooperate, and she risked letting her fingers leave the wall in order to flick a light switch.

Clumsily, she hit both at once, and the overhead bulb came on at the same time as the softer ones embedded around the mirror above the sink.

Damn. She shrank back instinctively, shielding her sensitive eyes with her other hand until they adjusted to the fierce glow. *Those nut-jobs turned me into a vampire, probably.* She peeked out from behind her hand and found that she could see without squinting now, but she still hesitated, afraid to face the mirror.

"I can't just stand in the doorway all night," she announced reasonably, and then shuddered: her voice wasn't noticeably higher or lower, but it was absolutely different: the same note produced by a new instrument. More curious than afraid now, she pulled herself forward into the bathroom, lurching to a graceless stop in front of the lit mirror.

She's so tall, she thought, half-hysterically. *I am, I mean.* Her new body had at least eight or nine inches more in its legs and torso than her old one had, but not noticeably more weight to go around. Her new, model-esque height came with pointed shoulders, small ripples of breasts, a long, flat stomach, and stretched-teardrop hips. Above her sharp collarbones, her face was unexpectedly girlish. Her jaw was wide, her cheeks short and round. She had a plump bow of a mouth and sparkling black eyes, which matched her straight, shoulder-skimming black hair perfectly. Most striking, though, was her skin. Jane, who had spent her life with the kind of hopelessly unfashionable peaches-and-cream skin that showed every blush and burned if she even thought about sunlight, ran a walnut finger across her walnut jawbone in wonder.

I wonder where I'm from, she thought idly; between her coloring and the slight almond turn to her eyes, she was distinctly racially ambiguous. *I just have to decide where I want to be from. And what my name is.*

The choices to be made from the seemingly endless possibilities in front of her suddenly felt almost overwhelming, and her breath caught in her throat. *I need some help with this,* she decided. She didn't know how long she had been unconscious, but surely Dee would want to see the outcome of their bizarre spell. She was probably still awake, in fact, and Jane pushed herself away from the mirror to go show her how their efforts had paid off.

She had barely stepped into the hallway before she smelled hot sugar and butter bound together by flour, and she forced her still-wobbly legs to pick up their pace. *She's awake* and *baking,* she urged her limbs. *Please hurry!*

She entered the living room just as Dee was leaving the kitchen, with a telltale piece of cookie in her hand. Dee stopped and stared at her in shock. She was still wearing the black lace top and baggy black cargo pants that she had had on for the spell, but they looked wrinkled and tired . . . as did Dee's face.

"It's me," Jane told her unnecessarily. "It worked." *The sky is blue and Lynne's a witch.*

"Oh my God, Jane, I thought you were—" Dee stopped, apparently trying to make a huge mental adjustment. "It *worked*?"

Jane glanced quickly at her hands; they were still the same glowing shade of brown. The half-moons under her nail beds stood out in even brighter contrast than Dee's. "Didn't it?"

Dee waved her cookie dismissively. "Of course, it's just . . . we kept checking on you, and then Misty had to go, but I kept checking, and you still looked like you the whole time. And you wouldn't wake up, and now it's— Oh, you must be starving."

"Are those hazelnut?" Jane asked helpfully, tilting her new chin toward the cookie.

Dee looked at it as if she had no idea how she had come to be holding it, then shook herself all over. "White chocolate–cherry," she corrected with a little more of her usual confidence. "But samosas first, and— Well, there's a lot, actually. I cook when I'm worried. And for God's sake, Jane, you haven't eaten in two days."

She disappeared back into the kitchen, leaving Jane frozen in place this time. She cleared her throat; it seemed to take longer than it did in her real body. "I haven't what in *what*?" she called out to the doorway that Dee had just vacated.

Her friend's tangle of black hair reappeared, although the rest of her body remained occupied by the stove. "I know you didn't touch the food I left before the spell, and then you were out all day today. We were really starting to panic, you know."

"I don't . . ." Jane whispered, then raised her voice again. She could hear the note of hysteria in it, but felt that a little panic was probably in order about now. "*Today?*"

Dee reappeared fully in the doorway, this time holding a plate. Jane could smell oil and the soft, low note of chickpeas, and her taut stomach growled fiercely. Dee opened her mouth to say something, but a loud, bell-like chime interrupted her. Her amber eyes darted to the front door and then back to Jane. "Shit," she whispered. "Jane, I really thought we needed—"

Today? Jane walked automatically to the front door, her mind still trying to wrap itself around this new information. She heard Dee frantically trying to apologize for something or other behind her back, but she couldn't focus on that right now: someone had come to their apartment in the middle of some unspecified night.

Feeling a little reckless (she had, after all, just pulled off a seriously empowering amount of magic), Jane swung the door open without so much as checking the peephole.

He's not so tall anymore, was her first thought, but the rest was still the same: the short, coppery curls, the dancing green eyes, the long, lean muscles that made a leather jacket look better on him than on just about anyone else she could think of. "Harris." She breathed, and stepped—almost fell—into his arms. He stayed perfectly still, and at first she imagined that he must just be surprised to see her.

It was only after she had been clinging to his unresponsive body for a good ten seconds that she realized that he had no idea who was hugging him. Apparently, the spell had left some things the same, though, because the tiny currents of electricity that curled under her skin whenever she was close to him were responding just as emphatically as ever. Jane pulled herself gently away.

"Excuse me," she improvised. "I'm from, erm, Brazil. We hug." She stepped back and shot a pleading look at Dee. The fact that Harris was here at all suggested that Dee was starting to have second thoughts about concealing Jane's whereabouts, but a new face gave them a chance to keep her secrets. "Please come in."

Dee had been gesturing frantically to Jane, but stopped as soon as Harris could see her. She opened her arms and accepted his hug while Jane chewed the inside of her cheek; theirs looked a lot more enjoyable than her one-sided gaffe had been. ". . . At this time of night," Dee was saying.

What time? Jane wondered. She inched to where she could see the digital clock on the oven. She assumed that it was broken when she saw 12:14, but then remembered that she was in America, where they used twelve repeating hours instead of twenty-four. *After midnight on Saturday, then . . . or actually Sunday, I guess.* She had slept through Saturday. And of course, she realized, Dee had called Harris when Jane had headed into hour twenty-four of her magical coma. She could hardly blame her friend for that. And as the son of a son of a witch himself, raised on his grandmother's stories and lore, Harris was a pretty smart choice to call for help.

"I don't think I've officially met your . . . friend," Harris said, and Jane's eyes snapped over to him as if they had a mind of their own. It was as though the air around him were somehow brighter than in the rest of the room.

"My roommate," Dee corrected as Jane started forward with her right hand outstretched for a more formal greeting than her first one. "She . . . um . . . Ella. This is my roommate, Ella."

"I've heard all kinds of nice things about you," Jane told Harris automatically, hoping this was enough of an explanation for her greeting him by name. And body-check.

"Charmed," Harris replied, turning her proffered hand to kiss the back, and Jane felt her unfamiliar lips curve up into an unfamiliar smile.

She searched her empty brain for some sort of nonchalant reply, but just then Dee appeared between them with a plate of lukewarm samosas. "It turned out to be nothing, of course," she told Harris conversationally, and Jane admired her coolness. "Our downstairs neighbor came home drunk and tried to get in here. It woke us up, and we'd already Netflixed *Paranormal Activity* earlier, so we were a little freaked out. I decided to stay up and cook a little, and then I guess the guy came back, because there were all kinds of weird noises and scratching at the door, and it completely freaked me out."

To her surprise, Jane felt the skin on her arms rise in goose bumps even though Dee was making the whole thing up. *She's really good.* "You should have called the police," Harris told Dee gently, rubbing her upper arms reassuringly. Jane clapped her hands over her own upper arms. "But of course I'm always happy to come play hero for the two of you," he added, flashing his wide, easy smile that never failed to make Jane want to smile back.

His bright green eyes met hers and narrowed curiously for a moment. Jane inhaled and looked away as casually as she could manage, feeling a familiar heat rising in her cheeks. *He's so close,* a rebellious part of her thought, and she felt an intense longing to just tell him who she was.

"We know," Dee assured Harris, moving the plate out to the side and leaning her body a little closer in to his. "Thank you so much."

"I guess, now that we're all safe again, I'll go back to bed," Jane made herself say. *Normal people have normal lives, and I want that for them. And once I fix things with Lynne, I'll be able to have that, too. Or something more like it, anyway.* The thoughts sounded hollow, and she shrugged her shoulders irritably, feeling a dull ache in their tired muscles.

"I should, too, actually," Dee admitted guiltily. "This Kate woman called earlier; she's starting a catering company and heard I did pastry." She glanced back at the food-covered surfaces of the kitchen. "I guess we can call tonight 'interview prep.'"

"That's great!" Jane told her warmly. "I had no idea. Let me know if I can help at all." *Like lend you clothes that we're both a little too tall for now, or act like a stranger off the street who adores your cakes, or snuggle with your new boyfriend. Or anything.* She smiled ruefully at her hopelessly one-track mind. It would get better once Harris and his pesky magical blood were a safe distance away, and then, she knew, she would be able to be properly happy about how Dee was getting her life together post–Hurricane Jane. Right now she could settle for ignoring her baser impulses and acting the part of a good friend.

"I'll let you two sleep, then," Harris offered gallantly, heading for the door but detouring toward the kitchen. "Although, if you could spare a little something for the long, lonely subway ride . . ."

"I'll wrap the cookies for you," Dee suggested, and Jane had to fight the urge to kick her in the shin. Following a short flurry of activity in the kitchen and a good-natured wave, Harris was gone. When Dee closed the door behind him, Jane felt her body finally relax.

Dee turned and raised an awkward black eyebrow at Jane. "Ella?" Jane asked, a little incredulously. "Like *Ella Enchanted?*"

"Like 'she,' in Spanish," Dee admitted sheepishly. "My mind went blank. But use the 'enchanted' thing if you ever write your memoirs or something, okay?"

"It's a deal," Jane promised, making a long-overdue beeline for the kitchen.

Chapter Ten

THE HEAVY, CARVED-WOOD DOORS OF NUMBER 665 SWUNG open, and Jane jolted to attention. She had been staking the place out from a Starbucks across the street, set a little bit back on Sixty-Eighth Street, from about nine that morning, but so far hadn't seen a single useful thing. A couple of the youngest McCarrolls, the grandchildren of Lynne's cousin Cora, had left with a nanny shortly after Jane had started watching. Blake Helding, the son of Cora's twin, Belinda, had staggered in around ten thirty in what looked an awful lot like last night's clothes. But between then and almost noon, she had seen nothing but comings and goings through the staff entrance, and she was starting to feel both discouraged and over-caffeinated.

Jane leaned forward toward the window, checking automatically to make sure her sunglasses were still in place. It was probably overkill, since she had acquired a completely different face and body since the last time she had seen anyone who lived in the Dorans' mansion, but a habit was a habit. *Besides,* she reflected, *if I'm trying to act like I belong in their circle, getting recognized as "that chick who was stalking the house" would probably be counterproductive.*

The woman who emerged from the dark stone archway was so thin she looked brittle, with massive sunglasses like Jane's and a telltale head of completely implausible highlights. *Laura.* Blake Helding's wife—probably distinctly irritated with her husband's so-late-as-to-be-early arrival home—was striding away down the block, and Jane nearly knocked over her stool in her hurry to get outside and follow her. She stayed behind her onetime almost-friend and across the street, careful not to get caught at a corner by the changing traffic signals. She guessed that Laura would have taken one of the family cars if she'd been planning on going far, and three short and one long block later, Laura proved her right.

Sunday at noon—brunch time, Jane realized belatedly as she watched Laura saunter into 212. She chewed her lower lip thoughtfully and considered the merits of staying right where she was. She only had twenty-eight days, one of which was half-gone: an abundance of caution was not what was called for here.

She stepped out onto the street, first nearly breaking an ankle in her viciously pointy, strappy shoes and then narrowly missing getting hit by a delivery truck. Crossing the rest of Sixty-Fifth Street more carefully than she had begun, she checked to make sure that a couple of crisp fifty-dollar bills were readily available in the pocket of her vintage, chain-strap Chanel minaudière.

She strolled past the line of waiting patrons as if she couldn't see them; she was busy locating Laura and her three trophy-wife friends, anyway. "One for brunch," she told the host in the bored, lofty tone that she had learned from the Dorans.

"Do you have a reservation?" he asked pointedly, his wispy blond mustache twitching strangely.

Jane pulled the bills deftly from her purse and rested them on his wooden stand, still folded between her slim mahogany fingers. "The banquette near the back is fine," she told him softly, releasing the bills. They drifted down across his reservation book like a rumor, coming to rest just above his pale, dry hands. He hesitated briefly, and then they were gone before Jane had even seen his fingers move.

"This way, please," he told her diffidently, leading her to the white-draped table she had suggested. She thought she heard an annoyed murmur from the line behind her, and she made herself remember to strut rather than slink.

She slid along the soft brown leather of the bench; he moved the table in a bit closer to her and hurried back to his post. She saw his right hand move to his left sleeve as he went, and then to his inside jacket pocket, and smiled: Malcolm would be so proud of her. A shrill laugh pierced her reverie, drawing Jane's somewhat jittery attention to one of Laura Helding's friends, a woman with slick, professionally straightened hair, whom Jane faintly remembered as the wife of some athlete. Her bare bronzed shoulder was so close that it almost touched Jane's. Laura herself was seated across the table from Jane's neighbor, but Jane still felt sure that, if she wanted to, she could reach over and touch Malcolm's second-cousin-in-law.

So close, she thought tensely, *but now what?*

As if in answer, a waitress arrived at Laura's table with three Bellinis and a Bloody Mary. *Now I wait,* Jane realized with a sudden flash of insight. *Now I let her get a little tipsy.* Laura had always been even more outgoing than usual when she had a cocktail or three in her angular body.

Jane suited action to thought, setting her purse on the table and picking up the menu. Over her fluffy Niçoise omelet (which was barely an omelet and not remotely Niçoise, to Jane's authoritatively French eye, but was absolutely delicious all the same), she thought she noticed Laura eyeing the beading on the minaudière, and reminded herself that she wasn't going into this mission completely blind. She knew a lot about Laura, after all: the woman liked private sales, loved one-of-a-kind anything, and loathed her husband in a good-natured sort of way.

Jane took a sip of her water and then a sip of chardonnay, reached into the tiny purse, and dug around for her new Vertu Constellation phone. It had been expensive—shockingly, heart-stoppingly expensive—but during the nerve-racking days of choosing the spell and locating the Forvrangdan orb, Dee had managed to convince her that she needed a power accessory. At the time, Jane had grudgingly written it off as retail therapy, but now it was practical in a whole new way: it was exactly the sort of accessory that Ella, socialite acquaintance of the Doran clan, would have. And since she couldn't wear her engagement ring around the Dorans, of course, she would have to get comfortable spending money on other eye-catchers. *Plus, so pretty,* she cooed silently, stroking the smooth ceramic of its keys.

Laura noticed it, too, out of the corner of her heavily lined eye, and Jane thought she read approval in her expression. *So far, so good.* But glances weren't invitations, and Jane gritted Ella's small, even teeth and dialed Dee.

"I'm on my way to the interview with that caterer," Dee answered crisply. "Is everything okay?"

"You're late," Jane drawled, forcing herself not to hush her voice the way she normally would. The real players didn't worry about who heard them. She tried to copy the light, lovely accent her old friend Elodie had spoken with: a mix of British English, Haitian French, and boarding-school Swedish. The memory of the week the two girls had spent in the Dessaixes' posh London home crashed over Jane like a wave, but she twisted the edge of the cream-colored tablecloth between her fingers and fought down the nostalgia.

"No, it's at—" Dee initially sounded confused, but then stopped abruptly and Jane guessed that she had caught on. "Oh my God, which of them is there?"

"I don't even care about your stupid excuses," Jane insisted, raising her voice a tiny bit more. "I can tell that you're hungover, anyway."

"Well," Dee pointed out reasonably, "you *did* keep me up past midnight with your coma drama. Who wouldn't drink, with such a crazy roommate?"

Jane had a fleeting moment of regret that she had called Dee instead of their answering machine, which probably wouldn't have distracted her with wiseass remarks. But it was too late now, and she determinedly soldiered on. "Do you think I couldn't just check with Alfred and ask when he drove you home? Do you think he keeps your secrets when I sign his paychecks, you idiot? But, you know, it's not even worth my time; I don't care enough."

"You're *so* mean." Dee pretended to pout. "Also, I'm not sure if I'm supposed to be your ne'er-do-well lover or your bratty teenager."

"Just get your things and get out." Jane sighed. "Forget brunch, forget us, forget everything. Be gone by the time I'm back from Garren, and don't bother the staff with carrying your crap."

"Bitch," Dee remarked good-naturedly. "And to think I was going to make enough dinner for *both* of us."

Jane clicked her phone shut with a disgusted snort and signaled to one of the ubiquitous blue-clad waitresses. "Champagne," she mouthed broadly.

To her barely containable delight, Laura snapped her French-manicured fingers briskly to get the waitress's attention before she could fill Jane's request. "Bring the bottle," she ordered, and then turned to Jane. "On me, of course. It sounds like you've had about enough of freeloaders for the day." She smiled at Jane, who had a momentary pang of guilt at using, arguably, the nicest adult associated with the Dorans. But, she reminded herself, when she brought Annette back to her family, everyone's life would get better, including Laura's. It was a deception but not really a betrayal: Lynne would probably *thank* Laura for bringing "Ella" into their lives. *And then Ella will disappear for good, and all the loose ends will vanish with her, and Malcolm will be safe and I can go on with my life.* It was almost easy to smile and raise her quickly produced glass in a toast when she kept all of that in mind.

"To cutting dead weight," Laura suggested archly. The five women clinked their glasses high above the table and sipped.

"I don't know what it is about men," Jane sighed tragically. "The moment they get comfortable, they turn into little children. Do they not know how terribly unattractive that is?"

"You should see mine," one of Laura's friends agreed, rolling her lash extensions skyward. "You'd think the entire world revolved around poker night."

"You *did* see mine, at the ASPCA thing last week," another pointed out. "And he thinks *I* should 'get a little work done'? I can tell you that whatever I 'have done' will *not* be for him. It'll be for that adorable boy who delivers for our florist, who actually takes care of his body."

"Blake came home this *morning* from Oliver's bachelor party," Laura admitted in a tiny voice, swallowing the rest of her champagne. "And we have to smile and be nice tonight for that harpy." Jane automatically poured more into her glass and leaned in. "Oh, sorry," Laura added, apparently remembering that Jane wasn't already in her loop. "My mother-in-law's cousin—it's kind of sick, you know, how they all live together, like it's a tiny town in Iowa no one ever leaves—anyway, she's talking to these weirdo Europeans about some kind of merger. I get it, you know: the family businesses pay for my Manolos. I'm totally on board with helping things go smoothly. But do we really all have to go to every stupid party and event and pretend like we're the world's most perfect people in every way? Not *one* night off since they got here last week, and I'm supposed to take the woman to Bendel's tomorrow. It will literally be the *least* fun that I have *ever* had while shopping."

Laura twisted a lock of hair that bore no relation whatsoever to her natural color and swallowed half of her refreshed champagne. Jane, however, was afraid to touch her own in case she got too loose-lipped in her excitement. *Lynne's distracted,* and *the Dorans are having parties every night!* She couldn't have found a better time to get herself invited into the mansion.

"Think of it as charity," Jane suggested, eyeing a ring that she knew Laura had been proud of acquiring. She searched her memory for every detail she could remember about it. "Everyone should be so lucky as to get to shop with someone who knows where to find authentic Laliques. I'd heard a few pieces went up at the Elaine Ausprey estate auction a few years back, but I thought it was just a rumor."

Laura giggled happily and sipped her champagne again. *I'm in,* Jane celebrated silently, and bit her lip to keep from grinning. "You should try shopping with that beast and see if you can stay so positive," Laura teased, "but I won't inflict that on you. Here." She reached across the table and scooped up Jane's Vertu between her white-tipped fingernails. She plucked her own topaz-encrusted phone and held the two beside each other, tapping diligently with her thumbs. "We'll think of something else to do; you'll thank me later."

I want to thank you now, but I'll wait, Jane cheered to herself, the grin finally breaking across her new face.

Chapter Eleven

JANE SIPPED HER MANHATTAN CAREFULLY BEFORE SETTING IT
on the glass table beside her. Less than an hour after settling in
to her new home at the Lowell Hotel—not quite ten blocks from
the Dorans' mansion—Jane had decided that it was time to *really*
get into character. Two days into her twenty-eight, Ella finally
had a last name: Medeiros. Unfortunately, she also was allegedly
Brazilian with an English-French-Swedish accent, and had impulsively tacked on the title of "baroness," which, she suspected,
created even more uncertainty about her origins. So Jane had
decided to take a few minutes in the lobby bar to figure out who
Ella really was, and had realized almost right away that even this
presented problems: Jane drank chardonnay whenever she had
the option, but what did Ella drink?

After an uncomfortably long hesitation in front of the patiently impassive bartender, she had remembered Maeve's sweet-

bitter-dark drink from the night of the disastrous cocktail party at MoMA. It had been stronger than Jane had really wanted, but she also remembered the way a borrowed sip of it had steadied her nerves, and she decided that Ella would probably love them. She also loved bright colors (the pastels and even some of the neutrals in Jane's closet had made her look dull and lifeless), high heels even though she was already tall, dogs more than cats, and the partly unbuttoned shirt of the unfairly tall, dark, and handsome man in the corner armchair. Jane had never really gone for the brooding, dangerous type, but to Ella it was hot as hell.

I can totally do this, Jane decided, letting the heat of the whiskey spread outward from the pit of her perfectly flat stomach. Dee, still giddy from her promising job interview the day before, had convinced Jane that she needed to go all in to shore up her disguise. After all, she couldn't risk the Dorans knowing where she actually lived, but if she wanted to hang with them, she couldn't very well pretend to be homeless, either. She might need a place to let Laura see; an address to hand out on the calling cards that the printer swore would be delivered by four o'clock at the very latest.

There was the sound of footsteps on the pale marble tile, and Jane turned instinctively to see if it might be the printer, finished ahead of schedule. But it was just a bellhop, studiously working not to struggle under the weight of about thirty shopping bags. Most were from Barney's, which was conveniently nearby, but Jane also spotted a few from Fresh, Teuscher, and Jo Malone.

I think Ella prefers Annick Goutal, Jane decided as the young man passed behind her chair, *but the rest is good.* Every sip of her cocktail made it easier to feel decisive, and she took another to celebrate the latest conclusion she had drawn about her temporary persona.

"'Garden' apparently means something different to you from what it does to me," an icy-cold voice announced, and Jane swiveled again on her black leather chair to see what the disturbance was. She tracked the voice across the shiny marble floor and past the polished brass of the revolving doors to the deep cheery finish of the reception desk. "I will be happy with your complimentary upgrade once I have been able to inspect the new suite," the woman standing at the desk continued in a tone that made Jane feel absolutely positive the "upgrade" in question had not been intentionally complimentary. Jane took in the complaining guest's close-cropped black hair and her sinewy, deeply tanned calves, and guessed that she was the source of the mountain of shopping bags that had just disappeared with the bellhop behind the doors of the service elevator.

The conciliatory-looking desk agent handed the unhappy woman a new key card, mouthing what looked distinctly like profuse apologies. Jane rolled her eyes and fished the cherry out of her drink. Was Ella the type of person who made a scene to get stuff for free? It would distinguish her from Jane, but hopefully there were enough other differences between them that such desperate measures wouldn't be necessary. She bit into the cherry, letting the soft burn of the liqueur spread to every corner of her mouth.

The woman at the desk spun on one totally-overkill-for-daytime stiletto and headed for the bank of elevators on the far side of the lounge, and Jane's gasp caused half of the cherry to lodge in her throat. *Mystery Witch*. Even without the sunglasses, there was no doubt: the woman who had been stalking Jane all over Manhattan was now in her brand-new hotel. Jane tried to inhale, but couldn't, around the cherry. She coughed instead, which helped, and then glanced around for the closest emergency exit.

But how is she even doing this? her mind complained. *Did Lynne hide some kind of tracking device under my skin?* The theory was a little too plausible to laugh at, especially now that Mystery Witch was bearing down on her at an alarming rate. *Screw this. If she can find me here, I'm just going to have to fight her and be done with it.* Jane turned a little in her chair and started pulling in her magic. She didn't have as much time as she had had for the last week's prepared spells, but she had the major advantage of fury working for her, and she had a respectable amount of power burning before her eyes before Mystery Witch had drawn even with her. *I should question her first,* Jane realized in alarm. *Also, fighting to the death is so not appropriate in public.*

As she hesitated, Mystery Witch swept past her and into an open elevator, leaving a cloud of L'Air du Temps in her wake.

What the—?

Jane looked around, completely baffled now. Mystery Witch hadn't even seemed to see her . . . *because I'm not me,* she realized finally. Her stalker hadn't followed her all the way to the Upper East Side; Jane had moved to the Upper East Side and stumbled across her stalker. At her hotel. By chance.

Jane finished her drink in a hurry and signaled the bartender for another one. Following Laura to brunch had been a lot of good planning combined with a lot of good luck, but this was just pure serendipity, and it was hard to wrap her mind around. She was literally right under Mystery Witch's nose, and the other woman had no idea. With a little ingenuity, Jane could find out who had sent her and what she wanted, and figure out her next moves accordingly.

Her fresh drink arrived, and Jane reached for it eagerly. The rim of the glass was at her lips before she noticed that it had come to her in the hands of Tall, Dark, and Handsome from the corner. *Ella really is one lucky girl,* Jane decided, smiling coyly at the stranger. From this close she could smell the rich, musky leather of his bomber jacket, and she inhaled deeply, letting its phero- mones saturate her brain.

"When I saw you here, I thought, *This beautiful woman must be having a very bad day, or else a very good one,*" Tall, Dark, and Hand- some told her softly. His voice was low and soothing, with just a trace of an accent that made Jane hope he would speak more. "So I felt I must come to you and ask you which it was."

Jane nodded to the chair across from hers, and the man slid into it with the controlled grace of a panther. "It's been a bit of both," she told him honestly, running a finger around the rim of her glass.

"Improving, I hope," he offered with raised eyebrows that sug- gested thoroughly insincere humility, and Jane smiled a little. Something about him reminded her of the men she had flirted with in France, before she had met Malcolm. *I wish I could place the accent,* she mused.

Every movement and gesture of his said "Old World," and Jane automatically copied her friend Elodie's cool confidence along with her borrowed accent. "I suppose that depends on how good the company is," she told him, leaning back slightly in her chair as she sipped her Manhattan. This one didn't burn her throat on the way down, and she guessed that she was already tipsier than she had realized through her adrenaline haze. *Good thing I don't have to fight, after all,* she decided, *although flirting with this particular man might be nearly as risky.*

Her stranger's name turned out to be André, and after the brief- est of hesitations, he added that he was visiting from Romania.

André was in town on "business," but declined to add more. Jane, who suspected that he was deliberately trying to make her curious, refused to take the bait, instead chatting with him about the chic Upper East Side lifestyle that she decided Ella led. It was easy to fake both the experiences and the attitude after the time she had spent living with her impeccably upper-crust in-laws, and she even managed to spare some of her attention for evaluating her companion. The set of his jaw told her he was frustrated that she wasn't swooning over his secretiveness, but she couldn't help but be impressed by how still and neutral the rest of his body was. It reminded her of a cat, waiting and watching, and she felt flattered to be the object of such unwavering attention. Sure, most of it was due to her new body and face, but she reminded herself that her personality, her wit, and the way she carried herself were still her own. And André, no matter what had drawn him to her in the first place, clearly enjoyed all of those things as well. *Besides, it's not like I was so painfully homely before,* she admitted to herself. Lynne Doran may have come up with a hundred inventive little ways to call her fat, but curvy, blond Jane had never lacked for male attention. *It's just weird getting it for being someone else. My looks were* mine.

"Baroness Medeiros," a timid voice whispered in Jane's ear, and she startled a little. Fortunately, she had already swallowed enough of her drink to keep it from spilling over the sloping sides of the glass.

She set it down carefully on the table between her and André, and although he stayed as still as ever, she was fairly sure that his eyes slid to the neckline of her raw silk tank when she leaned. *And me without my cleavage,* she griped silently, but André seemed to approve thoroughly of Ella's smaller, more delicate breasts. Smiling a little to herself, she turned to the anxious-looking concierge hovering by her shoulder, who was quite plainly trying not to wring his hands. "Yes?"

"Something has arrived for you," he managed to force out, holding out a single piece of creamy, heavy card stock in one lightly trembling hand. *That's definitely not my calling cards.* As soon as Jane touched it, she recognized it unmistakably as Doran stationery. She had received dozens of notes like this in the mansion: phone messages, appointment reminders, and invitations/summonses from Lynne herself. Jane's fingers began to tremble a little, too, as she took the card, but the handwriting inside was upright and loopy and totally unlike Lynne's. She steadied her breath and made herself read.

> *Dear Ella,*
>
> *Ran by Cenzo's Papiro for my daughter's birthday invites, and he was in the middle of engraving some absolutely gorge cards. I recognized your name, and would love to be the first to welcome you to the neighborhood! Please meet me for dinner tonight. My number's in your phone!*
>
> *—Laura Helding*

Jane fought the temptation to turn the card over, backward, upside-down. But it wasn't in code and there were no hidden messages: she had just made it one step closer to her goal. *I wonder if "dinner" is at the mansion,* she thought, but quickly reminded herself that she'd already had more than her share of good luck so far, and twenty-six and a half days to go with her disguise.

"'Baroness Medeiros'?" André purred, and Jane flushed.

But my new skin shows it less, she reminded herself sternly, and folded Laura's note into her purse. She fumbled clumsily with the buckles, which she didn't remember being nearly so complicated, and realized that she might be heading past "tipsy" by now. She pushed the edges of the purse closed and turned her attention back to André. "It's just 'Ella' among friends," she told him lightly, remembering just in time that real royalty shouldn't be self-deprecating. "Speaking of which," she went on, "I'm afraid I have some business to attend to this afternoon, and I really need to get going." *Such as a cold shower, a hot cup of coffee or three, and picking out the perfect dinner outfit,* she added silently, but if André was going to be coy about his business, then she could be coy, too.

The planes of his olive-skinned face registered what looked like genuine disappointment, and Jane felt a deeply pervasive desire to stay. But she had more pressing things to focus on than romance—or lust—and so, she reluctantly stood and brushed the lace layers of her skirt smooth. "I hope I will see you again while we are here," André told her, his black eyes following her movements intently. "It would be a crime to ignore *all* pleasure in favor of . . . business."

Jane smiled; he had a point. She really couldn't spend every moment stalking the Dorans, anyway. "I couldn't agree more," she told him sincerely before turning on one heel and sauntering toward the elevators, allowing her long legs to pull her hips into a gentle sway that she knew he would be watching. As the doors closed behind her, she felt a smile tugging at her lips. *Being Ella has definite perks.*

Chapter Twelve

"So *then* he acts like he doesn't even remember me telling him about the opera—not just that it was that Friday, but *at all*. But if he really didn't, then why did he think we weren't going to that vapid Nathan girl's insufferably dull soirée in the first place? But that's just the way he thinks: *his* plans are important, and if he didn't make them then he must not have any. No, no; if we're not going to his precious Nathans', then he must be free on Friday, so he can get smashed with those frat-boy friends of his and wake the whole house up on his way back in. *And* very nearly damage some antique sideboard thing that's been in the family for about a gazillion years."

"And *that's* how he fractured his shin?" Jane asked hopefully. It wasn't that Laura didn't have valid complaints about her husband's behavior. She just had a *lot* of them, and Jane was beginning to realize that she'd only ever heard the tip of the iceberg during her stint as Laura's soon-to-be second-cousin-in-law. They had barely started the main course and Jane could already feel her eyes glazing over. She had come to dinner prepared to Be a Good Friend to Laura, but hadn't realized that nodding and making sympathetic noises was virtually all that would be asked of her.

That and eating well, Jane admitted to herself, twisting a couple of strands of squid-inked linguini around her fork. The restaurant Laura had chosen featured five-star cuisine, twenty-seven varieties of vodka, and the priciest commodity in Manhattan: elbow room. The high, vaulted ceiling emphasized the sheer extravagance of the space around them, which was dotted with tables with yellow tablecloths set just far enough apart to seem truly private. Although she was aware of the low buzz of conversation around them, there was really nothing nearby enough to compete with the long string of Blake-bashing coming from her dinner companion.

"So he says," Laura snorted inelegantly, taking a sizable sip of her cabernet.

Jane, who had no idea what her new friend's skepticism was even implying (was the shin not fractured? fractured in some other way?), fought the temptation to do the same. She had, after all, started unusually early with her Manhattans, and she needed to stay relatively sharp now. "Men." She sighed ambiguously, rolling her eyes and hoping that the gesture would be enough to prove she had been listening. A woman in a low-necked blue dress about a hundred yards away looked faintly familiar, and Jane amused herself by trying to imagine her striking features framed by tabloid headlines. *Game-show hostess? Reality-show personality? Weather girl?*

Laura's Nars-glossed lower lip stuck out in a sudden moody pout. "I know," she agreed dejectedly, "but I really just don't know what else I could do."

She really didn't, Jane realized sadly. Even with Ella's (fictional, but empowering) example, it would never in a million years occur to Laura to simply pick up and leave Blake Helding. Jane had always assumed that she stayed for the money, or the connections, or even out of fear of Belinda Helding. But now she was seeing a new side of Laura: one that thrived on the drama. She might find a happier relationship than her current one, but that happiness could never make up for losing her license to complain and curry sympathy from her friends. And since, as far as Jane could tell, Blake felt roughly the same way about his wife, they were pretty much stuck with each other.

As if responding to some cue only she could hear, Laura straightened up sharply, her whole face brightening at once. "So tell me about *your* love life," she demanded.

A bow-tied waiter discreetly deposited a fresh roll on Jane's bread plate with a pair of silver tongs. She tore it open, releasing a little cloud of steam and flour. *Well, I'm married to a co-fugitive I haven't seen since our wedding because I found out he was a murderer, and I kind of had a crush on this guy whose sister was nearly killed because of me, so I'm avoiding him and now he seems to be dating my roommate anyway, and then there was this hottie at the bar this afternoon who definitely was flirting with me. No, no, and yes.* "I actually met someone interesting today," she began awkwardly, but didn't get any further before Laura pounced.

"Oh my *God*! Already? You don't waste any time, do you? Tell me everything. What does he look like—wait, did you meet him on the Upper East? I might know him. I mean, I assume he's, you know . . . *our level,* right? Oh, tell me you're not rebounding with someone totally inappropriate; it's so cliché, really. Although I have to admit that the fling I almost had with this *adorable* pool boy in St. Barth's was so hot it *still* gets me through some long nights, so maybe there's something to be said for inappropriate, as long as you don't go doing anything silly like marrying him, or leaving a marriage, or bankrolling his 'dancing' career." She sighed, her pale, watery eyes far away.

Finally, a story I want to hear! Jane leaned forward a little in her chair, but this apparently only served to remind Laura that Ella hadn't answered her barrage of questions yet. "So? What's he like?"

"Different from my ex," Jane answered carefully, sweeping some imaginary crumbs from the yellow tablecloth; that much was certainly true. "I met him at my hotel, actually. So it was in your—our—neighborhood, but he's not from here."

Laura clicked her tongue against her laser-whitened teeth. "Not local. Bad sign. Unless, of course, he's from somewhere fabulous and you two could split your time between here and there. I've always wanted to try Dubai, haven't you?"

"We just met today," Jane pointed out sensibly, "so I think planning our second home together is a little premature. Besides, he's from Romania. Love the accent, but aside from that, no thanks, you know?"

"Romania?" Laura was sitting up straight again, her glass frozen halfway to her lips. "About thirty, thick black hair, moves beautifully, wears a little too much leather for an American but it totally works on him?"

"He looked a little younger than that, I thought," Jane offered lamely, but the rest of Laura's description sounded suspiciously accurate. "He said his name was André."

"That's it!" Laura cheered, drawing surprised looks from some of the closer tables that she seemed completely oblivious to. "André Dalcaşcu. I met him last week, and then my mother-in-law basically *forced* me to take his sister shopping yesterday after brunch. Let me tell you: I *needed* that champagne we all had! That Katrin woman barely speaks in full sentences, and she *never* smiles. I mean, I'm all for feminism and all that, but it's possible to go overboard with the 'I am woman, hear me roar' crap, don't you think? But she goes stomping around like she's in the middle of World War III. It wouldn't surprise me if she carried a *gun* in that giant clunky purse of hers, although she'd probably prefer a machete. They don't let you carry those in New York, do they? Prawn?"

Jane blinked rapidly, trying to sift through the tangential mess of words. She could rule out the offered prawn right away, which she did with a shake of her head and an "I'm full" pat of her stomach. Laura had definitely mentioned something during brunch the day before about a dreaded trip to Bendel's, but Jane hadn't been paying enough attention to remember the context. *How the hell am I supposed to know when she's telling me something important?* For all she knew, it could eventually become a matter of life and death to know whether New York allowed one to carry a concealed machete—or maybe to know that Laura had never been to Dubai. But it was impossible to retain every detail of Laura's stream-of-consciousness revelations, so Jane suspected that she would spend most of her time just trying to keep up. "You know André, then?" *I think she said that, somewhere in there.*

"Oh, *he's* a catch," Laura confirmed, nodding sagely. "Maybe not for long term, because you wouldn't want to be stuck with that battle-ax of a sister, but he seems to have inherited *all* the charm in the family. I spent pretty much their entire welcome party just watching that man work the room. Of course, Auntie Lynne spent it fuming that after we'd gone all-hands-on-deck—like, they called Ford McCarroll back from fucking Sri Lanka—the Dalcaşcus only sent two people. *Two!* But then she decided that it wasn't so much an insult as a sign that they were less . . . they couldn't afford to send more. And it works for us if they're, um, cash-poor, I guess, so then she was all happy again. Which I was already, because instead of trying to control every little thing in the world I was just focusing on André's ass in these fabulous leather pants he had on."

I totally get that, Jane thought fervently, but just then a memory clicked into place. "Welcome party? So he's on the other side of that merger thing you mentioned yesterday, along with the woman you had to take shopping?"

She clutched her fork so hard that the handle bit into her palm, but Laura was too busy chatting to notice. "Yeah, that's Lynne's big thing. It's really like she can't cope without a giant project. There was Malcolm's wedding for a couple of months, and then, well, you probably know all about *that* fiasco. And she's still in the papers sounding all panicked about it, but not even two weeks had gone by before she was completely focused on this wild intercontinental merger business. She's just dropping quotes to reporters now and then, but behind closed doors she's totally over it. Honestly, can you even blame her son for taking off? I mean, I'm totally against drugs, but who *wouldn't* have some problems, growing up like he did? Obviously Belinda screwed up Blake about thirty different ways, but his poor cousin probably got it even worse."

Jane felt almost winded by the time Laura finished speaking.

Why isn't Lynne worried about Malcolm—does she know something about where he is? Does Laura really believe the drug nonsense? Who the hell are these people, and how did I find myself needing to get even more mixed up with them? "Malcolm, um, Doran?" she asked casually, although she felt fairly sure that the fork would leave a permanent welt on her palm. "I think I read about some drama he had last month. I assumed it would all be settled by now, though."

"Not at *all*," Laura countered, leaning forward conspiratorially. "Lynne's bribing half of South America for information, but so far he's still missing, and the wife, too. And after she threw that wedding! My parents could barely bother to sober up for mine, and God knows Belinda was *no* help. Meanwhile Lynne's flying in caviar from the Caspian and orchids from Cuba, and she'd only known the girl for, like, a month. Blake and I dated for *years*, and . . ."

Jane bit her lip as Laura went further and further off the topic that Jane cared about the most. *South America?* Did Lynne think that he was there somewhere . . . or did she know it? Was Malcolm pinned down, or was he still staying well ahead of the pursuit? Jane had no idea, and she had no way of finding out unless Malcolm came through with his promised e-mail. She checked her phone compulsively, but so far that day all she had gotten was an update from Dee about her awesome first day of work at her totally perfect new job, three ads for cheap Canadian medications, nine requests from total strangers to add Ella Medeiros as a Facebook friend, and yet another discount offer from theknot.com, which apparently was the only entity in the world that hadn't already heard about Jane's disastrous wedding.

She longed to shake Laura until the woman's brassy highlights rang and demand to know what the South America stuff was all about. But she had a plan, she reminded herself firmly, and she didn't have enough time as Ella to screw it up. She had to get into Lynne's house, and no matter how friendly she got with Laura, Laura was just one stepping stone toward the front door. André, however, could turn out to be even more useful, so it was only prudent to keep working on both angles . . . and leave Malcolm out of it altogether.

Jane set her fork back down on the yellow tablecloth, smoothing a stubborn crease in the heavy fabric. She heard the song of clinking crystal somewhere off to her left, and she inhaled deeply and looked up again. "I'll admit, we only just met, but I'm in dire need of a really good rebound, and André could really hit the spot. Do you have any idea what he looks for in a woman? Does he have any hobbies? Is he close with his sister? Should I try to be nice to her, too?"

And, most important, does the next merger-related event call for a plus-one?

Chapter Thirteen

JANE ARRIVED BACK AT THE LOWELL CLOSE TO MIDNIGHT, HER head buzzing with a little too much alcohol and way too much of Laura's gossip. *Some of it was useful,* she reminded herself as she narrowly avoided colliding with the white-jacketed door-man. His face remained impassive, but she noticed that he stood behind the glass door rather than beside it as she passed through. *Occupational hazard,* she guessed, placing one careful ribbon-tied wedge in front of the other on the slick marble floor.

She made her way slowly toward the elevators, but she really wasn't in a mood to sleep yet. Late as it was, she had a lot to think about, and the prospect of doing so in her empty hotel room was not especially appealing. A movement in the lobby bar caught her eye and she turned. The bar area was darker than it had been during the afternoon, lit mainly by little tea-lights on each table. André was seated in an armchair like a delicious sliver of fate, nursing the last few drops of what looked like a snifter of cognac. He had chosen a chair at the edge of the shadowy zone, facing out, and Jane felt absolutely positive that he had been waiting there in the hopes of running into her again.

The certainty mingled with the whiskey in her stomach and warmed her all over, and she pivoted confidently to approach him. The difference in lighting between their two parts of the lobby made her feel as if she were on a stage, crossing it under a spotlight while he watched from the audience. His black eyes followed her every movement appreciatively, and by the time she reached the chair opposite his, she felt as though she might burst into flames. "You should be careful," she told him, folding her long body into the blue-cushioned chair across from his. "I might think that you never leave here."

Laura hadn't known a ton of useful information about André, but it was more than Jane had known before. Unfortunately, all of it added up to "Trouble with a capital *T*," but Jane reminded herself that she wasn't looking for the love of her life while living undercover.

He smiled slowly before raising two imperious fingers in the general direction of the bartender. "I find the company more pleasant here than any place I have been in New York so far," he told her with a courteous nod. The bartender deposited two fresh snifters of cognac on their table, then discreetly retreated back into the shadowy, wood-paneled bar.

Jane's better judgment suggested that she should avoid the golden-red liquid in front of her. But André raised his glass in a toast and waited expectantly, and wasn't she supposed to be getting closer to him? Besides, she didn't really want to do any more thinking at the moment, and besides *that*, it had been months since she had had a proper glass of cognac, and the sweet, earthy smell wafting from the glass told her unambiguously that this was the good stuff. She raised her glass and tapped it briefly against André's, sending a soft, chiming note through the empty bar, and sipped. It was sweet, smoky, and strong, like almost-burnt caramel, and she let it spread across her tongue and down her throat hungrily. It tasted just like home.

"It's always inspiring to meet a man who enjoys his own company," she observed tartly once the burning of the cognac had passed. She and Laura had both concluded that André was the type of man who enjoyed pursuit all out of proportion to his enjoyment of the woman being pursued. Flirting with him, she guessed, would mostly be about resisting the force of his attention long enough to intrigue him, and if there was one thing France had taught her, it was the vital importance of being intriguing. She had gotten a slow start in the art form under the watchful eye of overprotective, thoroughly American Gran, but Elodie and her other Parisian friends had been more than happy to provide remedial classes until Jane was nearly as expert as they were.

André smiled and leaned back in his chair, all signs pointing to intrigued. *Not that I have to guess what he's thinking,* Jane realized abruptly. *I'm a freaking mind-reader, right?* It wasn't a talent she had ever been very comfortable using, especially on people she knew and liked. But, however likable she found André at the moment, this was still business; it was only masquerading as pleasure. *And a convincing masquerade it is,* Jane admitted, sipping at her cognac and continuing to banter on autopilot. *But I really need to remember that I know better.*

She inhaled steadily and began to pull at the threads of her power, but although she could feel its strange hum in her veins, it was hard to find; harder to hold on to. *It's late,* she reminded herself, conveniently ignoring the other plausible culprit swirling in the cut-crystal snifter in her right hand. She reached again and missed; it was like trying to lift water in an open hand. Still, there was no harm in trying, so she focused the scattered sparks of magic on André's mind, opened her own, and listened hard.

Nothing.

She felt herself almost physically repelled by his brain, or, rather, by something just in front of it, keeping her away. She rallied her power and tried again, but there was just a smooth wall and no way in. Jane sat back in disappointment, and had to remind herself sternly to keep smiling; keep flirting; keep playing hard to get. Suddenly, *André* was the uncatchable quarry.

It's late, she repeated to herself, *and I've been drinking. But still, I should be able to see something in there, even if it's just what's in the front of his mind right this moment. Unless he's a witch, which is genetically impossible, or ... related to some.*

Jane almost laughed aloud as the realization struck her. "*Magic calls to magic,*" Malcolm had told her. The overriding, unthinking chemical attraction between two people with magic in their genes made it hard to think about anything else. It felt like true love, like soul mates, like meeting someone made just for her. The feeling was so basic and primal, so instinctual, that it never seemed to occur to her it might be supernaturally enhanced. She had felt it with Malcolm, then with Harris, and Malcolm's crazy brother, Charles, had obviously felt it with her. *Of course,* someone she found as appealing as she found André couldn't be anything but a son of a witch. *Is there anyone in this damned town who isn't?*

Still, she decided, her mind starting to drift pleasantly from the alcohol, there was no reason to run the other way. So the Dalcaşcus were magical. This was definitely an important piece of a bigger puzzle that she needed, at some point, to try to fit together. At some point when she was sober, preferably. But in the meantime, André himself was just a man, no matter what strangeness ran in his blood. He might be magical, but the rules were the rules: he couldn't *do* magic. *I can just enjoy this moment now, and then worry about strategy and implications and all that crap afterward,* she decided thickly, remembering almost too late to chuckle throatily at a double entendre of André's.

She stood, stretching to her full height and trying to ignore the gentle spinning of the room. "The company here *is* good," she declared boldly, "but I'm getting tired of the view. Any suggestions?"

André stood as well, stepping gracefully around the table between them to offer her his arm. "The view from my suite is exceptional," he murmured, his breath sending shivers down the back of her neck.

She let him steer her into the still-waiting elevator, where his arm unlinked from hers and slid around her waist. His hand traced the hem of her emerald silk halter top, finding and exploring the space where it met her skirt. His warm, rough fingers brushed the smooth skin of her waist and she closed her eyes. When the elevator stopped, she started forward, eyes still closed, André's hand pressed against the small of her back.

His suite looked something like hers, but a bit smaller and with its parts rearranged into an unfamiliar pattern. His sitting room was to the left of the hall rather than the right. She saw the cloudy gray marble of the kitchen a bit farther along, and caught a glimpse of the down comforter on his king-size bed through the open door at the very end. It looked inviting, and she knew it was probably just as comfortable as hers. But she was enjoying herself, and she wanted to draw these moments out. Her shoes tapped gently a few times on the chocolate-colored floorboards before she stepped onto the thick, pale carpet of the sitting room. In the darkness, the low couches and the heavy walnut coffee table created obstacles that made her move even more slowly and carefully. The hairs standing up on the back of her neck told her that André was navigating the room just as slowly a few steps behind her. She drifted toward the tall windows that faced tree-lined Sixty-Third Street; the lights along Madison Avenue were just visible through a corner of the glass panes. André caught her wrist and spun her toward him, and she forgot all about the view outside. She was too busy taking in his thick eyelashes, the shadow of stubble under his olive skin, the half-amused arch of his eyebrows that was echoed in the turn of his lips that were moving steadily, inevitably, closer to hers.

He kissed her softly the first time, then again with more intensity, and then she felt the magic in her blood catch fire as he drove her back against the window with so much force that she briefly wondered if the glass would crack. His tongue parted her lips as his fingers found the hem of her top again. This time, when he found it, he pulled it up roughly, breaking their kiss just long enough to pull the scrap of green silk over her head and drop it somewhere behind him. Fortunately, the rest of their clothes could come off while allowing their mouths to stay locked, and for a long moment Jane found herself pressed between the cool glass behind her and André's smoldering body in front of her, both touching every inch of her bare skin. *Not mine,* she reminded herself, *Ella's. Who cares who's scandalized?*

But André apparently had a bit more of a sense of decorum left.

He whirled her away from the window, twining his leg around hers so that she lost her balance and her weight was entirely in his arms. Then he set her down on the nearest taupe couch, and followed her body hungrily with his own. He entered her immediately, without hesitation or warning, but she found that her body was fully ready for him, and her back arched so hard that she thought she might leave the couch entirely. Then he was driving her back down into the thick fabric of the cushion, his mouth roaming across her neck and collarbone as he thrust. Her hands glided across his back, and then she felt a sudden spasm of heightened pleasure and her fingernails bit into his skin as her back tried to arch up again. He caught her wrists deftly, one at a time, and pinned them gently above her head.

In the darkened room, she could still see his even darker eyes and the hint of a smile on his lips. Acting on impulse, she drove one heel into the back of the couch and flipped him, their still-interlocked bodies free-falling to the ground. He grunted a little as his back struck the plush carpet, but the smile was still in place, and she pulled herself upright to straddle him, her body shining in the moonlight, her now-freed hands winding ecstatically in her own hair. He came with a final series of powerful thrusts, and the change of the rhythm triggered shockwaves in her own body, and she leaned down again, kissing him helplessly, until they passed.

After a long few minutes, she rolled to the side, separating from him. He stayed where he was, breathing deeply, but his hand snaked out and circled her wrist again, this time in a much firmer grip. "Don't go far," he murmured forcefully, and then released her.

Chapter Fourteen

JANE KEPT HER OVERSIZE SUNGLASSES ON UNTIL SHE REACHED the door of her Greenwich Village apartment. When her retinas were assaulted by the sun streaming through the living room's massive wall of windows, she wished that she had kept them on, but she reminded herself that she had earned every stab and throb of her hangover and soldiered on.

"J— Ella!" Dee squealed happily, poking her head out from the kitchen. Jane winced at the noise, but the smells wafting through the doorway made her cautiously optimistic about her ability to keep food down.

"You will not *believe* the day I had yesterday," she told Dee, keeping her own voice intentionally soft. "But before I go there, is there coffee? Mine's gone." She waved her empty Starbucks cup pointedly: the venti Americano had lasted her about two cross-town blocks in traffic. "Next time I'm *so* just taking the subway.

But changing trains in these shoes—have you *seen* these shoes? They're—"

She eventually stopped rambling when she realized that Dee was waving frantic complex signals at her with one hand: the hand, Jane realized, that was hidden from the rest of the kitchen by the doorframe. "Hi, Ella," Dee supplied in the awkward sudden silence, her throaty voice as cheerful as possible while pointedly emphasizing Jane's cover name.

"Hi," Jane began again. "Um . . . coffee?"

"We were just having some. There's toast, too, which you look like you could use."

We? Jane frowned a little, then more as the wrinkling made her headache even worse. "Hi, Harris." She sighed as she rounded the corner to find him sitting at the spindly kitchen table. *Duh.*

He waved a slice of bacon at her cheerfully, his mouth already full of what looked like French toast. He wore jeans and a white V-neck tee that had a couple of pinpoint holes in it from frequent laundering. His usually sparkling green eyes were still a little puffy and bleary. *He slept here,* she realized. He looked like a natural part of the apartment, as if he were completely comfortable there. *Didn't take him long to make himself at home,* she thought shrewishly, then grimaced at her own meanness.

Dee pressed a mug of black coffee into her hand and Jane finished nearly half of it in one scalding swallow. "Long night?" Harris asked amiably, having finally finished chewing.

"Apparently those are going around," Jane replied loftily. Under his light dusting of freckles, Harris blushed. *Leave it alone,* Jane told herself, but part of her was quietly gleeful at his embarrassment.

"Harris took me out to celebrate my first day of work," Dee inserted between them, not looking embarrassed in the slightest, and this time her pointed emphasis was on Harris's name. "Ella, have you ever been to Masa Bar? It blew my mind. And then, of course, we went and finished the job with tequila."

"I'm so sorry I had to miss it," Jane told her, more or less sincerely. Even if it stung a little to watch Dee and Harris together, she knew she should be there for her friend. At the very least, she should *want* to. "My work ran really, really late."

"Clearly," Dee agreed, her amber eyes raking over every wrinkle in Jane's clothes. Jane, who had fished them off a still-sleeping André's floor just an hour before and was painfully aware that they looked a little too "lived-in" for eight in the morning, scowled at her. Dee's eyes came to rest on a substantial bruise that was starting to surface under the bare, dark skin of Jane's left arm. Jane, suddenly and vividly recalling the splintering crash against André's coffee table that had put it there during Round Three, decided to scowl at her plate instead.

Harris's green gaze flickered back and forth between the two women, watching them like an approaching storm cloud. He stuffed two more pieces of bacon into his mouth while Jane and Dee both sulked in their opposite corners of the narrow kitchen, chewing and swallowing in record time. "I should go," he declared abruptly, pushing his chair back and depositing his plate in the dishwasher in one elegant movement. "I just need my . . . um . . ." He flushed again, glancing at Dee but studiously avoiding Jane's eyes.

"In front of the couch," Dee told him, as discreetly as she could manage with Jane sitting right there.

Harris kissed her quickly on the cheek and then strode away into the living room, where he scooped a pale-green button-down shirt off the floor. He fastened it as he moved toward the door. He kept his head down, but Jane could still see his blush. When he was halfway through the door, he politely hesitated to call, "Bye, Ella, nicetoseeyou," before pulling it shut behind him with a solid thud.

"So," Dee said, turning a black rubber spatula over and over in her tawny, calloused hands.

"So," Jane echoed, swirling the dregs of her coffee in the thick white mug and wishing for more.

Suddenly Dee was a flurry of tangled hair and long, golden limbs, and within seconds Jane was facing a plate piled with French toast and bacon. "So my new job is *awesome*," Dee went on, apparently deciding to go first. "Way better than the bakery, because our clients want all kinds of things and I'm completely in charge of the desserts. More variety *and* more responsibility, and Kate—I told you about Kate, right? You never really know with start-up caterers; half of them are just bored home cooks who have no idea what they're doing. But I can actually *learn* from this woman, and she was showing me some of her past menus and I couldn't believe it. So then we spent all day prepping for this huge birthday thing on Wednesday, and I was watching her work and it was incredible! I guess the birthday girl has a house in Bali, and so her sister wanted a 'tropical theme,' so I'm sitting there doing my little pineapple custards like it's 2002, and Kate's like, 'Okay, now I'm going to brine this suckling pig.' In Manhattan; seriously."

There was more—a lot more—but Jane tried to tune it out with her chewing. She was happy that Dee was happy, really. And Kate the Caterer sounded awesome. And, she reminded herself, Dee had had to leave her job, her apartment, and her life thanks to Jane in the first place. She had helped Jane when Jane had needed help, and she had paid a heavy price for it. *But do I have to hear every single detail of how the woman rolls her own noodles at this hour of the morning?*

Jane chewed the inside of her bottom lip between bites of breakfast. *I'm jealous again,* she realized with a pang. It was certainly true that Dee had lost a lot because she had helped Jane, but Jane had lost a lot, too. And, unlike Dee, Jane still had a ton of difficult and dangerous work to do before she could hope to return to any kind of normalcy. *Meanwhile she's got a cute boyfriend and an awesome new boss, and I'm drinking half the day and sleeping with a completely unsuitable guy I'm trying to use for access to my mortal enemy's fortress.* It wasn't Dee's fault, she knew, but it wasn't fair, either.

"So, um, do you want an ice pack or anything?"

Realizing that Dee had apparently finished the rundown of how great her own life was, Jane glanced up. *My arm,* she realized. *Good thing she can't see my hip. After we broke that vase . . .* "I'm fine," she said out loud, grateful for the change of topic, at least. "I met a guy."

Dee, ignoring her refusal, wrapped a bag of frozen peas in a dishtowel and pressed it against Jane's arm. It stung, then ached. "An enemy?" Dee guessed sympathetically.

"A means to an end," Jane replied grimly, and told her everything she had learned about the Dorans and the Dalcaşcus. She sketched her plan to manipulate both families through André, drawing patterns in her maple syrup with her fork in order to avoid eye contact. She had made real progress, surely, but instead of confident, she mostly felt uncomfortable.

Dee looked concerned, but she refrained from commenting on Jane's recent redefinition of "unsafe sex." "Well, you have a plan," she mused delicately, although her distaste showed in the tension of her full mouth. "Two, actually, because befriending Laura could still totally work." Jane twisted her own mouth into a noncommittal shape. "Okay, but as long as you're . . . involved . . . with this André guy, I guess we'd better get the most out of it. I mean, he must be newsworthy in his own right, right?"

Jane frowned. "I'd never heard of him."

"You'd never heard of the Dorans, either," Dee pointed out patiently, "but that doesn't mean that the tabloids hadn't. And if Lynne is dealing with André and his sister, then they must have something she wants but can't just throw her weight around and take. So they must be on her level somehow, which means there's a good chance that Page Six will be interested in what they're up to, where they're going, and who they're . . . dating."

Jane winced at the euphemism but mostly had to agree. "You think gossip columnists would be interested in me if they think there's an 'us'?" She felt a tingling in her biceps that spelled the beginning of numbness, and she set the bag of peas on the edge of the table. A fat brown sparrow settled on the windowsill above the sink, tapped the brick with its beak a few times, and then took off again.

"I think they'd be interested in you anyway, *Baroness*, but they've never heard of you before, since you didn't exist before. And if you had a debutante ball for yourself or whatever and tried to publicize it, they'd probably have a lot of questions about your background that we can't answer. But if you're just *with* someone who's already tabloid-ready on his own, you're in the story without being the story. And it might even make the Dorans curious to meet you, which I'm sure André will be happy to help them out with."

Jane steepled her fingers together on the table, examining the pale half-moons that stood out against the dark skin of her nail

beds. "Shouldn't you be off masterminding a coup d'état somewhere in Africa?"

Dee chuckled hoarsely, and Jane felt a slight lessening of the
new awkwardness between them. "Their puff pastry leaves something to be desired," she replied airily, and then sat up straighter.
"Although Kate showed me this thing where you just take a spray
bottle filled with tap water, and . . . it's a revelation, seriously.
Anyway, I can call a couple of tip lines and say I'm an employee
at the hotel or something. I know the kind of rumors they like to
print: I'm pretty sure I can get some press about your . . . relationship."

"Thanks," Jane told her, sincerely but with renewed stiffness.
She wished that she could relax more, but it still felt like there was
a short circuit somewhere in their usual, easy rapport. *I've got a
silly crush on her new boyfriend, and she's worried I'm in over my head with
mine,* she pointed out to herself gently. *We'll both get over it.*

"We should probably be ready for you to get invited to the
house anytime; that part could be hard to predict," Dee went on
pragmatically. "And we don't know how much time you'll have
alone to go looking for Annette's old room or her things, so I was
thinking you might need some magic ready to help you look. I
don't know any spells that would help, but we could go by Misty's
when I'm done with work, and—"

"That's okay," Jane told her abruptly. "I've got nothing but free
time. I'll go over to Book and Bell myself in a little bit. Misty'll
probably want to inspect her handiwork, anyway," she added in
a not-quite-successful attempt at levity, waving her left hand to
indicate her face and body.

Dee's smile was a fraction too late and too wide, but Jane told
herself there would be plenty of time to shore up their friendship

later. She had made huge strides in her crazy mission already, but there was still a long and difficult road ahead: getting into the mansion, finding something of Annette's, finding Annette herself, and then bringing her home. *And then I can focus on being as happy as she seems to be lately, instead of being all grouchy about it.*

In the meantime, the best thing she could do would be to put some physical distance between herself and Dee. And if she got some research done in the process, so much the better.

She pushed her chair back from the table and slid her syrupy plate beside Harris's in the dishwasher. She crossed through the living room, studiously not looking at the spot on the pale-gold boards of the floor where Harris's shirt had been, and moved with relief into the relative darkness of the hallway. Her entire body ached in one way or another. Research would have to wait; her top priorities were a long bath and a short nap.

Chapter Fifteen

THE UNEVEN FLOORBOARDS SQUEAKED UNDERNEATH THE THIN red carpet of Book and Bell as Jane stepped inside. A tiny bell jangled above the door, and Misty turned her cloud of frizzy blond hair toward the sound. The Wiccan's face didn't register any kind of familiarity, though, and Jane reminded herself that she wasn't herself—literally. She had opened her mouth to explain when she noticed a college-age girl with skinny jeans and punk-short black hair leafing through a copy of *Tea Leaves and Chicken Bones: A Modern Girl's Guide to the Secrets of the Universe*. The girl didn't look like the type to be following tabloid drama, but Jane still hesitated to broadcast her real name within earshot of strange New Yorkers.

She sidled up to the pressboard counter instead. As she approached, Misty's right hand disappeared beneath the counter. The older woman's eyes remained calm, but fixed unwaveringly on Jane. She realized that Misty either had a panic button back there, or something more sinister and supernatural waiting for people who came into her store looking as cagey as "Ella" probably looked right now.

"Misty," she blurted out, and the shopkeeper's blue eyes narrowed suspiciously. "I'm Dee's new roommate," Jane rushed on. "My name is Ella. We were supposed to meet this weekend, but you had to leave the party before I got home." She set her own left hand on the counter for emphasis, and saw Misty's eyes dart to the plain silver ring that had held Celine's magic until Jane had arrived to inherit it. It looked like a perfectly smooth band with beveled edges, but she would also once have sworn that it was covered in ancient carvings. Lynne and Malcolm had both recognized it on sight, and Dee had noticed something strange about it before she had even known for sure that witches were real. Jane felt certain the ring would vouch for her among people who knew magic, even if she couldn't exactly say why.

Misty nodded curtly, her right hand returning to rest on the top of the counter, and Jane relaxed a little. "Well, any friend of Dee's is more than welcome to come browse anytime, but I get the feeling that you're looking for something a little more specific." She glanced at the punk-haired girl, who didn't look up or indicate that she was paying any attention to them at all.

But then, Jane thought, *isn't that exactly how an eavesdropper would act?* Fortunately, she had spent enough time in the shop to know that there was a simple solution to the problem. "I think you keep what I'm here for in the back room," she announced casually, and Misty smiled in apparent satisfaction.

"Things are a little disorganized in there right now," she answered, swishing toward the curtain divider in a cloud of curling hair and gypsy skirts. "I'll show you where to look."

Jane followed, her mind full of her previous trips to the shop's tiny back section. It had the same worn red carpet as the front of the store, but instead of the attractive displays of crystals, candles, and silver jewelry that cluttered the main selling floor, every inch of the wall space in back was devoted to books. There was a small triangular table in one corner, and a few sturdy wooden chairs that reminded Jane of extra pieces from a public school. She had come here with Dee and Harris and learned to use her magic deliberately for the first time, back when it had been a cool new secret and she hadn't realized just how scared she should have been. She sighed a little at the memory, and Misty spun to face her.

"Seven hells, Jane," she half-whispered. "Dee said it worked, but this is amazing!" She stepped a little closer, examining Ella's face. Her scrutiny bordered on intrusive, but Jane reminded herself that her curiosity was natural—and she was entitled to it, and more, after all of the help she had given. "I thought for sure there would be something to recognize," Misty murmured. "Something around the eyes, maybe. But even when I know it's you, I can't tell."

"Neither can anyone else so far," Jane confirmed. "You found exactly the spell I needed."

Misty's un-glossed lips pressed into a smile. "Something tells me that my reward for such good work is another try at a wild-goose chase."

Jane blushed a little. "Dee and I were talking about the next few steps of the plan," she admitted, "and she did suggest that you might be able to help me plan ahead, spell-wise."

"Of course I can," Misty agreed amiably, pouring tea from a cast-iron pot into a waxed paper cup. She folded out the handles and passed it to Jane. "But that's not why you're here."

Jane sat heavily in one of the wooden chairs. It was a little lower than she remembered, and she was a lot taller, so she had to spend a few seconds wobbling and trying not to spill her tea. "Things are just a little out of control already," she admitted, "and while I've made all this progress in just a few days, I feel like I'm getting dragged along. And then I go home and realize that I'm still so, so far away from getting back to a safe, normal, happy life. Besides," she added guiltily, sipping her tea, "on top of all of it I've got a hangover. So."

"You sound like you could use more than a couple of 'Blessed be's,'" Misty agreed wryly. "I'd offer to spike your tea, but your aura's not exactly calling out for hair of the dog. What you need, my dear, is a project."

"I really just came for a spell," Jane pointed out hesitantly.

Ignoring her feeble protest, Misty poked her head around the black curtain divider into the shop's front room. Apparently satisfied that no one was stealing or waiting for help, she returned her full attention to Jane. "In that case, there'll be a project for each of us. I'll look up your spell, and you'll read these." She pulled a stack of loosely bound manuscripts from a high shelf.

When she set them on the table, Jane knew at once whose cramped, vertical handwriting she was looking at. "Rosalie Goddard's diaries," she gasped. The pages were yellowed and cracked, and looked exactly as she'd always imagined valuable, old, magic-related documents should look. Rosalie Goddard had literally written the book on real witchcraft before being institutionalized by her horrified family. She had lived and died in the 1600s, but as far as Jane knew, her book still contained the highest fact-to-myth ratio of any that were available to the general public. Some of it was nonsensical and plenty had to be just plain wrong, but enough of Goddard's claims checked out to make Jane trust the long-lost author instinctively.

"We'd been using it to find some of her source material," Misty reminded Jane, "but there are all sorts of interesting things in there that didn't make it to the published book. It's not organized at all, but you might find something that helps you. And looking for those bits and pieces will help you to get centered again, which, truthfully, it sounds like you need."

Can't really argue with that, Jane agreed silently, pulling the closest manuscript to her and turning it right-side up. "Thanks," she remembered to say as the other woman swirled back through the curtain to watch over the main part of the store, leaving Jane alone with the diaries.

"And if magick is not a tool of the devil or a trick of charlatans, but rather a simple talent of some who walk among us like singing or drawing or shooting?" she read, her mind already settling into the familiar stillness that usually came when Dee talked her into meditating.

> We all know that there's meant to be marks on witches, to show their evil to the world, but evil is, I believe, usually better hidden than all of that. They say that a witch will show its power rather than die, yet while I know of enough executions, I know of no one who has survived by means of visible magic. I can only conclude, therefore, that we huddle like children in the dark, convincing each other that we will know the strange when we see it. There is undoubtedly magic in the world, but why should those who cannot wield it have the power to detect those who can? Should they

not more reasonably be a higher order among us, in plain sight and yet all unseen?

Mother dislikes this new project of mine, but I think Father secretly enjoys my scholarly efforts. He would never say, much less since it would mean to contradict her, but tonight I found a new sheaf of paper in my writing desk that I know was not there in the morning. Either he wishes to help me a little, or perhaps some witch has already learned of my studies and is guiding me in secret. I hope I have been too discreet in my inquiries thus far for the latter, but time will tell.

"'Time' indeed," Jane huffed under her breath, sliding the manuscripts out in a fan. The dates on them spanned six years, and Goddard was already showing signs of being long-winded. But Jane's huffing wasn't entirely sincere: the subject of discovering magic was certainly important to her, and there was something about Goddard's voice that she liked. The second part turned out to be especially useful when it came to maintaining her new calm, because for most of the first volume of diaries, magic barely came up again at all.

Rosalie Goddard was still interested in magic, of course, but she was also a young woman with a lot on her mind.

The preparations are under way for my wedding feast. I know I am of age, and I know John Goddard is a good man and pleasant enough, but even with Mother fretting about the dowry every day I cannot quite believe it is real. My sisters are jealous: Lizzie in particular dreams of being a wife every night, and often during the day while she wakes as well. But this is the only life I have known, in which I am a studious child and John Goddard is the sweet boy down the road who can never quite keep up with us when we run about and play at adventures. He is not even of a height with me yet, although Lizzie feels sure he will grow as tall as his own father. Of course, she also thinks she is a misplaced princess of some faraway kingdom, so—

Jane flipped a few pages, then moved on to the next book. Rosalie was still talking about her life, but now her life was getting more interesting, and Jane read avidly.

"Petru" is not a Nordic name, of course: he says his real father isn't Mr. Thorssen at all, but rather someone from his mother's homeland. She came from somewhere well east of where my family was from in the Old World, before she sailed here with Petru and married. She won't talk about it, and makes us all call him "Peter," which Erica Carter says is because her people are gypsies and she doesn't want people to know now that she is married to a respectable man.

Petru loves Mr. Thorssen like a father, but sometimes I think it must make him sad that his mother never wants to talk about her life before. He was too little to remember anything, and if his mother wishes her former life to be forgotten then he may never know even the smallest details. Sometimes he seems so sad and far away that I wish to take his face in my hands, and I have to remember that a far more appropriate match has already been made for me than a fatherless boy from a nameless country.

It goes without saying that John dislikes Petru intensely, but he is even more baffled by my interest in Sabina Thorssen. She is so lovely and so mysterious, and sometimes I think that even the way she distrusts me makes me more curious about her life on the other side of the ocean. Petru hinted once that her people back there had magic of their own, and Erica insists that gypsies are all just thick with it. I don't know about that, but if I close my eyes and imagine a person who could command unnatural forces, it would be Mrs. Thorssen. Petru says she prays in a language he cannot understand, that she never taught him. Anyone might pray in their own language, of course, Father Rexford says, but Petru says that sometimes he is almost sure she is saying something else.

John jokes that she is a witch all right, but I know he doesn't mean it the way I do. Perhaps I really am as foolish as he says: perhaps I am using these ideas I have become fascinated with to explain my fascination with the Thorssens.

"Spoiler alert: she marries lame-ass John anyway," Jane muttered, a little disappointed. Petru and his mother sounded far more interesting and far less likely to allow their relatives to commit Rosalie to a mental institution down the line when her book tarnished their family's reputation. Jane remembered when, shortly after she had started working at Atelier Antoine, Elodie had discovered just how restrictive Jane's upbringing had been and spent three long months catching her up on the pop culture she should have gotten as a tween. She had the same feeling now as when they had screened *Titanic* in her cozy studio with the (sometimes partial) view of Notre Dame: maybe the story would end differently this time. Maybe Rosalie would live happily ever after; maybe the boat wouldn't sink. *But that's not the way it happened.*

She skipped a few more volumes and opened to a page at random. A familiar name leaped off the page at her instantly. *Ambika.* There must be more than one in the world, but Jane knew immediately in her bones that Rosalie was writing about the one whose name was also carved into marble on the Dorans' wall: the mother of all the witches in the world. The legend was that she had had seven daughters, and left her magic to them when she died. One of those seven had become Jane's ancestor, another one had been Maeve and Harris's, and one had begotten Lynne and her cabal. Jane closed her eyes and pictured the family tree in Lynne's parlor, but she didn't really need to: the first name below Ambika's had definitely been "Hasina."

Jane's eyes swept across the pages, trying to pick up the thread in the dense forest of vertical handwriting. Rosalie was married now, to John, just as Jane knew she would eventually be. And Petru was gone. He had grown up angry and increasingly reckless until he had fled the colonies under a cloud of suspicion related to the mysterious death of a trapper. In the privacy of her diary, Rosalie allowed herself to wonder if some of his newfound violent temper had anything to do with her reluctant refusal to have an affair with him, and her guilt tied her firmly and finally to Sabina Thorssen.

Although Petru's mother had never admitted to being a witch outright, the myths and stories that she told Rosalie to ease her sorrow over her lost son sounded an awful lot like the true ori-

gins of magic in the world. Admittedly, most of Jane's understanding had come from Rosalie's own book and source material,
but enough of the details had been corroborated along the way
by Malcolm, Harris, Gran's letter, and Lynne's marble wall to convince Jane that Rosalie had found her first major lead.

Sabina had taught Rosalie all about Ambika: the only child
of a powerful warlord, who faced ferocious challenges from her
father's subjects when he died. But the gods had touched her,
Sabina said (Rosalie quailed at the plural), and the shamans had
all agreed when she appeared before them glowing with magic
that she should be their queen. The lesser warlords had taken
a little more convincing, but they had fallen into line quickly
enough when Ambika had raised floods and earthquakes to deci-
mate their armies.

However, old age came sooner back in those days, and although Ambika had had seven sons and seven daughters, she
hadn't been able to choose any one of them as the next ruler. So
she had divided her land among her sons and her magic among
her daughters, and then she had closed her eyes and died. Her
daughters, Sabina Thorssen had explained, were as different
as the days of the week. Jane wondered whether she was more
likely the descendant of the one who had used all her power to
manage the weather around her tiny farm, or the one who had
constantly bewitched men into attacking, on her behalf, the
lands that her brothers had inherited. One of them was widely
known as "Amunet the Vengeful." Several had adjectives tacked
on to their names, in fact, but Lynne's ancestress's reputation
was a bit of a puzzle. Although she hadn't lived any longer than
anyone would have expected back in prehistory, according to
Sabina Thorssen, she had been known as "Hasina the Undying."

"But she *did* die," Jane argued with the yellowed page. "You said so yourself. Why would people keep calling her that after they'd buried her? Or is it a figure of speech—like Lynne still has to keep a shrine to her memory somewhere in a closet or something?"

But Rosalie's words couldn't rearrange themselves to answer her questions, of course. Feeling a little silly and a lot more poised than she had that morning, Jane pushed away from the triangular table, replaced the journals on their shelf, and headed out to the front room to thank Misty and return to her mission.

Chapter Sixteen

Two nights later, Jane snuggled closer against André's solid shoulder as the city flashed by in a neon blur. She inhaled his musky cologne, which made her feel almost light-headed. *Must keep watching the street signs,* her brain told her lazily, and she forced her eyes to flicker out the window occasionally. They definitely weren't going to the Dorans' mansion, she realized with a small pang of frustration; that was only a couple of blocks from the Lowell. But the trip was already long enough for her to really feel the effects of André's nearness. She straightened her spine a little, trying to shut out her magical attraction and focus on her plan.

That morning, a note had been delivered to her suite practically begging her to give André something to look forward to by agreeing to accompany to him to a terribly dull work party. Jane had, of course, agreed immediately, although she had waited a cool ninety minutes to inform him of that fact. Playing hard to get for two days while enduring an unexpectedly physical craving for André's company hadn't been easy, but it had definitely been worth it. *And it's worth keeping up now.*

She forgot her strategy for a few blocks in the lower Thirties, when his hand found its way onto her knee and then began a purposeful slide upward, toward her spangly silver minidress. It suddenly felt both too short and too long at the same time.

"You blind, buddy?" their cabdriver shouted belligerently to the driver of a city bus in the next lane, and both Jane and André jumped a little. The bus driver responded by flipping the cabbie off with an exaggerated flourish. Their spat escalated quickly from there, ending in vague threats and the suggestion of a drag race that was so ludicrous André lost his focus long enough for Jane to regain her own.

She emerged from the taxi in the East Village feeling as though she had just surfaced after nearly drowning, and she pulled the humid city air deep into her lungs as the cab sped away. "This way," André murmured, his lips brushing her hair, and for a moment she thought she might begin to sink again into the animal scent of him.

She turned her head away carefully as they made their way across the street: she felt sure she would need her wits about her. André steered her to a nondescript doorway, which opened as they drew close to it. A massive bouncer nodded politely, and then closed the door with a soft but firm click when they had passed. Jane continued forward into the glass-walled elevator that waited invitingly in front of them, and André joined her, sliding his thumb idly along the small of her back.

The elevator rose smoothly and swiftly, and when it came to a rest, Jane stifled a gasp. They were on the roof, covered only by a

glass-and-wrought-iron canopy that would keep out rain. Tucked
into many of the iron joints were a number of the cylindrical heat
lamps that made Jane think of Parisian cafés. The April air was
still damp and chilly, but under the canopy it felt like a sultry
summer night. Ivy curled up trellises and around the wrought-
iron frames of white-cushioned couches that dotted the flagstone
roof. At the center of it all was the epitome of elegance and charm
herself: Lynne Doran, in a high-collared garnet dress, her chestnut hair forming a perfect twist, a sparkling martini glass in one
hand.

The air rushed out of Jane's lungs, and for a brief moment it felt
as though André's hand on her back was all that kept her upright
and moving forward. *She can't recognize me,* she reminded herself
sternly, trying to shake her muscles out of their rubbery inertia.
She isn't even looking at me.

It was true: although a black-shirted waiter had made a beeline
for the party's newest arrivals, no one else seemed to have noticed
them at all. *It's my job to notice them right now,* she reminded herself,
turning slowly until she had taken in the entire roof. Although
there were plenty of people whom she didn't recognize, familiar
faces dotted the party like fireflies, each one catching Jane's attention in a quick flare. *Blake Helding, Andrew McCarroll, Rolly Mc-
Carroll, Cora McCarroll, Laura Helding* . . . it was like the mansion at
665 Park Avenue had turned itself inside-out on top of this downtown club.

Jane's glance darted warily back to Lynne, but her nemesis
was deeply involved in conversation with a tall, thin woman in a
severe black pantsuit, who had her back to Jane. There was something familiar about her posture, but Jane couldn't place her.

While André made small talk with a distant Helding cousin,

and Jane smiled vapidly at his wife, she sent the tendrils of her mind out toward the woman talking to Lynne. Jane concentrated hard, pushing mentally past the people milling in between, and finally found the woman's mind. Or, more accurately, found the blank wall where the woman's mind should be. *I keep forgetting other people are witches,* she griped silently, and turned her probing attention to the trophy wife directly in front of her. The woman was making an extremely emphatic point about some congressman's recent sex scandal, but the inside of her mind was as firmly barred as the first woman's had been.

Officially weird, Jane decided. Of course, it was possible for this woman to be a witch, too, but she wasn't that much older than Jane, and probably a bit younger than Malcolm. If a practicing witch of his age had been available to marry into the family, Lynne never would have let her wind up with some third cousin. Breathing a little more shallowly now, Jane prodded André's mind, and then bounced her attention to Andrew McCarroll's, then to a stranger in a plum Armani shirt. *Walls, walls, and more walls.* Had she lost her power somehow? With a burst of inspiration, she shot her focus toward a waiter who was winding carefully through the crowd.

The man flinched almost physically under the force of Jane's mind, and she saw everything: his worry over his dog's illness that morning, his grocery list, his shirt size, the way he took his coffee, the phone number one of the guests had just slipped into his pocket. She could see the three friends he had gone to see Aerosmith with, and how much he had lost in an Atlantic City casino the next night, and the mountain of crab legs he had crammed into his mouth at the buffet to try to make up for it. By the time she pulled free, she knew him almost as intimately as she knew herself, and she gagged a little at the unintentional violation of his privacy. André turned toward her, curious and concerned, but she waved his attention away. "I inhaled some bubbles," she explained awkwardly, waving her glass of champagne. André frowned, and she pasted on her old party smile. "Excuse me, please," she added to the cousin and the trophy wife, backing out of their little circle and heading for the fresher air outside of the canopy.

She reached the wrought-iron railing, and leaned out slightly over the busy street below. *It's a business event thrown by two magical families,* she mused, the thoughts snapping into place like interlocking blocks. *Anyone whose mind could be read is a weak link.* It would only make sense that the active witches present would protect their own family members' minds from being read. *No wonder Lynne was annoyed that the Dalcaşcus only sent two people. Her side is stuck blocking the minds of half of Manhattan, while André is the only one his sister has to worry about.* Most of the attendees probably had at least a little magical heritage, Jane guessed, which would make them harder to read than most people to begin with. But it still must have taken a huge amount of power and concentration to render their minds completely unreadable.

It seemed like an awful lot of effort, actually, for people as rich and powerful as the Dorans. No matter how alluring the prospect of a good deal was, couldn't they do as well, or nearly as well, without dealing with other witches? That way they would have a major advantage, which was how Lynne preferred to conduct all her business.

Unless, Jane's brain continued on briskly, *it's not really about that kind of "business" at all.* It would undoubtedly be better to treat with nonmagical companies when the stakes were purely financial. And Lynne didn't need more money; she needed more witches.

Young, female witches who could be brought into her family so that she could continue her magical legacy the way she had once tried to do through Jane. *Except this time, instead of murder and seduction, she's inviting their relatives to swank parties,* Jane thought bitterly, kicking at a scuff mark in the flagstone. But her feelings aside, she knew she had hit upon something. *"Cash-poor," Laura called them, but they've got plenty of money. She meant magic.* Lynne had magic, so the Dalcaşcus must have witches. It wasn't a merger at all: it was an alliance.

And I'm stuck right in the middle of it, she realized suddenly, feeling more than one pair of eyes on her. She looked up and saw Laura look quickly away and move off into the crowd. From one dark corner, Belinda Helding was staring at her thoughtfully, but unlike her daughter-in-law, she didn't bother to hide what she was doing when Jane met her cold, pewter gaze. Jane's eyes located Laura's asymmetrical taupe cocktail dress again, this time next to Lynne's sleek garnet one. The two women were whispering, their shining coiffed heads so close they were nearly touching.

Laura is suspicious, Jane decided in a panic. *She met me, and now I'm here, and she knows something's up.* There were at least three witches between Jane and the elevator. She gripped the railing so hard that her knuckles went white, but the interested tilt of Lynne's head was telling her something important, and she concentrated hard. *Dee got me and André onto Page Six,* she reminded herself, feeling a sudden space of calm in her mind. *They can't read my mind, so they'll think André's posse is protecting me, too, which would mean I'm important. They'll be curious, and I can use that.*

Lynne stepped back from her tête-à-tête with Laura and turned her dark eyes to rake Jane over from head to toe. Jane pushed away from the railing before she could talk herself out of it, and

sauntered across the roof toward Lynne. She was amazed at how
steady she felt; even her champagne stayed level in its flute as she
closed the space between them.

"Lady Baroness," Lynne greeted her with an arched eyebrow
that briefly took Jane back three months.

"Mrs. Doran," she replied politely, inclining her head a fraction
of a degree.

"You've made quite the entrance in New York," Lynne observed,
her voice smooth as a polished diamond. "I'm told that André normally goes for women who are more . . . interchangeable."

"Perhaps he's trying to impress you," Jane shot back coolly,
enjoying the fleeting twitch of surprise on Lynne's face. Being a
mystery was much more fun than being the prey, she decided.

"That could be it," Lynne agreed impassively, brushing back
an imaginary stray lock of hair into her flawless twist. "Although
at the moment I'm rather more interested in what *you're* trying
to do."

Out of the corner of her eye, Jane watched the shifting pattern
of people: Laura moving toward Belinda; Cora and André close
together while the naggingly familiar woman in black, still facing
away from Jane, drew nearer to the huddled pair. The woman
in the black suit kissed André quickly on both cheeks, but Jane
still couldn't see her face. Cora and Belinda found each other in
the crowd: identical gray twins in identically unflattering gray
gowns.

"I'm sure my goals wouldn't interest you," Jane answered carefully, "unless I could help you with yours, that is." The slight tension around Lynne's peach-lipsticked mouth told her that her
message had been received clearly.

"While I'm sure you have André wrapped around your lovely

little finger," Lynne drawled with the hint of a threat in her soft voice, "my business is with his sister, Katrin. I'm sorry to say that if you wanted to put your hand into our dealings, you've seduced the wrong sibling."

God, what a world she lives in, Jane thought with a shudder of disgust. *What a world she imposes on the rest of us,* she corrected herself, because technically it was true that she had seduced André to get to Lynne. The fact that her motives were far more personal than Lynne apparently suspected, and that André had been more than willing to cooperate, didn't make it all that much better.

The fact that she murdered my grandmother does. Jane's jaw clenched; she refused to feel any kind of guilt in front of this woman. "Your 'business' with Katrin is your own," she told Lynne firmly, searching her brain for anything that would pique her mother-in-law's interest. *I certainly can't risk mentioning Annette yet.* "I'm more interested in a mutual friend we have. In South America," she added, remembering what Laura had said about Malcolm over dinner the other night. She bit her lip uncertainly; it felt unpleasantly like a betrayal. *But the information ultimately came from Lynne in the first place.* Whether it was true or not, it was nothing new to Lynne, but Jane guessed that it would still get her attention.

Lynne's dark eyes snapped wide, and Jane recoiled instinctively. *Too much attention, maybe,* she quailed, but there was no undoing it now. All she could do was pretend to be holding a better hand than she really was, and that started with not showing weakness. She straightened her long spine and set her shoulders squarely. "First, of course, I have some questions for *you,*" she improvised, hearing an authentic note of boldness in Ella's unfamiliar voice.

A large hand closed painfully around her arm and jerked her back, away from Lynne. For a moment, she saw Cora McCarroll whispering frantically in Lynne's ear, but André spun her around and was half-shoving her toward the glass-walled elevator. "We have to go now," he hissed in her ear, and pushed her inside.

He loomed in front of her, filling her field of vision, but as the elevator started to descend, Jane saw Belinda Helding glaring after it from off to the left. Beside her, Jane saw the tall woman in the black pantsuit, her face obscured by a heat lamp. Laura Helding stood alone to the right of the elevator, and she, too, stared intently at Jane. *I've been made,* Jane realized with absolute certainty, reading her friend's face expertly. She had been naïve to assume that no one would notice that her mind wasn't supposed to be unreadable; someone had.

They know I'm a witch. The elevator doors slid open, and André propelled her out to the street, his face a mask of fury. *He knows I'm a witch.*

It's over.

Chapter Seventeen

JANE OPENED HER EYES AND GLANCED OVER TOWARD THE FRONT door of her suite. She breathed a sigh of relief when she saw that her barricade was still in place: a taupe couch stood on its end behind a walnut hutch, two armchairs, and a rolltop writing desk. The pileup had been a compromise of sorts: her initial instinct had been to flee the hotel, the Dorans, and her assumed identity, and never look back. But although the cab ride back to the hotel with André had been strained, to say the least, he had spent most of it trying to pretend that things were normal.

"Those parties are *so* dull," he had declared in a lousy imitation of a casual tone.

Jane had nodded along, her mind racing. He knew she was a witch, and the information had clearly rattled him. But he seemed determined not to show it. He had even kissed her good-night in the elevator—a long, slow, deep kiss that sent two completely dif-

ferent sets of shivers down her spine and into her legs. She had
ridden the last two floors alone, breathing as hard as if she had
just sprinted a mile. By the time she had stumbled into her suite,
she had decided to wait and see . . . behind a well-reinforced door.

A soft tapping came from the other side, and Jane realized that
it was the sound that had woken her up. "Housekeeping," a tenta-
tive voice warbled from the hallway.

Jane popped out of bed, on the alert and ready to read the mind
outside the door. *Although it's not like I could let her in, anyway,* she realized quickly, and rolled her eyes at herself. The barricade might
realistically gain her a moment or two if angry witches were at
the door, but for anyone else it was just an inconvenience. "Come
back in an hour, please," she called through the door, and heard a
shifting noise as the woman moved along down the hall.

Out of the corner of her eye, Jane saw movement in the bathroom, and she flattened herself against the wall beside the door. It
had been a person, she was sure: tall, with shoulder-length dark
hair. *Like me,* her brain supplied. *Now, anyway.* She sighed heavily;
she had gotten so used to the sight of her new face in the mirror
that it didn't usually startle her anymore. *Will I jump at first when I
see the old Jane again?* she wondered sadly, peering around the doorframe into the bathroom just to be completely sure there was no
one there. Ella's dark, almond-shaped eyes blinked back at her,
and she straightened and returned her attention to her makeshift
barricade.

"All right," she murmured to herself, eyeing the taupe couch
resentfully. "You first."

It took much longer to put her sitting room back in order than
it had to demolish it. Jane felt sweaty and disheveled by the time
she had finished, but with the door unblocked, she felt perversely

unwilling to turn her back on it long enough to take a shower. *I'm losing it,* she decided, but after the previous night's drama it was hard to get her thoughts in order. *But if that's what it takes to relax long enough to brush my teeth . . .*

Something rustled just on the other side of the door, and Jane jumped in the air, stifling a scream. But instead of the wood splintering to reveal a horde of angry witches, a thick ivory card slid anticlimactically under the door of her suite. She clenched her hands into fists, focusing on her breath until her heart stopped racing. Finally, she crouched and scooped up the card, fumbling until it was out of its envelope and right side up. It was unmistakably Lynne Doran's stationery, but it took Jane a moment to make sense of its contents. Instead of the handwritten notes she had grown used to at the mansion, this was a printed invitation. *I guess that's a message all on its own,* she thought, tracing the slightly raised lettering. Lynne had invited Ella to a cocktail party the following Friday . . . at 665 Park Avenue.

"I'm in," she whispered. "How the hell am I in?"

She paced the hall, her bare feet padding on the plush runner. André had clearly intended to bring Ella to the party as titled and tabloided arm candy to impress the Dorans—a tactic Lynne had apparently seen through. Once Jane arrived, though, someone on André's side—maybe the "battle-ax" sister that Laura Helding complained about—had pegged Jane as a witch. The Dalcaşcus couldn't have known at first whether Ella was a Doran spy or a free agent with an agenda, but they had obviously realized quickly that it had been a mistake to allow her anywhere near the pending "merger." But it had gotten completely out of their control, Jane realized thoughtfully, right around the time that she had obliquely mentioned Malcolm to Lynne. Lynne's interest made

Ella too valuable to attack or even just cut off. André would have to keep her close now . . . and his family would be waiting for any chance to turn the tables on her. This wasn't the time to give up on her disguise; it was the time to work it for all she was worth.

She had to be Ella—and only Ella—for a little over a week, and then she would be in the mansion and on to the next step in her search for Annette.

Jane stepped into the dim, sticky-floored bar where she was supposed to be meeting Dee. Jane would be heading into the lion's den tomorrow night, and Dee had agreed to collect the locator spell that Jane would need from Misty and then meet her at a bar near their apartment to explain it to Jane. *Just like the old days,* Jane told herself, recalling all the times the two of them had met secretly to work on Jane's magic, although somehow she didn't quite feel it.

She peered around the dark space doubtfully. The slim triangle of a familiar torso caught her eye almost immediately. "Harris," she blurted out, trying to keep her face as cheerful as possible. *This is her version of being extra-discreet?*

Harris turned and stood, smiling politely, and waited for Jane to sit before he returned to his own stool. "Hi there, Ella," his cool voice rippled. "Hope you don't mind me tagging along on girls' night." He smiled a little more broadly this time, and Jane felt the corners of her own mouth tugging their way up, but inside she was furious. Dee clearly hadn't spilled her secret, but to Jane's whirling mind that made it even worse that she had brought a date.

Hanging around with Ella Medieros right now is nearly as risky as being friends with Jane Boyle was, she thought uncomfortably. Harris's sister, Maeve, had been run down by a taxi for the heinous crime of trying to help Jane, and her recovery had been slow and painful. Yuri had tried to kill Dee in the alley behind her apartment, and Lynne had even brutally beaten her own son when she found out that he had changed sides. Jane had felt awful, even though all three of them had known about the danger . . . and Harris wasn't able to make the same kind of informed decision at the moment.

"Hi," Jane replied awkwardly. She tried to shoot a meaningful glare at Dee, but try as she might, she couldn't seem to catch her friend's eye. Instead, Dee, radiant in a red cowl-necked sweater that was more stylish than anything Jane had ever seen her wear, laughed at Harris's jokes, invented completely unnecessary reasons to touch him, and flipped her tangle of black hair over her shoulder at every opportunity. She must not even know how dangerous it had been to bring him to their meeting, Jane realized sadly as she watched Dee gaze longingly after Harris when he shoved his way to the bar to get them a round of drinks. *That right there is the face of a serious crush, and crushes make people careless.*

There was probably a message in there somewhere about her and André. She had been a little nervous about seeing him after their hasty exit from the rooftop party, but, if anything, the new tension between them improved their already sparkling chemistry. It was as if they had a shared secret now—one they were keeping from each other. It was an unconventional basis for a relationship, but since they spent most of their time in bed anyway, Jane didn't much care about the basis of anything. The thought was interrupted when Dee suddenly leaned forward and pressed a crumpled baggie into Jane's hand.

"The spell is really easy," Dee rushed hoarsely, pushing back her thick hair in an entirely different manner from when Harris was still at the table. "Just mix all of these together, picture her while saying her name seven times—before or grown-up, it doesn't matter—and then spread the powder on your lids like eye shadow. There's enough here for an hour."

"Eye shadow?" Jane asked blankly.

"It should wind up sort of gold," Dee assured her. "Not great for you, but definitely plausible. Just keep it in mind when you pick your outfit."

"Thanks," Jane said numbly, leaning down precariously to shove the baggie into her purse. *Apparently, Dee isn't so much "careless" as she is "a much ballsier undercover agent than me."*

An AC/DC song began to play a little too loudly on the jukebox. Harris returned with a Manhattan and two bottles of Brooklyn Brown Ale. "So, Ella. Dee says you've been working around the clock lately. Between that and the fact that trying to pry her away from her new job is like trying to shove a cat into a kitchen sink, I barely see either of you anymore. Tell me honestly: is it me?"

His green eyes were mischievous, but his smile was cool and sweet, and Jane took it in like oxygen. "I can see why you'd be worried," she told him playfully, "but Dee's been completely ignoring me, too. I've been so neglected that it's driven me to work overtime; can you imagine?" In the back of her mind, she wondered what Ella's job was supposed to be—had Dee already made something up? *This is why you don't bring plus-ones,* she decided. First André and now Dee had demonstrated vividly why it was a bad idea.

But Jane had been taking plenty of risks of her own, and her relief at being among her real friends again was so soothing that she had a hard time being too upset about Harris's presence. She didn't even really mind when Dee began rhapsodizing about the perfection that was Kate's consommés. *Ella's life may be fabulous, but Jane's doesn't suck, either,* she reminded herself wistfully. She felt an overwhelming longing to be herself again, but thought instead of the invitation on her rolltop hotel desk and the spell in her purse. It wouldn't be long now.

"Dee said your sister was in some kind of accident last month," Jane blurted out, ignoring Dee's wide-eyed glare of protest. "I hope she's feeling better now."

Harris's face warmed perceptibly. "That's very thoughtful," he told her, and Jane felt her body lean a few millimeters closer to his. "The physical therapist just signed off on less frequent sessions, which she's thrilled about. But our parents are still freaked about the whole thing, so she's been staying with Grandma and Aunt Charlotte upstate, and they're driving her crazy. She can't wait to get back to city life again."

He smiled, and Jane smiled back. Belatedly, Harris turned to include Dee in the moment, and Jane looked quickly down at her drink. After a pause, Dee began chatting rapidly about vol-au-vents, and Jane risked looking back over to see if Harris was following along. He had been looking at her as well, and their eyes locked for a strange, happy moment before Jane looked quickly away again. "So, Ella," Dee asked levelly, "how are things going with that handsome Romanian of yours?"

Jane blushed, but knew that between her walnut skin and the dim lighting, no one would be able to tell. She focused on keeping her voice level. "I wouldn't exactly call him 'mine,'" she demurred. But there was no point in denying what she had already manipulated the gossip columns into writing about. Harris's family occasionally featured in the same ones. *He might well have heard about* "us," and if not, then at least he can help spread the rumor, she argued to herself, but there was something about this particular lie that made her even more reluctant to tell it. I don't like using Harris, she told herself, but that wasn't quite it, or at least not quite all of it. "Things with André are going great," she said firmly, watching her knuckles go white around the stem of her glass. She might not like it, but she only had one chance to get it right. "I've never met his sister, though, and apparently the Dalcaşcus are pretty close, so that might be a problem."

She flicked her eyes nervously at Harris, and was surprised to see him rigid on his stool, his face even paler than usual under its light dusting of freckles. He can't be jealous, Jane chided herself. Can he? "Dee didn't tell me you were seeing that André," he said finally, his voice quiet and strained.

"You know him?" Jane asked, nonplussed. He might, she guessed: all the surviving magical families seemed to at least know of one another. And he had certainly known (and disliked) Malcolm well before Jane had ever come into the picture. It seemed a bit too coincidental that he would have an ugly history with both of the two men that Jane had shown an interest in since they had met, but Jane reminded herself that she quite obviously had questionable taste in men.

"Only by reputation," Harris answered, clipping off each word with a tensed jaw that Jane could see even in the low light. "It's none of my business, but if you don't mind some unsolicited advice . . ."

"Not at all," Jane encouraged him. "I'd like for the relationship to go well," she added, hating that keeping up her cover made Harris's mouth set into such a cold, tight line.

He hesitated, and Dee looked around as if she were trying to find a way out of the conversation that she had started, but finally

Harris found his voice again. "His family comes first," he told Jane with conviction, "especially that sister, Katrin. She practically raised him, and according to my aunt, they almost seem to share a brain. He won't ever, ever go against her wishes, so if she doesn't approve of you—and she doesn't like most people, by the way—you probably shouldn't get too attached. He'll let you down."

"Sisters are important," Dee offered softly.

Jane thought about Annette, Katrin, and Maeve, and the way Dee had become almost like a sister to her, even if their bond had gotten strange lately.

"They really are," she agreed, her voice barely above a whisper. She raised her glass in a half-loving, half-melancholy toast, and Dee and Harris followed suit. "Thanks for the perspective."

Chapter Eighteen

JANE STUDIED THE HEAVY STONE ARCHWAY OF THE DORANS' house. It struck her all over again that, squatting gloomily between 664 and 668, the building shouldn't really have been numbered 665 at all. *Were they superstitious,* she wondered, *or afraid that using the right street number might give something away about them?* The greenish-gray mansion easily rose eight stories from the street, but there was nothing graceful or sleek about its height. Even though her inner architect, which tended to see things in blueprint form, insisted that it was vertical, it seemed to almost be looming over the sidewalk. The windows, although moderately sized, were set deep back into the thick stone. She remembered how little daylight penetrated the fortress, even on the higher floors. André typed a short code into a discreet keypad to the right of the entrance, and a massive wooden door swung open on silent hinges. They stepped through the enormous arched entryway into the foyer.

An icy shiver ran down the length of Jane's spine at the familiar marble and gilt. *That's where Cora fell when I hit her with that ball of magic . . . That's where they re-paneled the wall after I nearly killed Malcolm's father by accident . . .* It was a nerve-racking trip down evil memory lane. *No one will recognize me,* she told herself with as much conviction as she could muster. And it was true that Gunther, the ancient uniformed doorman, barely opened his bleary eyes as they passed by. Although her return to the mansion was momentous for her, to everyone else she was just another slinkily dressed invitee.

The atrium was full of those, Jane noted when the wood-paneled elevator let her and André off on the eighth floor. The eighth floor had always made Jane a little uncomfortable. Although normally she liked airy spaces—of which there were few enough in the Dorans' massive house—something about the floor-to-ceiling glass that ran all the way around the building made her feel as though the mansion might try to throw her out. The view was spectacular, somehow avoiding taller buildings to create a sightline from Central Park to the East River, but Jane hugged the solid interior of the hollow square, reassured by the cool wall at her back.

Her first instinct was to locate Lynne and then the twins. The semi-familiar woman Jane had noticed with them at the last party was nearby, apparently deep in conversation, but Jane felt sure she was keenly aware of André and Ella's entrance all the same. *That must be André's sister,* Jane realized. She couldn't see much of the woman's face in its one-quarter profile, but there was a similarity in their coloring.

She doesn't want me here, Jane thought, her smugness at getting in tinged with anxiety. *But I don't really want to be here, either, so once I get what I came for we'll both be a lot happier.*

Unfortunately, getting what she came for seemed to be a lot easier thought than done. It required slipping away from the party, for starters, and although Katrin Dalcaşcu seemed determined to spend the evening with her back pointedly turned to Jane, the resident witches were a lot less inclined to lose sight of her. Lynne, in particular, kept her dark eyes riveted on Jane. Her scrutiny was so intense that Jane kept feeling the urge to check the artful folds of the black fabric of her sheath dress to make sure nothing had slipped. She had been going for "elegant but understated," hoping it would help her blend in to the shadows, but that wouldn't help if she couldn't even get to said shadows unnoticed.

André's arm circled her waist possessively, and Jane jumped a little. *A whole floor full of people keeping their enemies closer.* At least André's presence seemed to keep Lynne away, and Jane felt a tiny sliver of relief at not having to make up more information about Malcolm.

She sipped at her champagne, then took a longer drink of it. *Maybe everyone will just get drunk,* she thought hopefully, tracking the movements of a small army of silent waiters bearing trays laden with full flutes. At her current rate, she would probably be pretty tanked herself by the time any of the other witches got tipsy enough to leave her alone. *At least Ella has a higher tolerance than Jane,* she thought anxiously, raising her glass and then self-consciously lowering it again. Even without the curves she had lost, the eight extra inches of height allowed for more food and drink than her old body could comfortably handle.

"André, I've just been *dying* to get a moment with you. Would you excuse us, dear?"

Jane blinked; Cora McCarroll had seemingly come out of nowhere, and deftly inserted herself between Jane and her date. She linked her arm in his and led him away before he could even open his mouth to protest. Jane froze, feeling as exposed as a deer in headlights.

Halfway across the room, one corner of Lynne's peach-lipsticked mouth twitched up, and then her black-and-white Chanel dress began to move purposefully toward Jane. Jane glanced around for some sort of cover, but saw nothing except a crowd of unfamiliar faces in her immediate vicinity. The plain, recessed wooden door that led to the back staircase was only a few yards away, practically taunting her with its nearness. Jane scowled at it, then turned back toward Lynne.

But the vintage Chanel was no longer in view, because someone had directly blocked Lynne's path. The sharply muscled planes of the woman's exposed back and her severe black haircut were instantly recognizable: Katrin had put herself between Lynne and Jane. Jane held her breath expectantly for a short moment, but Lynne's face did not reappear around Katrin. She was obviously eager to discover what Ella knew about her son, but not so eager that she would alienate the Dalcaşcus in order to find out. *Careful woman, keeping all her options open until one of them works out.*

Jane backed quickly toward the staircase door. The last thing she saw before she reached it was André, striding back to the place where she had been moments before, his face nearly as angry as Lynne's. Jane shivered at the sight of him, feeling a moment of real fear. Her hands felt numb, but she forced them to work with the handle of the door until, finally, it swung open and she all but fell through.

Jane's breath rasping was the only sound in the suddenly silent air. She fumbled with the catch on her clutch, forcing it open with wooden fingers and fishing out the crumpled baggie inside. It contained four smaller plastic bags, and Jane turned one of them into a makeshift mixing bowl for the rest. *Annette Doran,* she thought fiercely, closing her eyes. *Annette Doran. Annette Doran.* A vision of the girl's square jaw and dirty-blond waves of hair floated in front of her. *Annette Doran. Annette Doran. Annette Doran.* The girl's dark eyes stared out of her golden skin and bored into Jane's closed ones. *Annette Doran,* she thought violently, smearing the combination of powders on her eyelids.

The stairway looked exactly the same when she opened her eyes again, and she fought off a wave of disappointment. The spell wouldn't work until she saw something that belonged to Annette, so there was no real way to tell whether she'd performed it correctly. But Jane felt a strange, eerie tingling in her fingertips and eyelashes, and decided that magic was definitely happening.

She tapped down the stairs as quickly as care allowed, stopping at the seventh floor. That floor was mostly bedrooms, including the one she had shared with Malcolm, so it seemed like the best place to start. Her heart pounding audibly, Jane entered the same code André had used for the main entrance, and was relieved when the door swung open. It was possible that the Dorans could have gotten more paranoid since her great escape the month before, but all the keypads apparently still responded to the authorized codes. Jane, scanning telepathically for all she was worth, stepped into the corridor.

It was dark and silent. Jane felt one of Lynne's thousands of Oriental carpets beneath her feet, and she moved quietly to the nearest door. *Linen closet,* she realized disappointedly, closing it again quickly. The next one was closer to what she was looking for: the door revealed a high four-poster bed, a teak armoire, and a few overstuffed chairs near a mosaic-inlaid fireplace. The bed was perfectly made, the armoire looked empty, and the dim yellow glow of the streetlamps outside didn't reveal a single personal item to Jane's eager stare. She blinked again, hoping her magic eye shadow would do something—anything—but her vision remained unchanged. *It's a huge house,* she reminded herself. But four sterile, empty guest rooms later, she began to have real doubts. Lynne was conscious of the past, but she wasn't especially sentimental: the Lowell Hotel was homier and more personal than the mansion's vacant rooms.

A creaking noise sounded somewhere in the maze of dark hallways, and Jane whipped open the closest door and jumped inside. She pulled the door most of the way closed, avoiding the snick of the latch. Her heartbeat pounded so hard she felt dizzy, and she rested her head against the painted wood of the door until it began to slow. She didn't hear any new noises, and she exhaled all of the air in her lungs. She glanced around quickly at the room she had hidden in. It was much smaller and plainer than the others, with a window no wider than Jane's shoulders. *Sofia's room, or someone else on the staff,* she realized. With a disappointed sigh, she slipped back out of the little bedroom.

I'm thinking about this wrong, Jane decided. *Lynne plays the media like a fiddle, but her real self is super-private; she wouldn't leave Annette's things out for just anyone to see. Malcolm felt like he had to hide his own memento away in a bank vault.* She groped her way back along the hallway toward the wooden door that led to the stairs. *But she still might have kept hers close by.*

Jane knew—theoretically—where Lynne's bedroom was on the sixth floor, but she had never been inside. She held her breath as she turned the polished-brass door handle, but it didn't give off so much as a squeak. Her eyes adjusted slowly to the dark interior of the room. A king-size four-poster bed resolved itself first, and eventually Jane was able to make out a few chairs, a low table, and a massive armoire. *No windows—does she combust in direct sunlight?*

She closed her eyes, listened hard for any nearby minds, and flicked on the light switch. The room was almost as spare and cold as in the dark: the wallpaper was a steely charcoal color that reminded her of the twins' flat pewter eyes. The pattern on it showed twisting vines of the same color, winding their way toward the ceiling but never reaching it, and the depressing theme was repeated on the bedspread and pillow shams. *The devil has pillow shams.* Jane shuddered, but even with the warm light of the wall sconces to supplement the spell on her eyelids, nothing in the room seemed the slightest bit out of place. There was, however, a door in the far wall that Jane hadn't been able to see in the dark.

It's just a bathroom, she tried to tell herself, even after she noticed the open door to a gray-marbled bathroom off to her right. *It's nothing.* But her black Swarovski-studded peep-toes were moving as if of their own accord, carrying her toward the closed door. The honey-colored floorboards creaked faintly when she was halfway there, but it was too late: no one was listening and no one came to stop her, and within moments her hand was on the doorknob. *This is a terrible idea,* her brain told her as she pushed the door open.

All of Jane's senses heightened as soon as she flipped the lights on in what could only be Lynne's private office. A massive teak desk squatted in front of the deep-set window, and a couple of teak-lined file cabinets stood against the left-hand wall. Jane's gaze ran along the walls, whose paper matched the bedroom's, looking for a cliché along the lines of a painting hiding a wall safe, but there was nothing. Lynne apparently liked a thoroughly spartan working environment; her desk was as uncluttered as her walls. *She's obsessed with her family's history; I know she is,* Jane thought anxiously, tugging at a drawer of one of the file cabinets. It opened easily under her hand, and she shut it again with a little more force than she needed, reaching for the next one before it was fully closed. The second drawer wasn't locked, either, and Jane worked her way quickly around the room. Nothing stood out, and nothing was locked.

Who the hell is this woman?

Jane's breath sped up. She couldn't stay away from the party forever, but what was she supposed to do now? Her whole plan had been based on the assumption that something of Annette's must still be in Lynne's possession, but what if she had been wrong all along?

She stumbled as she made her way back toward the immaculate bedroom, a vicious cramp knotting her stomach. Her fumbling fingers flicked off the light, and then the one in the bedroom as well, and then she was in the hallway. As she pulled the door shut behind her, she realized that she hadn't closed the office door, but her blood was pounding in her ears, and her entire body was wracked with the awareness of her failure, and details like that didn't seem to even matter anymore.

Two more weeks as Ella, and then I can go back to being hunted as Jane. Even if Annette's things were still in the house somewhere, it was a huge house, and hadn't Malcolm once told her that the families who lived there had divided and redivided it as needed? Ariel McCarroll could be sleeping on Annette's old pillow, for all Jane knew, but there was no way she could search all eight floors in one evening without attracting the wrong kind of attention.

She leaned against the wall of the hallway, closing her eyes and feeling blank with disappointment. She wanted to rally, to think of some new plan, but her brain just felt hollow. Not knowing what else to do, she pulled herself away from the wall and made her slow way back up the stairs.

She stood up and pressed two fingers hard into the space just below each cheekbone, allowing the pressure to pull her together. "Okay," she whispered, starting forward, but she hesitated just as her hand was on the door that led back to the atrium. *They call it an "atrium," but it's not really,* her inner architect observed. Its light came from the glass walls around the four sides of the house and an enlarged skylight in the center, but there was still one level above it, shaped like a hollow square. And so the staircase behind her led down to the floors that she had just explored, but another set led up, as well, to the real top floor of the mansion.

The floor where she keeps her nasty secrets.

The memory of pain and fear shot through every nerve of her body. But a flood of absolute conviction followed close behind it, and Jane knew where she had to go.

Chapter Nineteen

THE STAIRS TO THE ATTIC WEREN'T CARPETED, AND JANE CARE-fully set each toe and heel down together to avoid unnecessary noise. The scent of pine and dust filled her lungs, and she was sure her hair would smell musty by the time she returned to the party.

The first door at the top of the stairs led to what looked like a child's playroom, but Jane knew better than to get excited just yet. *It may look like it's for a child, but I know it's for Charles,* she thought ruefully. She blinked her spell-covered eyelids a few extra times, just in case. She knew she had guessed right when nothing stood out to her enhanced vision, but she still felt a pang of disappointment.

The next room was set up like a classroom, with just one lonely student desk under the sloping roof. *I wonder if they brought in teachers,* Jane thought idly, trailing her fingers across the dusty chalkboard. Charles had spent his entire life in this attic. The household staff knew about him, of course, but would Lynne have allowed in outsiders? Jane imagined Sofia, the Dorans' tiny, bulge-eyed maid, standing at the front of the room lecturing a drooling Charles on geography.

Of course, he probably would have needed a doctor sometimes, too, Jane realized pragmatically, and, as if the attic were attempting to answer her questions, she opened the next door to find what looked like a hospital room transported into an Upper East Side attic. *Man,* she thought, shuddering and hurrying along, *when Lynne decides to keep a secret, she doesn't screw around.*

The next room, opening to the right rather than straight ahead, contained a massive flat-screen television, a squishy-looking couch, a floor-to-ceiling shelf stacked with approximately every board game ever invented, and Charles. His stringy brown hair hung over his eyes, which Jane remembered as flatter, duller copies of Malcolm's. His intimidating bulk was crammed into a corner of the couch as if the other three-quarters of it were off-limits, and his meaty hands were full of Stratego pieces. At the soft creak of the door opening, he looked up, and another piece fell out of his slack mouth.

"Jane," he announced happily. "My friend Jane."

Jane flinched at the sound of her name, and held her hands up to her face. The long, sturdy fingers were still the same walnut-brown, and her hair was still in its longish, smooth bob. Her fingers fluttered over her cheekbones, nose, and lips, but they all seemed to still be firmly Ella's. Her disguise hadn't suddenly disappeared . . . Charles just didn't see it.

"Charles," she said levelly. "You remember me?"

He jumped heavily off of the couch, and she reached behind

her to make sure the door was still open in case she needed an escape route. But he shuffled away in the opposite direction instead, and after a moment of counting all the things that could go wrong, Jane clenched her hands into fists and followed him. Charles was both unpredictable and not fond of bathing, so she kept her distance, but he seemed entirely focused on his self-appointed mission.

When they reached what had to be his bedroom—all the toys that money could buy, but shabby with madness and neglect—Charles became a little more agitated, rooting around in the top drawer of a sturdy white dresser and sending a few pairs of socks flying. With a triumphant-sounding gurgle, he pulled out the object of his search, and Jane blushed furiously: he was holding the lacy red thong he had accepted as a bribe for helping her escape from the attic the last time she had been up here. "Jane," he repeated fondly, stroking the scrap of lace like a cat.

"I told you I would come back," she improvised, although she couldn't remember if she had ever actually said that. Charles was watching her intently, and she had no idea what those empty-looking eyes might see.

"Charles," she began again, sending a probing finger of her mind toward his, "I need your help again. You helped me so much last time, I know you can do it again."

"Friends help," he mumbled, ambling over to sit on his twin bed. But he wouldn't look at her, and Jane, filtering through the top layer of his mind, realized that Lynne had been furious with him after Jane's escape. She clearly hadn't suspected that Charles could have helped Jane intentionally, which had probably saved him some real pain, but she was still his mother, and her rage had been painful enough for him on its own.

"It won't be like last time," she assured him, hoping fervently it was the truth. No matter how badly Charles had frightened her in the past, she didn't want him to suffer. "I just wanted to know about your older sister. Can you tell me about Annette?"

"I have a brother," Charles told her uncertainly, sliding one hand into his pocket. Jane remembered that he liked to carry around the old Yale key chain Malcolm had given him, and sincerely hoped that this was what he was fumbling around with in there. "He had a sister."

They never even met, Jane reminded herself; no wonder he didn't really understand that they were related. There would be no point in trying to find pictures of Annette in Charles's head; Charles had only been conceived in the first place because Annette had died. *Or so they thought.* "Did he tell you about her?"

Charles shook his head no and began rocking gently back and forth on his bed. Jane raced through his mind, pausing whenever a young version of Malcolm came into view, but she wasn't even entirely sure what moment she was looking for. She knew how Annette had looked at the age when she had supposedly drowned, but if Charles had ever seen a photograph of her, he had buried the memory deeply. *Of course, there's nothing remotely organized about his mind, anyway,* she thought testily. There were no connections between his thoughts that she could understand or follow, and his memories tumbled at her mind like plaster raining from the roof in an earthquake.

Suddenly, Charles jumped up off the bed, and Jane jumped back. But he just shuffled toward the room's other door, gesturing vaguely for her to come with him. She knew that she should be getting back to the party; she had already probably spent too long on this wild-goose chase. But she couldn't help herself. Now that she had come face-to-face with the sad, broken boy she had once thought of as a real-life boogeyman, she felt an overpowering need to see whatever he could show her. She stepped carefully around what looked like a pillow fort and followed him.

Two rooms later, they seemed to have left the part of the attic that was meant for Charles. *The room I was tied up in must be around here somewhere,* Jane realized with a chill. They had taken the shortest route to the stairs that time, which hadn't led through Charles's living space, but there was only so much attic left between where they were now and the other side of the staircase. *We'll take the long way back,* Jane promised herself absently. Then she noticed that Charles had stopped. At the sight of the room he had led her to, Jane stopped in her tracks as well and stared.

The walls were lined with shelves, which were filled with orderly rows of boxes. The boxes on the floor formed considerably less orderly stacks; there was probably room for a person to walk between them, but it didn't look entirely safe to try. Most of them didn't have lids, so the corners that weren't perfectly aligned sank into the boxes below, creating Tower of Pisa–esque stacks of cardboard that wound first one way, then another. Each one was labeled with initials, and Jane could see papers, ribbons, trophies, clay sculptures, and stuffed animals peeking out of the gaps between them. *Evil psycho witches keep crayon drawings?*

Apparently, they did: at least some of the boxes were marked "MWD." *Malcolm Walter Doran.* She held her breath as she dug one of them out of its stack, but although there was some dangerous wobbling, she managed to get to it without knocking anything over. A model of the solar system, a bunch of notebooks, and a single shin guard were inside; Jane spun Saturn thoughtfully. "They never throw anything away, do they?"

"Sister." Charles shrugged, digging with a yellow fingernail deep scratches into a corner of one of Blake Helding's boxes.

Jane smiled in spite of herself: in his own strange way, Charles kept coming through for her. *Plus it was kind of nice to be recognized, especially by someone who isn't currently trying to kill me.* She knew how important it was, and that it was quite temporary, but after two weeks of seeing a stranger in every mirror, her disguise was starting to get to her. If it weren't for Jane's face periodically popping up next to Malcolm's in various tabloids, she felt she might start to forget what she looked like: it was already hard to remember the contours of her real eyes.

"Do you know her middle name?" she asked hopefully, but she had already begun to search through the stacks. Charles was too busy widening the hole in his box to acknowledge her question, but it didn't really matter: Jane knew she would recognize two out of the three initials. She wandered haphazardly through the piles of boxes, trying to make sure she saw all their labels. They were all so similar that they blurred together, and she suspected that she was covering the same territory multiple times. One of the boxes even seemed to glow a little, and Jane blinked a few times. But her vision didn't clear: the box was brighter than the ones around it, as if lit from within. Jane craned her neck until she found the marking on it: "ALD." Jane spun around, trying to take in as many of the boxes as she could at once. Two others were glowing faintly as well, and she felt a silly grin break across her face. *Three boxes of Annette's things—things that she didn't intentionally give up—way more than I even need.*

She pulled one out and began rooting through it, but it was mostly clothes: practical shirts and shorts, stylish tunics and leggings, and a blue velvet dress with lacework that took Jane's breath away. "The world's best-dressed six-year-old," she muttered, replacing the box in its stack. Clothes probably weren't personal enough, she guessed: whatever she used had to be something that Annette would still have considered "hers" no matter how much time had passed. She pulled the next box off one of the shelves along the wall, and it was a gold mine: a leather jewelry box full of silver chains and stick-on earrings, two pairs of jelly shoes, a doll that looked homemade, five dusty, velvet-lined boxes with glass figurines in the same style as the unicorn that Jane's first spell had broken, and a stuffed rabbit so worn that it must have been laundered thirty times. There was even more underneath, but she didn't bother to dig through it.

"Thank you, Charles," she whispered sincerely. He stayed half-hidden behind a stack of boxes and still wouldn't look at her, and his shyness made her feel extra-brave. She tugged a pretty knot-work ring off her left pinky, held her breath, and tiptoed over to him. She thought she saw a faint smile on his slack face when she pressed it into his grimy palm. "I have to go now," she told him, backing away again and staring hard at the ring. *Not mine anymore,* she thought firmly, for good measure. *Not connected to me at all.* "But this is yours now, and I'll be back to visit as soon as I can. You're a really good friend."

As she heard herself say the words, she realized that she meant them. She ran lightly down the back stairs with her box, which she could hide just outside the back entrance and pick up later without being seen. She knew from experience that no one at 665 Park Avenue ever bothered with the stairs.

And then all I need to do is survive the rest of the party, Jane reminded herself cheerfully. Being glared at by witches and suffocated by André still wasn't her idea of a pleasant evening, but it suddenly seemed a lot more bearable.

Chapter Twenty

JANE RUBBED THE WORN GRAY FUR OF THE TOY RABBIT WITH ONE thumb. The box and the rest of its precious contents sat on the floor beside the closet, and she crossed her legs on her down comforter and tried to keep herself from bouncing in excitement. She had been so eager to examine her prize that she hadn't even bothered to change out of her black dress, although she had kicked off the glittery shoes at the earliest opportunity.

It had been even harder to shake off André after the party than it had been during it, but as soon as she had returned to the atrium, she had repeated the words "food poisoning" in every context and combination she could think of, and finally he had given up. *It couldn't be that hard to believe, after I'd run up and down all those stairs,* she admitted to herself. When they'd reached the mirrored hotel elevator, she saw just how thoroughly she'd failed to touch up her hair and makeup before hurrying back into the Dorans' party. *No wonder he let me off the hook; I wouldn't want to sleep with me tonight, either.* But all she could feel was giddy happiness: nothing was going to stop her from finding Annette now.

She dropped the rabbit gently onto the comforter, where it stared at her with one glassy brown eye. *Can I do this myself?* She hesitated briefly. *Maybe I should wait.* After all, the first time she had done this spell, she'd had two Wiccans, tons of crystals, and a vial of tasteless but potent goo. But she was keyed up and nearly bursting with magical electricity. There was no way she would be able to sleep tonight. As the power buzzed through her veins, it whispered to her that, as long as she had enough magic, everything else was just props.

She closed her eyes, counted seven deep breaths, and let her mind drift toward the small stuffed toy. Feeling slightly foolish but wanting to re-create what little of the original spell she could, she held her arms up, creating a circle around the rabbit with her hands meeting each other on the far side. She held the magic inside of that, spinning it around the circle's edges like water in a funnel. She couldn't remember what Misty had chanted, so she substituted a meditation mantra of Dee's, focusing on the rhythm rather than the meaning.

Although her hands remained raised, after a few minutes she could physically feel the synthetic fur, the plastic whiskers, the black glass of the eyes. She could very nearly feel the oil left behind in Annette's invisible fingerprints from every time the girl had picked up, hugged, or carried the bunny. Jane sent her mind along their tight whorls, following them to an identity. *Tell me where she is. Show me Annette.*

A buzzing noise so low that she hadn't noticed it at first intensified until she wished that she could cover her ears, and then her consciousness was wrenched violently away from her body. Although she had prepared herself for the pain this time, it seemed to have multiplied. *Should've drunk the goo*, she gasped mentally, wishing she were still in her body so she could be sick. But there was nothing she could do except wait for the pain to pass, because wherever she was, it was no longer the Lowell Hotel.

So where am I? Where is she? Jane tried to look around, but felt frustrated all over again by her inability to so much as twitch of her own volition. She had to wait for Annette to move, turn, hear, look. *At least this time I know whose body I'm in*, she reminded herself. Without the confusion and then the shock of discovering that she had mistakenly inhabited the body of a girl who was supposed to be dead, Jane felt sure she could stay there long enough to see something useful.

When Jane's vision cleared, Annette was slicing lemons into wedges. A cheap-looking paring knife cut methodically into the yellow peel over and over, separating it into quarters and then eights. *So "something useful" is still a ways off.* Jane tried to focus on her peripheral vision and could tell she wasn't in her dingy, depressing apartment; this space looked bigger and darker, although early morning light sifted through a small window in the background. A bar, she guessed, straining her eyes to see the corner of something that might be a jukebox. Annette swept the lemon pieces into a white plastic bin, and Jane tensed in anticipation. But the girl just pulled another lemon from a different bin without even needing to look up, sliced the fruit in half, and began again.

You've got to be kidding me, Jane tried to shout, but Annette's jaw didn't so much as quiver. *I pull this spell off all on my own, and you're going to spend the whole time doing* mise-en-place? She didn't know how long she would be able to stay this time, but lemons were too universal to help her one bit.

Annette finished her slicing, swept the pieces into the bin with the rest, and turned. Jane clenched every non-corporeal muscle, in her excitement, and then relaxed them into a disappointed heap: Annette was only looking for limes. They were a bit farther along the bar from the container that held the lemons, but as soon as she located them, Annette dropped one on her cutting board and carried on with her incredibly dull work.

I saw something, Jane realized after a few moments of watching the knife slide through the translucent green flesh. *There was something . . . look back!*

Annette finished cutting her lime, dumped the pieces into an empty white plastic container, and turned away from the bins and the cutting board entirely. Jane felt her own muscles pull and joints pop as her host body stretched hard, her hands clasped over her head and her back arching like a bow. Annette's field of vision was now largely consumed by rows of variously shaped glasses, fanciful bottles of liquor. Behind the bottles, she noticed a dusty, black-spotted mirror. It showed a dark room full of wooden booths and benches, as well as an outlined rectangle of white-gray light.

The window! she realized in a heart-pounding rush. It was backward, she knew, and her eyes were nearly closed; but it didn't matter: the silhouette outside was symmetrical and enough light filtered in that she could make out the general shape. *Two large windows, like halves of a split barrel,* Jane told herself rapidly, trying to memorize every detail. *Yellowish brick. A tower in the middle, with a little clock.* Before she was sure she had it, a large red blur passed in front of the window, blocking the entire building from view. Annette began to turn back toward her cutting board, and Jane mentally tugged at the girl's mind, trying to get her to slow down. But her magic evidently didn't work without her body, because Annette continued toward her work without any hesitation.

As she turned, though, Jane's eyes caught the thing that had nagged at her mind earlier. A folded newspaper sat on the polished bar beside the bin of limes, and this time Jane got a clear glimpse of it before she was stuck again with the sight of the citrus-stained cutting board.

The Times, it read quite clearly, with an intricate crest between the two words. It was a popular enough name for a newspaper, but Jane knew exactly what she was looking at. After all, she had seen the same crest every day for two years next to her desk at Atelier Antoine, because Elodie Dessaix, the daughter of a British diplomat, was a lifelong subscriber to *The Times* of London. *And that red thing . . . I'm almost positive that was a double-decker bus.*

Jane could feel her spirit starting to tug her away from Annette's. The sensation was mild so far, but she suspected that it wouldn't stay that way for long. She had done well this time, but the spell still couldn't last forever. She thought about trying to fight its pull, but the memory of being torn forcefully back into her own body made her feel faint. *And I'm exhausted,* she realized; her whole spirit felt shaky and weak. *I have to let go.*

Jane's will collapsed then. She blinked briefly and saw the plain white ceiling of her hotel room and felt the quilted bedspread beneath her folded body.

I quit, bounced hollowly around her brain. *I was there, and I just let it go.*

But all her energy was gone; she couldn't stir her muscles to sit up or even roll over to switch off the lamp. Instead, her mind swam downward toward darkness, forcing her into a sleep that was more like a temporary death.

Chapter Twenty-One

JANE WAS IN HER OLD FARMHOUSE IN SAINT-CROIX-SUR-AMAURY, but Gran was nowhere to be found. Jane moved through the house, running her fingertips over the depressing oil paintings along the stairway, and then across the round kitchen table with its bouquet of dead daisies in their familiar blue-glazed vase. She wanted to call out for Gran—it would have been the most natural thing to do—but her vocal cords wouldn't obey. She left the kitchen, an added sense of urgency hurrying her steps along, and moved quickly toward the living room. The hallway felt almost too short; she was afraid of arriving at her destination and wished for a longer delay, but the entrance to the living room was just ahead, and there was no avoiding what was waiting for her inside.

She tried to brace herself for what she would find, but it was hard to concentrate when Malcolm was banging on the farmhouse door. She tried, but it seemed that every step that brought her closer to the living room also made the pounding outside more urgent. *Can't he just let me do this?* she wondered angrily. *He's the whole reason I'm here.*

She wanted to go in and see Gran, but the knocking wouldn't let her think. She hesitated between the entrance to the living room and the front door; maybe it would be easier to see what Malcolm wanted first, then go and visit Gran. *But I need to see her,* she fretted anxiously; there was definitely a reason why she needed to see Gran before she let Malcolm in. But with the racket at the front door, it was impossible to remember why.

Come in, she whispered.

"Come in," she mumbled out loud, rolling over and shoving her face into her soft hotel pillow.

Then she sat bolt upright. The knocking came again at the door to her suite, and she realized that she had at least a few seconds to prepare for whomever might walk through the door. She swept the stuffed bunny underneath the frame of the bed, tugging the edges of the comforter down carefully to make sure it was covered. She swung her legs over the side of the bed and kicked the box containing the rest of Annette's things into the closet, pausing briefly to pull a terrycloth Lowell robe over her rumpled black dress.

By the time she reached the door of her suite, the knocking was as loud as it had been in her dream. She yanked it open. It wasn't Malcolm on the other side (*of course it's not,* she realized belatedly, with a pang of regret); it was André.

He seemed almost as startled to see her as she was to see him, and she wondered just how disheveled she looked after the previous night's marathon of stress and magic. But he recovered quickly, smiling his predator's smile and holding up a bottle of Pommery for her to see. "I thought I might invite myself to join you for brunch," he explained courteously. "So I come bearing gifts." His smile stayed in place, but his eyes flickered curiously over her shoulder, sweeping as much of the suite as he could see. His body slanted forward slightly, and she could tell he was eager to get inside for a better look.

I must have really rattled him with the strange behavior last night. He'd been suspicious of her since he had discovered that she was a witch; of course he wouldn't believe a lame upset-stomach excuse. But she had hidden the evidence of her real purpose in going to the Dorans' house, so she smiled as convincingly as she could and stepped aside to let him in.

"I'll call room service, but do we need orange juice or is there some in your kitchen?" he asked, his voice fading as he made his way into the living room.

"I don't have any," Jane replied, following him slowly. The full details of the night before were starting to filter in to her surprised brain. "But I'm afraid I don't really have time for room service, either. I have to make an unexpected trip today, so we should probably just save that bottle for when I get back."

The unmistakable pop of the champagne's cork startled her, and she flinched back into the hallway. André, as graceful and unconcerned as ever, fished two flutes out of the bar cabinet, filled them with careful, alternating pours, and held one out to her. Jane took it automatically, but André didn't let go. She glanced up to see his burning black eyes boring into hers. "Where are you going?" he asked, and there was nothing unconcerned about his voice.

Jane fought the instinct to flinch; André would notice any sign of fear or uncertainty. *Lynne's interest in me is a double-edged sword.*

He can't afford to scare me off, but he'll be scrutinizing every move I make. She closed her eyes as she sipped her champagne, drawing the moment out as long as she could to steady her nerves. She had already lied to André about nearly everything she possibly could, and it was doubtful he believed any of it anymore. What could it hurt to tell him where she was really going? London was a big place, and no one but her knew that Annette Doran was even alive. It was better to tell as much of the truth as she could than to risk getting caught over an unnecessary lie. "I have to go to London," Jane told him, deliberately turning her back on him to saunter to the taupe couch, "this afternoon. Some family business just came up."

André crossed the room in three swift steps and sank down beside her on the couch. The hairs on her arms stood up with the charge of his nearness, and she tugged absently at the cuffs of her robe. "You haven't told me about your family."

I can't fake a whole branch of a witch family to him, she decided frantically; if she made up concrete facts, he might check them out. It would be best to stay vague. "They're terribly boring," she countered, widening her eyes innocently. "But sometimes my twenty-year-old cousin gets it into her head to party like a rock star; she's been to rehab twice already. But it doesn't stick, so this time I got elected to talk some sense into her before she gets out of hand again."

André looked thoughtful. "London. Today."

She nodded, sipping her champagne and wishing he would relax enough to do the same. "I think the flights mostly leave in the afternoon, but I haven't even booked a ticket yet, so I have a busy morning ahead."

An amused smirk twisted his mouth. "Considering that it's almost noon, I would say so."

Holy crap. Jane whipped around to check the clock on the mantel. *No wonder he was surprised to see me in my bathrobe.* The spell must have taken even more out of her than she had realized; she had slept for over eleven hours. "Wow," she observed feebly. "The aftereffects of last night."

André nodded thoughtfully, and Jane hoped he was comparing her current disarray with her long, long absence from the party the night before. She suspected that they would add up, even if it was only a lucky coincidence. "Well," he said finally, "it seems I can be of service." Jane raised an eyebrow curiously, encouraging him to explain. "I had an ulterior motive in coming here this morning," he confessed self-deprecatingly. "I planned to tell you that I needed to leave town for a while as well, and hoped you would forgive my absence. It's unavoidable . . . but now I think the timing is better than I had thought."

"Oh," Jane blurted out, and then stopped, confused. "Where are *you* going?"

"Mainland Europe," he purred, and she guessed that he didn't intend to get any more specific about that. "But I had also been thinking of making a stop in London, and suddenly that seems like a much more appealing prospect. So," he finished in a businesslike tone that caught her off-guard, "we will take my plane. The pilot is on notice for five o'clock, which gives us plenty of time for brunch."

Jane blinked. *Well* that *happened fast.* "I couldn't possibly impose," she began, knowing as she did that protests would be useless.

"Nonsense," he told her, just as she had expected, and then he reached over and held her chin in his fingers, forcing it up gently until she met his eyes. His pupils were dilated, and she felt uneasily as if she might fall in. "I will not take no for an answer."

"Well, then," Jane said slowly, licking her lips involuntarily. "I guess the answer is yes."

He smiled wider then and raised his still-full glass in a toast. As she clinked hers against it, her head was racing with excuses. She opened her mouth to backpedal, but before she could speak, he covered it with his own. Her objections slipped out of her mind as his kisses grew more insistent, more demanding.

He pushed her back on the couch and pulled her terrycloth robe open, glancing only briefly at the cocktail dress she still wore underneath. His large, capable hands found its invisible zipper without the slightest hesitation, and her body rose up to meet his hungrily.

Danger, a tiny part of her brain whispered, but the tension just sent a deeper thrill through her.

I don't care.

Chapter Twenty-Two

SUNLIGHT GLIMMERED OFF JAMAICA BAY, REFRACTING INTO A million bright pieces in the airplane's cabin. Jane had always heard that private jets tended to be less glamorous than they sounded, but this certainly was not true of the Dalcaşcu's plane. Heavy, gold-embroidered curtains worked as movable dividers to create as large or intimate a space as was needed, and André had opted for something fairly intimate. There were two over-size seats for takeoff and landing, and a low couch along the opposite side that was as deep as a bed. More curtains doubled as wall-hangings, obscuring the usual gray plastic of the plane's shell. It wasn't to Jane's taste, exactly—the Romanian siblings favored bloodred leather and velvet and a clutter of luxury over the clean, open spaces she preferred. But there was no denying that the thing was swank, and once their climb slowed and gravity relaxed its downward pull, it was as easy to believe that she was in a sexy lounge as thousands of miles up in the sky.

Complete with sexy strangers, she thought, glancing coyly at André, who was buckled in beside her. Two weeks would normally be enough time to at least start to get to know someone, but their bizarre double-double-agent game ensured that she had no real idea who the man sitting next to her really was. *It's just as well,* she decided. She didn't really want a romance and certainly couldn't afford another entanglement right now. So if by some miracle André turned out to be a genuinely good and likable guy, she would really prefer not to know about it. And if, as she suspected was far more likely, he was as evil and soulless as Lynne Doran, she'd rather not know that, either. It was far more palatable to be sleeping with a stranger than with the enemy.

He blinked against the slanting sunlight, his long black eyelashes settling briefly on his olive skin, and Jane nearly sighed out loud at the sight of him. It was definitely better to just enjoy the moment and not ask too many questions. As long as she didn't make the mistake of actually trusting him, he was the perfect companion.

André's eyes were open a slit, and slanted toward her small, perky breasts. Jane had been pleased to realize that she no longer required a bra at all, and André seemed to greatly appreciate that new direction in her wardrobe. But they were both distracted by a subtle-but-noticeable light that flashed on over the cabin door, and Jane cleared her throat and sat up in her red leather seat. "Does that mean the plane's going down?"

"Not the plane, no," André leered, his accent a little thicker than usual. But he pressed a button on the wall, and the door opened to reveal a stewardess wearing what Jane could only describe as a black leather bustier.

Seriously?

The woman swished in with all the swagger of a professional dominatrix. Jane automatically pressed herself back against her chair, but all the woman did was drop a scrap of glossy paper in her lap, another one in André's, and sashay through the cabin door again. "Dinner," André explained curtly, and if Jane wasn't mistaken, he was blushing a little as he held up his piece of paper to show her the menu printed on it.

Bet the flight attendant does more than just waitress duty, if asked, Jane realized, blushing a little herself. She clenched the menu in one hand and read it over and over until a few of the words made sense. *Should you ever order oysters on a plane? How about on this plane?*

The meal, of course, turned out to be every bit as flawless as the ones she had enjoyed back on land when she had been a Doran fiancée. In addition to the oysters, there was caviar with toast points, red snapper tartare, medium-rare quail, and a boeuf bourguignon that rivaled Gran's. The flight attendant swished in periodically with new plates, expertly matched glasses of wine, and the occasional lingering smile that made Jane feel uncomfortably as if her clothes had suddenly gone see-through.

But eventually the meal was done, the sun was setting behind the Atlantic Ocean, and she was alone in the red-draped cabin with André. Coincidentally or not, he was also watching her in a way that made her wonder if she was still dressed . . . and how strongly she felt about staying that way. Even though she had never been able to read his mind magically, thanks to Katrin's blocking mojo, she had a fairly strong intuition about what sorts of things he might be thinking. *There are still hours and hours left in the flight,* she reminded herself, stretching her long body languorously.

"The 'fasten your seat belts' light is off," he told her, echoing her thoughts. "Perhaps now you would like to see the rest of the plane?"

Jane unbuckled her seat belt obligingly but stayed in her seat. "What sort of things might I see?" she asked archly.

"There is an office," he told her idly, running an olive forefinger along her arm and making the fine hairs stand on end. "A small one, anyway. Very boring. And a little half-kitchen near the back, in case you want just a snack and not a five-course meal."

"Well, we just ate," Jane murmured, turning her body toward his. "So I don't think we need that."

He gently tugged the shoulder of her top down her arm. "Maybe, maybe not," he replied softly. "I have learned a thing or two about you, Ella, and I know you are a woman of considerable appetites." His finger began tracing her collarbone, which seemed to be directly connected to the electrically warm place between her legs.

Impulsively, she slid out of her seat and turned so that she was straddling him. His hands gripped the small of her back, pulling her down and closer so that she could feel the hardness of him. "I was hoping to hear about a bedroom," she told him seriously as his lips touched her throat, "but you kept talking about everything else and wore out my patience."

"Hmm," he murmured, his voice muffled by her warming skin, "I would never wish to upset a guest, but I do enjoy testing the limits of your patience." He reached up and began unfastening the small, iridescent shell buttons of her top. It was a brick-red satin sleeveless thing that would have made the real Jane look both blotchy and lumpy, but on Ella it looked divine, and Ella was the one who coyly slid André's leather belt out of its buckle. He smiled when he reached her last button, and pulled the top just partway down over her arms, so they were caught behind her in the fabric.

Then he surged up and spun her back into her own chair, pinning her there with his body. Jane wriggled a little, experimentally. She was pretty sure she could work her arms free of her top with a little effort, if she wanted to, but then André began to kiss his way down her body and she discovered that she really preferred to stay exactly where she was. After a brief pause to flick his tongue gently around her nipples, he moved downward, his mouth sending shivers radiating out in every direction.

The waistband of the long, swishy broomstick skirt she was wearing—another piece that wouldn't have flattered Jane's real, much shorter body—was elastic, and André rolled it down turn by turn. His mouth explored each inch of newly exposed skin, and Jane moaned happily. *Good food, great wine, the setting sun turning the tops of the clouds all gold, and an incredibly sexy man who can't get enough of my body,* she counted in her head: it was a lot of blessings at once. *Even if I am in near-constant danger, including right now.*

André moved fractionally lower, and a shiver that was neither entirely pleasure nor entirely danger shot up her spine. She didn't know the specifics of the Dalcaşcus' negotiations with Lynne, but she could only assume that discovering that one of Lynne's top-two most-wanted fugitives was in their possession would astronomically improve the siblings' bargaining position.

If he finds out who I really am, I'll be even more trapped than I am right now. Between the top around her arms, André blocking her into the seat, the sealed doors of the airplane, and the fact that the only nerve-endings of hers that seemed to be working at all were the ones directly under his tongue, a sudden escape would be pretty much out of the question. The fear began to coil around her arousal like a pair of snakes, but both somehow grew stronger by being locked together.

"More," she heard herself whisper, her voice rasping in the dry, thin air. "I need more."

She felt rather than saw André's smile. *I'm in so much trouble here,* was her last coherent thought before he pulled her out of her chair entirely, setting her down with unexpected gentleness on a velvet-covered couch. She saw him in fragments: dark hair falling over his eyes, the decisive cut of the muscles just above his hips, dark stubble just below the strong planes of his cheekbones, a mole on his rib cage that looked a bit like a heart. It was still, but hers was racing, racing, as he bore down on her and gave her exactly what she had asked him for.

Chapter Twenty-Three

A BLACK CAB RUMBLED BY, AND JANE HUGGED HER PLAID BUR-berry trench coat closer to her body. Patches of warm light spilled onto the sidewalk every few yards from crowded pubs and elegant shops, but their inviting glow just made Jane feel colder.

I thought London was supposed to be foggy, she griped to herself. *I didn't realize I was in for constant drizzle.* Having finally managed to get a few hours away from her extremely attentive traveling companion, though, she supposed that she couldn't really afford to be picky about the weather.

Since they had landed, André had been so cagey about where he was going after London, and why, that Jane was starting to wonder if he had made the whole trip up as an excuse to stalk her. He had begun by expressing extravagant concern for her train-wreck of a younger cousin, and insisted that he had nothing but time to be supportive of Jane while she searched for the fictional party girl. Jane, who had no idea where she was going but certainly didn't want André accompanying her there, had invented excuse after excuse. They had spent a day and a half in a stalemate, and instead of looking for Annette, Jane had accomplished nothing but dining, sightseeing, and sleeping with André.

Over beet salad at Texture, he had finally, if reluctantly, told her that they would have to spend the afternoon apart, and Jane's heart leaped. *He must actually have had business to attend to here*, she smiled to herself, spearing a leaf of frisée cheerfully. Then it had occurred to her that this might just be a new kind of ploy on his part, and she felt a little sad that it actually made sense now for her to be so paranoid.

In spite of herself, Jane glanced over her shoulder. From the thin crowd behind her, a dark-haired man in a brown leather jacket ducked into a used bookstore. Jane clenched her fists and hurried on. She had already seen him twice since she had left their Kensington hotel. He was wearing something different each time and never paid the slightest bit of attention to her, but her heart still thundered in her rib cage.

She lit a cigarette, inhaling deeply and waiting for the smoke to calm her down. But her jitteriness remained, and her hand was even colder than it had been before. She stamped out the barely smoked cigarette on the sidewalk and stuffed both hands back into her pockets.

If André *was* leaping from rooftop to rooftop and following her every move, she admitted ruefully, at least her movements were both boring and unintelligible. She'd spent nearly an hour wandering along Hyde Park until it emptied into Green Park, and then St. James's Park, and if it weren't for the occasional massive monument or statue, she might almost have forgotten that she was in a majorly crowded city at all. But the impressive stretch along the Thames was livelier, and she wandered aimlessly up the bank. She felt an urgent need to look seriously and systematically for the building she had seen in her vision of Annette, but it was more difficult than she had allowed herself to expect.

There's so much here, she thought anxiously, clenching her jaw tightly. She had visited London three times, all with Elodie. The Dessaixes had a spectacular house, whose top floors overlooked the river, and a suite of its rooms had remained exclusively Elodie's for years after she had moved to Paris. *If I'd had to find something belonging to her in her parents' house, it would have taken, like, two seconds,* Jane realized ruefully. But now that Jane was in this supposedly familiar city alone, with nothing but a glimpsed shape to go on, she realized how dramatically she had managed to oversimplify the task ahead of her. *I could wander for weeks. I might even pass it and not notice.*

Jane had both an innate and a well-trained eye for architecture, but there were an awful lot of buildings in London. It was a bit like looking for a needle in an oversize haystack. She knew what the roof she was hunting for looked like, but she didn't know which side of the street it would be on, or how high it would be. She had to swivel her head back and forth and up and down constantly, and she was starting to get seasick after covering less than 1 percent of the city. *And if she's in some other city . . . some other country, working in an expat pub that gets* The Times *for its nostalgic clientele . . .* She couldn't bear to think about it.

All the evidence had pointed her here; the newspaper had only been one piece of it. Annette had been watching a sitcom on the BBC, and Jane was almost sure she had noticed an electrical outlet beside the girl's bathroom mirror with the serious, flat-footed triangle of UK sockets. And the double-decker buses that occasionally rolled past her on the street really did resemble the blur of red that had rushed by the pub's window in her vision. While none of this was conclusive, Jane's instincts had all told her the same thing. And shouldn't a witch's instincts count for something? *Maybe if I start walking with my eyes closed, my magic will just... walk me there.* She blinked a few times experimentally, took half a step forward, and then jumped back as a white-striped Mini thundered past where she had just been standing. *Not such a good idea with this traffic,* she decided, flipping her collar up against the damp chill.

"I hope you *are* watching, André," she whispered petulantly as she passed a towering, four-sided obelisk. It was covered in columns of large hieroglyphs so old that some of them almost seemed to be melting into the stone. "I hope you're just as confused by what I'm doing as I am."

Just then, something looked familiar, and she spun around to look more carefully. It wasn't the cylinder-and-steeple roof that she was looking for—not even close—but she had definitely seen it before. *I was here,* she realized after a moment. *Elodie and I had tea right across from here, and I saw those gables and thought about what it would be like to live there. I wondered if I could get a work visa, or be licensed as an architect in England with my French degree.* She and Elodie had giggled and evaluated each handsome man who passed by for his potential as a lover, or possibly a husband. Jane had wondered aloud what Gran would think of her living so far away: moving to Paris had already enraged her cautious guardian as it was. With her usual buoyant confidence, Elodie had insisted that Celine Boyle would be happy as long as Jane was, and, for an afternoon, Jane had let herself believe it.

She threaded a path through some cobblestoned streets, still following the course of the river but no longer in sight of it. This time, it wasn't her magic she was trusting to guide her: it was her memory. She knew she had never seen the mysterious roof from her spell before, but she felt lost and alone and she suddenly desperately needed to be somewhere familiar. Gran was gone, Malcolm was missing, Dee and Harris were an ocean away together, and Jane's friendship had already cost Maeve far too much to ask for more. *I have no one,* she sighed, biting her lip. She longed to feel sure and in control of her steps, and to belong somewhere without having to feel like she was walking a tightrope with an inner-ear infection.

Her feet moved faster as she started to recognize more and more of her surroundings. The buildings were set farther back from the street now, behind walls and gates, and at least half of the women on the wider sidewalks reminded her of Elodie's excruciatingly well-dressed mother. Occasionally, a colorful flag hung from over a gated doorway, signaling an embassy or consulate of some distant nation. She knew the area was popular with diplomats, and although she couldn't remember the exact order of streets, she guessed that she was getting close.

Two cross-streets later, she noticed an extremely familiar flowering cherry tree, turned instinctively back toward the river, and found herself half a block from the Dessaixes' house. She drifted toward it almost involuntarily. Elodie's parents had always invited Jane to visit the house whenever she wanted, and she felt a bone-deep longing to be inside, nursing a cup of orange tea in their sun room. She could see the corners of a couple of its glass panels from where she stood. A gust of wind blew some cold drizzle down the back of her neck, and she felt tears well up in her eyes.

No time for that, she told herself sternly, squeezing them shut until the feeling subsided. A nondescript black sedan raced past her and then skidded to a stop in the middle of the block. The driver hopped nimbly out of the car and held one of its back doors open, and a long pair of legs in immaculate camel-colored trousers emerged. They were followed by a pretty, paint-brushed-looking blouse and a wide fuchsia straw hat. It covered its wearer's eyes, but Jane would recognize Elodie's mother's style anywhere. A quick glance confirmed that the woman's husband had reached the street on the other side of the car, and Jane froze indecisively.

From the still-open door behind Mrs. Dessaix, another long pair of legs appeared, thigh-high boots first. They could have been an aggressive look for the middle of the afternoon, but their somber color and the floaty, demure top paired with them made the look edgy but still appropriate. The girl had espresso-colored eyes and a springy black bob.

"El!" Jane shouted, her feet flying across the damp pavement, oblivious to traffic, so happy that her voice broke in a sob. "Elodie, oh my God, I can't believe you're here!"

She crushed her old friend in an overjoyed hug, but Elodie shrank back, her entire body rigid and unwelcoming. Jane stepped back, too, confused. If anything, Elodie looked even more confused: there was nothing friendly in her usually warm brown eyes. "Excuse me," she said coldly, in the same British-Haitian-Swedish accent Jane had borrowed for her new identity.

It hit her in a split second: Elodie had just encountered Ella.

"I'm from Jane," she whispered desperately in her friend's ear. "I'm a friend of Jane's, and we need your help, and I can explain if you just cover for me now, please?"

Elodie stepped back and Jane held her breath, uncertain for

a moment whether her Hail Mary would work. But after a fractional pause, Elodie smiled brightly and turned to her curious-looking parents. "Mom, Dad, you remember me telling you about Marjorie, right?"

"Pleased to meet you," Jane mumbled awkwardly, shaking their offered hands. "I'm so sorry to just show up here, but I'm having a bit of a crisis, and I need to borrow your daughter for a couple of hours. If that's okay." *Mr. and Mrs. Dessaix, can your twenty-four-year-old daughter come out and play?*

Mrs. Dessaix's head was inclined toward Elodie's face, her clear brown eyes scrutinizing her daughter's. "Go on, dear," she ordered, and although outwardly her husband maintained what Jane assumed was his professional unreadability, she suspected that if she read his mind, he would be as surprised as his wife was. "It sounds important, Daniel," Mrs. Dessaix added with a gently reproving note in her voice, confirming Jane's guess.

"I don't know how long this will take," Elodie admitted cautiously, her eyes flickering from her mother to Jane and back again. "I can try to meet you at the Finnish consulate later on, though—"

"Nonsense," Daniel Dessaix rumbled in his rolling Haitian accent. "You didn't come here to spend all your time doing my job, *chérie*. Enjoy yourself, help your friend, and don't worry about the Finns—just do try to make it to the garden party on Wednesday; that one will be more fun for you anyway. It was a pleasure to meet you, Marjorie."

With that pronouncement, Jane and Elodie were clearly dismissed, and the Dessaixes made a prompt retreat into the gated compound. As soon as they were out of sight, all the fake friendliness ran off of Elodie's face like a bad batch of dye.

"I haven't heard from Jane in months," she pointed out flatly, and Jane felt a pang of guilt. She had never intended to drop her old friends so completely, but her new life had turned out to be unexpectedly confusing at first, and then downright perilous. "I read the gossip columns, though," Elodie went on, "and I have a *lot* of questions."

Jane nodded, swallowing a few times to try to clear the lump from her throat. "Not here," she croaked finally. "Let's get over to the water, and I'll tell you everything."

"You'll have to," Elodie replied fiercely, and Jane winced.

She felt almost more alone than before she had spotted her old friend. Now Elodie was right beside her, their shoulders nearly brushing, but they were strangers. *Another thing Lynne Doran has taken from me,* she thought viciously, kicking at a bit of gravel. But although Elodie's presence couldn't give her much comfort, it did give her some hope: the life that Jane had lost was still out there, waiting for her.

I just need to get back to it.

Chapter Twenty-four

"MY NAME IS ELLA," JANE BEGAN, BUT ELODIE APPARENTLY wanted to get all of her questions out before she would even consider listening to answers.

"Where the hell is Jane?" she demanded, kicking the heel of one of her boots against the stone bench they had commandeered for their talk. "She's supposed to be missing, which is ludicrous. Because she does *not* do drugs, and although I was mad as hell that that Prince Charming playboy dragged her off to the other side of the world, I don't believe that he does, either. And that leaves me with this absurd 'amnesia' story, which I don't think I even need to dignify with a— I mean, how do two people get amnesia at once and then *both* manage to disappear off the face of the Earth? But then why is that mother-in-law pushing such crazy nonsense? And since when does Jane—my Jane, who shared a tandem desk with me for two years and couldn't even pick out a first-date dress without me—get married with five hundred people there and I find out about it in *People*?"

Jane started to speak, but Elodie waved her off. "Look, I don't know what kind of 'help' you came to me for, but you're not getting a thing from me until I'm satisfied that Jane actually *wants* me to help you. She's clearly gotten mixed up with some shady people, to say the least, and I refuse to go along with *anything* that isn't in her best interests."

"You're a good friend," Jane managed to choke out finally, when Elodie had spent a few seconds glaring but not speaking. "You're— I'm— She's really lucky."

"She's *missing*," Elodie hissed furiously, her dark eyes huge with emphasis. "She's married and missing and apparently suspected of murder. Who the hell are you and why are you here?"

"I'm here because I need your help," Jane told her truthfully. "I'm here because you're such a good friend." She felt perilously close to crying, but her mind kept doggedly turning possible stories over and over, testing them for holes. It was hard to tell what sort of lie Elodie might find convincing, and she had obviously spent enough time following Jane's adventures in the tabloids that Jane wouldn't be able to just make up a whole story from scratch. She probably couldn't have even if she'd wanted to, she realized, because suddenly she was feeling deeply, draggingly exhausted. There had been so much lying and so much subterfuge, and now that she was sitting with a true friend and gearing her brain up to do more of it, she found that she was just too tired.

I can be tired, but not stupid, she decided finally, and pulled in a few slippery shoots of her magic. She felt terrible doing it—invading someone's mind was unfair and distasteful—but she had to be as careful as humanly possible. She pushed the magic reluctantly toward Elodie, who was tapping her foot impatiently again.

It was difficult at first to make much headway, because Elodie had a whole lot on her mind, and nearly all of it was about Jane. Nearly every moment when their paths had crossed in Paris spun by in a disorientingly nonsequential cascade, and it was thickened and complicated by all the gossip items Elodie had pored over to try to keep track of her after she had moved to New York and fallen out of contact. Elodie had timelines and suspect lists and all kinds of wild theories, but what she didn't have, as far as Jane could find, was any contact with the Dorans. Or the Dalcaşcus, or any witchy associate that Jane could recognize, or anyone who seemed to be the slightest bit sinister.

Jane pulled her magic back in, studying her friend for a moment with her regular vision. When she looked closely, she could see the powdery texture of extra concealer underneath Elodie's eyes. In spite of it, the skin looked a little puffier than usual, and Jane felt touched. Not only was she not in league with Jane's enemies, but Elodie had been losing sleep worrying about her.

"I'm Jane," Jane blurted out, and then snapped her mouth shut in surprise.

Elodie looked quite surprised herself. She stayed frozen on the bench for a long moment, then crossed her boots at the ankle and leaned back on her hands. "Go on," she prompted evenly.

Jane sucked in a breath of drizzly air. "I'm Jane. I'm a witch. Gran was, too, and it turns out that Malcolm's mother and her cousins are also witches. Except they're evil and I'm not, and they were trying to get me to have a daughter with Malcolm so they could kill me off and have another baby witch to raise as their own. It's this whole pride-and-legacy thing, apparently. Malcolm felt guilty and tried to help me escape, but it went wrong and now we're both on the run. But I didn't want to do that forever, so I started poking around, and it turns out that Malcolm's supposedly dead sister isn't dead at all; she lives here. And if his family gets her back, then they won't need me, and I can go back to being me. Oh, and I'm in disguise, in case you hadn't noticed. And Malcolm killed Gran."

Elodie cocked her head thoughtfully. "What color were those fuzzy socks I got at Galeries Lafayette?"

"Green. And you got gray ones for me. And it wasn't *at* Galeries Lafayette, it was from one of those vendors right outside."

"What did Antoine say about the real Marjorie's first drafting project?"

"That it looked like she spent her entire time at university screwing guys who couldn't draw, which is probably true."

Elodie smiled a little and ducked her head to hide it. Jane's heart jumped in her chest: how was it that everyone she liked turned out to be either thoroughly evil or amazingly cool? But Elodie wasn't done testing her yet. "Show me some magic."

Jane frowned. She didn't want to admit to being able to read Elodie's mind, since she already felt guilty about doing it moments before. And "Think of a number between one and a million" felt kind of gimmicky, anyway. *But telekinesis never goes out of style, right?* Jane checked discreetly around; while there were a few people who were technically within sight, none of them seemed to be paying any attention to the two girls on the stone bench. Many were holding umbrellas and most were hurrying along; they were about as private as they were ever going to be in a public place.

She pulled at her magic again, feeling its sluggish reluctance to respond. *I know we're tired,* she told it soothingly. *Just a little now; I only need a little.* "Watch the tree," she told Elodie shortly, her voice coming out as more of a gasp. Elodie obediently turned to the crackly-barked acacia whose canopy spread almost to the space above their heads. Its leaves were still not much more than buds this early in the year, and there were even some of the edamame-like seedpods left on its branches. From Elodie's rapt posture, Jane suspected that she was waiting to see Jane magically make the entire tree dance or something, but she hoped her friend would settle for much, much less.

She tugged as hard as she could at one of the brown seed-pods closest to them, and it danced noncommittally on its twig. *What would Dee say?* she asked herself sarcastically, and pulled in a shaky breath to try again. This time, the seedpod came loose and began whirling toward the ground like a tiny little helicopter rotor. Feeling a little more comfortable with her plan now, Jane mentally caught it in midair, stopping its fall just above Elodie's black curls. She let it down slowly from there, turning it back and forth as if to display it. Elodie watched its unnaturally slow descent curiously, reaching up as if she might touch it and then pulling her hand back superstitiously. Jane made the pod bounce a bit in the air for emphasis, and Elodie, not taking her eyes off the hovering object, nodded. Exhaling all the air in her lungs, Jane let it fall. Elodie flinched to one side to avoid letting it touch her.

For a long, silent moment, Elodie looked at the seedpod by her feet. It wasn't major magic, Jane knew, but wouldn't it have convinced her six months ago? Finally, Elodie cleared her throat. "So you're Jane. And I was totally right that moving to New York was a god-awful mistake, and now you know never to ignore my advice again."

"You *loved* Malcolm before he proposed," Jane pointed out reasonably, ignoring her urge to sigh with relief. "You even loved him after he proposed; you just didn't love that he was from America. Which was, as it turns out, the least of his flaws."

Elodie's eyes softened, and Jane saw concern in the corners of her mouth. "He . . . really killed her? Your Gran?"

Jane nodded, her eyes finally filling with tears. "It's not that simple, of course. He was manipulated. There's a whole history, and it's all super-complex. Except that really, it is that simple. He murdered my only family, and now I have to reunite his just to stop them from murdering *me*."

Elodie drew her plump lower lip between her teeth. "This sister, who's in London. You must know more than that—haven't you even Googled her yet?" She pulled a sleek phone out of her faux-crocodile purse. "I can do it now; what's her name?"

Jane shook her head. "It used to be Annette Doran, but there's no way she's been living under that name for more than twenty years without being found." *How was she never found?* Jane's mind prodded at her; she still didn't have an answer, and she didn't have the time to try to figure one out. Annette was alive, and Jane had to find her; that was all that mattered right now.

Elodie put her phone away, then turned back to Jane. "So then how will we find her? There are a lot of women in London."

"I know," Jane agreed, "but we don't need to find a woman. We just need to find a building." She fished in her own purse for the little notebook and pen she had stashed in there in case she stumbled across any clues she needed to write down. She sketched the one real clue she had on it: the outline of the building she had seen outside the window of Annette's pub. "These parts were windows," she clarified, shading most of the two half-cylinders, "and the whole thing is sort of goldish brick."

But Elodie was already nodding confidently. "This is King's Cross Station. She lives at King's Cross Station?"

"She works across from it," Jane clarified. She felt a momentary stab of doubt; Elodie's eye for architecture was at least as good as hers, but Jane's drawing was cramped and marred by the lines on her notebook paper. "Are you sure?"

"Of *course* I'm sure," Elodie insisted, rolling her brown eyes in annoyance. "You disappeared to the States like all those girls who dump their friends for a guy, showed up on my doorstep like the world's most conspicuous protected witness, and then dumped all of these ridiculous secrets in my lap; the least you can do is believe what I tell you. Especially when your entire 'plan' apparently consisted of strolling around one of the biggest cities in the world looking for one building. Dolt."

Jane nodded, although she would have preferred to be dancing with glee. *She works across from King's Cross Station,* she tried out in her head. *Oh, Annette? Sure, she's at some little pub by King's Cross. I know just where she is.* "Okay," she agreed. "Well, look. I've heard of that station, so I'm sure it's on my map. I can't thank you enough for believing me and helping me. I promise you that once all this is over—"

"Seriously?" Elodie asked in a dangerously low voice. When she spoke again, it was nearly a shriek. "Seriously? So you go find this chick and I go to the Finnish embassy and that's it now?"

"Consulate," Jane corrected automatically, and then winced. "Look, El, I couldn't stand being responsible for getting you any more involved than I already have. It's not safe." The image of Maeve sleepwalking out into the middle of a city street flashed before Jane's eyes. She saw Lynne's malevolent stare, the taxi hurtling forward, Maeve's fragile body crumpling like paper. Then she saw Yuri, pinning Dee's helpless body to the ground and raising a tire iron for what would surely have been a fatal blow. Jane shuddered. "It's better for me to go alone."

Elodie pursed her lips, and Jane sensed trouble. "Like you went to New York alone? Like you fled the scene of your own wedding alone? Or came to London and started wandering around with no plan whatsoever until you cracked and told me your whole story, alone? Jane, honey, you're really not doing so well on your own."

Jane thought about pointing out that she had, technically, done the first two things on Elodie's list with Malcolm and the third with André, but she doubted that any of those corrections would support her point. Besides, she hadn't been able to even really talk with Dee during the last couple of weeks, and it was undeniably nice to have a close friend by her side again. "I'll be fine," she protested, but her heart wasn't in it.

"You haven't been so far," Elodie reminded her tartly, and hopped off the bench. She held out a hand to Jane, who reluctantly allowed herself to be pulled up to stand beside her friend. "Come on; I could use a pint after all this, anyway."

"Me, too," Jane muttered under her breath, but if Elodie heard that she ignored it completely.

Instead of responding, she linked her arm through Jane's, striding off so energetically that Jane stumbled a little to keep up. She checked halfheartedly over her shoulder to make sure they weren't being followed. Elodie's positive energy was so infectious, though, that for the first time that day Jane really didn't expect to see anyone there. *The old Jane didn't jump at shadows,* she realized with a new confidence. *I'm getting bits of her back already.* She squeezed Elodie's arm a little extra for good measure and turned her attention back to the path ahead of them.

Chapter Twenty-five

"YOU COULD TOTALLY SEE THE STATION FROM THERE," ELODIE whispered, pointing along the street. Tucked between a punk clothing store and an apartment building, a pub sat almost directly opposite the yellow-brick building Jane had seen in her vision of Annette. It was painted dark green, had a small dusty window on either side of its red door, and a sign hanging over the sidewalk said THE CHEEKY DRAGON. Elodie discreetly blocked her pointing finger from view with her other hand, looking around them suspiciously.

The stuff spies are made of, Jane thought, smiling. Once they had left the stately buildings by the river far behind, Jane was even happier to have company. She didn't exactly feel unsafe in King's Cross, but it definitely wasn't as nice a neighborhood as the Dessaixes'. Now and then, one of the men hurrying into or out of the station would glance up and stare at her in a way that made her wish she had worn a plain black raincoat instead of her rather flashy Burberry-plaid one. She was glad not to be there alone.

Ignoring the glances from passersby, Jane stopped across from the pub and took it in. The Dragon seemed to almost be squatting on the curb. A neon sign advertised Guinness, and a streaky chalkboard by the door listed food Jane was fairly sure would taste even worse than it sounded. *Why do these people insist on eating "kidney" when there's "foie" out there?* Besides, if the kitchen was anything like the rather grubby bar she had seen Annette working at, Jane suspected that she really should pass on dinner.

"Good, I'm starved," Elodie declared, dragging Jane across the street toward the red-painted door.

"Are you French at *all*?" Jane grumbled, but she good-naturedly let herself be pulled across the threshold.

A few older men—the same men, Jane recognized, who were in bars at five o'clock all over the Western world—were scattered around the dark room. One of the wooden booths was occupied by a twentysomething couple in cheap clothes; a small group of university-age students was gathered around a cluster of stools at one end of the bar. A very young-looking man in a stained white button-down shirt ran a grayish sponge along the bar. Jane twisted her fingers together: was this the right place?

Some parts looked familiar—the colors were right, and the general shape of the room—but she had seen everything from a perspective that she couldn't get to without drawing an impossible amount of attention to herself. *And I don't see Annette anywhere.*

"Sit. Down," Elodie hissed in her ear, and Jane's knees buckled cooperatively. Fortunately, there was a wooden bench just behind them, but she suspected that she would have some bruises on her rear end from the impact. *No big; André will kiss that all better,* she caught herself thinking, and blushed furiously. "Is she here?" Elodie asked so softly that she almost just mouthed the words.

"No," Jane whispered back. "And we're kind of overdressed." Elodie's stylish boots, expensive top, and obviously well-groomed hair stood out like a stoplight, and Jane imagined that her own sleek Burberry look wasn't much better. Three of the girls in the student-ish group in the corner, all in sweats and too-tight denim, had their heads close together in a gossipy pose. The young man behind the bar watched Jane and Elodie as though they were a pair of green, slimy aliens and didn't make any kind of move in their direction. Jane twisted her hands awkwardly together on the table, then moved them to her lap.

"They're just jealous." Elodie giggled, pulled out a tiny camera, and snapped a few random photos like a giddy tourist.

"I'm trying to be inconspicuous," Jane reminded her waspishly, kicking at her under the table.

"Can I get you something?" a British-accented voice asked them, and both girls jumped. A waitress was standing by their table, wearing faded jeans and a fitted white tee that emphasized her generous bust. Most important, she had wavy, shoulder-length dark-gold hair, an elegantly square jaw, and dark eyes like two deep pools.

Holy . . . Jane kicked Elodie under the table again, harder this time. Elodie winced, but rose to the occasion. "We'll both take pints of Guinness and fish-and-chips, please."

Annette pursed her lips in concern. "Kitchen's closed another half-hour," she told them carelessly, her voice the liquid-gold sister of Malcolm's deep rumble. "I can get you sandwiches, or you can just start with the pints and wait if you like."

"We'll do that," Jane agreed, feeling strangely out of her own body. Although she had used her own natural, American-English accent to talk to Elodie, she faintly remembered that "Ella" was supposed to sound foreign—in fact, she was supposed to sound just like Elodie. *Shape up,* she snapped at herself, correcting the sound of the words in her mind. "We'll wait, I mean," she clarified when she realized that both Elodie and Annette were giving her confused stares. "With just the beers, is fine."

Annette nodded crisply and moved off, although Jane caught her glancing curiously over her shoulder at their table.

"We sound like sisters all of a sudden," Elodie whispered sardonically.

"Um," Jane replied wittily, still watching Annette out of the corner of her eye. The girl had an athletic squareness to her, but her movement wasn't especially easy or graceful. She reminded Jane of an overgrown puppy still trying to get used to the new length of her limbs.

"It's a good idea," she went on. "No one has ever been able to figure out where I'm from."

"That was the idea," Jane confirmed. Annette was behind the bar, carefully pulling the Guinness tap over a tilted glass. "El, I have no idea what to do next." *I didn't actually think I'd find her,* she realized uncomfortably. Even at her most optimistic, her search had been so far-fetched that she hadn't been able to really imagine this moment. Everything had been hypothetical, but now she was just a few yards from a very, very real Annette.

Elodie rolled her eyes in a manner that Jane felt was unnecessarily exaggerated. "Well, you could lurk in the shadows and stalk the girl until either she notices and freaks out, or your clock strikes midnight, Cinder-Ella." Jane stuck out her tongue. "Thank God you didn't try to do this alone."

Jane opened her mouth to argue, but Annette was coming back. And she had to admit, Elodie was absolutely right. Without the prior knowledge she had used as an "in" with Laura Helding, or the casual confidence she had gotten from André's obvious attraction to her, she felt completely out of her depth.

It's not that I'm not personable, either, she sulked privately as Elodie effortlessly began chatting with Annette. *People like me plenty. I just don't really know where to start with a total stranger I have so much secret history with.* But Elodie evidently did, because Annette—or Anne Locksley, as she introduced herself—seemed willing to chat. She was even willing to pose for more of Elodie's obnoxious tourist photos: she obligingly leaned her head first near Jane's, then Elodie's as the camera changed hands, and smiled generically.

" 'Anne' is a great name," Jane jumped in while Elodie was fussing to get the camera back in its little case. "I love those really classic ones. Is it a family name?"

Annette (*Anne!*) seemed to almost-but-not-quite flinch. The moment was so quick that Jane nearly missed it, but a glance over at Elodie's concerned frown confirmed that she had seen the girl's reaction, too. "Anne" was already back to her casual self, though. "Don't really know," she admitted.

"Well, it's pretty," Jane offered awkwardly. Anne flashed a smile before whisking herself back to the bar.

"Nice," Elodie whispered ironically.

"Well what am I supposed to do?" Jane whispered back. "Show up out of the blue and ask her what happened in the Hamptons when she was six and allegedly died?"

Elodie chuckled. "I wasn't saying you weren't being direct *enough,* Jan— Ella. I think you scared her off."

"I don't have much time," Jane reminded her friend, taking a largish swallow of her beer and then self-consciously wiping the bitter foam off her upper lip.

"Don't be silly," Elodie told her in an exasperated tone. "We have these whole pints. And then at least one more, with food. And then two whole weeks, in case you need them."

Jane nodded noncommittally. After all of the unexpected twists in the mission so far, it felt impossible to just sit back and relax and let things take their course. She sipped her beer again, more carefully this time. She stiffened when she saw Annette—Anne—heading back toward them with green paper place mats and rolled-up silverware.

Elodie kicked Jane under the table with one of her pointy-toed boots. She mouthed something that looked a lot like *"Chill,"* and Jane obediently attempted to do just that.

"Thanks," she said when Anne had set their table. It sounded a little squeaky, and Elodie kicked her again. She seemed to be enjoying herself far more than Jane was.

Anne turned to leave. Elodie made an urgent face at Jane, who, fearing another kick to the shin, cleared her throat. "Um, so I just came in from . . . the train," she improvised, realizing belatedly that she had no idea where trains came into King's Cross from. "And my cousin—" she seized the opportunity to kick Elodie, who waved like a pageant queen, "—will be working all week and doesn't know this part of the city well, anyway. Is there anything around here you can recommend? For, um, sightseeing?" It was a long shot, if the sights on their way to the pub had been any indication, but at least Elodie kept her pointy toes to herself this time.

Anne pursed her wide lips thoughtfully. "Well, we're not far from Regent's Park, and that's pleasant enough, especially in good weather. There's a theater and a zoo. Madame Tussaud's is over there, too, if you like wax, but it's a bit eerie for me."

Jane shuddered in agreement: the silent, motionless, shiny-faced celebrities at the New York branch had made her distinctly uncomfortable. "The park sounds better." She nodded. "It's always good to get a local's perspective—or someone's who works here at least," she corrected herself, although this time her awkwardness was entirely faked. "I suppose you could live anywhere." *Could she have run away? Was she kidnapped? Did she just get lost?* Nothing made sense. The six-year-old's disappearance and presumed death had made national headlines for nearly a week. And her witchy mother had an even more effective way of finding her daughter at her disposal, as Jane had obviously demonstrated. Even now that Jane had found Anne, something major didn't add up.

Anne snorted a sarcastic laugh, leaning against the back of Elodie's side of the booth. "Don't know about *that*. You wouldn't believe the rent at Buckingham Palace these days." Anne waved her hand dismissively, and her follow-up sounded sort of like an apology. "I've been around here since I aged out of my foster place. I'd moved a bit, so I like sticking to just the one flat now. People rag on this neighborhood, but it's home, you know? Didn't mean to snip just then. I'll go see if the cook's in yet."

Jane smiled as warmly as she could, but Anne was already heading off again. *Does she even remember that she used to have a different home?* "Well, now I want to adopt her," she murmured to Elodie.

Elodie was craned around to watch Anne go. When she turned back, Jane could see that her face was troubled. "I wouldn't, if I were you," she whispered.

"Think what she must have been through," Jane urged as quietly as she could. "You don't know what it's like to grow up without parents—"

"Shh. You still grew up with family. Jane, I'm sure she's had it rough, but she didn't have your Gran keeping her in line, either. And she . . . I just get a weird vibe."

"She's a witch," Jane whispered, taken aback by Elodie's reaction. "We give off weird vibes."

Elodie looked doubtful but tried to hide it with another sip of Guinness. "I liked you fine."

Jane laughed out loud, prompting a new round of stares from the university kids. "And what's that supposed to say about your instincts? Look where that's gotten you."

Elodie smiled. "You, miss, needed my help. Obviously."

"And she needs mine," Jane retorted, but she had doubts of her own. *I can give her her family back. She seems to want to belong somewhere, and I can show her where that really is. But that means turning an innocent girl who's already had a tough life over to Lynne Doran. That's not what most people would call "help."*

Elodie seemed lost in dark thoughts of her own, and by the time their food came out—crispy, oily, and, most of all, hot—it was a merciful distraction from their gloomy silence.

Jane never could have predicted it, but finding Annette seemed to bring up yet more questions and problems—rather than solving any.

Chapter Twenty-Six

JANE POKED AT A SLIVER OF CORNISH MACKEREL WITH HER FORK, pushing it around her plate for a moment before remembering where she was and carrying it politely to her mouth. It was better than the oily, deep-fried fish she and Elodie had gulped down that afternoon, definitely. And any sane person would cheerfully have taken a late dinner at the celebrated Hibiscus with a dangerously sexy man over an early one of reheated standbys at a grimy pub.

Guess I'm feeling insane again, Jane admitted complacently. The gray, gold, and ivory tones of the dining room were soothing, the food was extraordinary, and the wine was plentiful, but her companion's obvious bad mood made it impossible to really enjoy.

"The white-onion ravioli is delicious; would you like a taste?" Tonight, André's accent sounded coarser somehow; instead of purring, it almost grated.

What are you still doing here and why won't you leave? Jane wanted to shout at him. She still had no idea where he was going after London, because, day after day, he just wouldn't *go*. And while she was sort of curious about the private guided tour of the Tower of London he had insisted on planning for the next morning, thanks to his near-constant attention, she was starting to feel more like a prisoner than a spy. She tapped her fork nervously against the rim of her plate. "No, thanks," she replied weakly.

He tilted his head in a fashion that suggested genuine concern for her mood and well-being, and Jane cursed her overly suspicious mind. Just because she and André were both lying to each other didn't mean they couldn't get along for the moment.

She smiled wanly. "I know I must seem like a bit of a drag today," she admitted. "I've been having a lovely trip so far, but my business has taken some unexpected twists." She and Elodie had eventually had to accept defeat earlier in the evening. The Cheeky Dragon wasn't much to look at, but apparently it was an extremely popular after-work stop for a lively blue-collar crowd. By the time they had eaten enough of their food to decently call it "finished," there was barely room to turn around. Having another pseudo-casual chat with Anne would have been impossible, so Jane and Elodie had agreed that they had done all they would be able to do right then. Jane would just have to return—during lunch, she thought might be better—and try again. "How about you—what's on your horizon this week?" she prompted, dipping her fork into a strawberry-balsamic reduction and sucking it thoughtfully.

"I believe passionately in unexpected twists," André replied with a twist of his full lips that Jane could practically feel on her own skin.

That's not an answer. "I don't mean to press, but I would at least like to know your travel plans. I might need to take a side trip to Europe, and it might be awkward to run into you on the street somewhere after you've gone through all this trouble to be mysterious." That was a lie, of course: she intended to be back on a plane to New York as soon as humanly possible after convincing Anne to come with her. But it was a pretty low-risk lie and well worth the trouble if André believed it.

He seemed frozen for a moment, although he continued to chew his ravioli and reach for his wine. But just as quickly, the impression was gone. "You haven't even told me what you're doing here," he pointed out reasonably. "Not the truth, at least. But you want to know where I'm going next? Ella, my dear, this is hardly in the spirit of our . . . arrangement."

Of course he didn't buy the hard-partying cousin thing. Jane sighed to herself. *Probably because I completely forgot to ever mention her again after the jet touched down.* André swirled his thick red wine inside the crystal balloon of his glass and watched her expectantly. She stared into his black eyes intently, trying to read something from them the way normal, non-witch women so often claimed that they could. *The last time I was in a Michelin-starred restaurant on this side of the ocean with a too-handsome man, he was playing me, too,* she recalled sadly. When Malcolm had swept her off her feet, she had imagined having a real family, a loving partner, and an unshakable place in the world. To an orphan who had been raised in near isolation by a grandmother so fearful that she had cut herself and her ward off from the world, those hopes had been irresistible. Even her six successful years in Paris hadn't been enough to allow Jane to shake off the lonely confusion of her childhood, but Malcolm's arrival had promised to finally do the trick. *But I'm not fooled this time, and surely I have more reasonable expectations than I did back then*, she reminded herself hopefully. *Now all I want is to be left alone.*

"I'm here about Malcolm Doran," Jane heard herself say, and felt momentarily dizzy with her own daring. She had no idea if it was brilliant or stupid, but the die was cast, so she finished the roll: "And Jane Boyle."

André stared at her for what felt like forever, while her heart tried to pound its way out of her chest. There was no mistaking the predator behind his handsome face this time; he looked as though he might leap across the table to go for her throat.

Emboldened by his total shock, Jane swallowed another bite of mackerel in a way she thought actually passed for nonchalant. "Do you know where they are?"

André finally seemed to collect himself, although he picked up his fork and set it down a couple of times for no apparent reason. After the third time, he set it carefully on the tablecloth, and Jane saw a real smile playing around his lips. "Ella, once again you amaze me."

"I figure they couldn't have stayed hidden so long without each other," she pointed out, hoping her adrenaline would pass for conviction. "After all, he's got all that money, and she's got . . . other gifts."

"And you think they're in London," André prodded, and then frowned. "But now you 'may' have to go to the Continent. Ella, darling, have you been playing me the whole time with this London nonsense?"

"Have you?" Jane countered. "You said you were thinking of 'making a stop' here—which I assumed was a convenient fiction anyway—but now, three days later, we're touring the city and sipping wine like we've got all the time in the world. I can't help but wonder if we're not following the same lead." *The same* fictional *lead*, she reminded herself sternly. *So keep it simple and vague.*

"Katrin and I have been looking for them as well, of course, for some time now," he admitted casually. He went on to say more—she could see his mouth moving—but a crazy roaring sound had filled her ears. It was as if she were standing directly under a waterfall.

Of course they have. She felt like she might laugh out loud, or burst into tears, or fall to the floor in a seizure. Katrin's sharp body and short black hair appeared clearly in her mind, but unlike the times when she had only half-seen André's sister, this time she knew exactly what the woman's face looked like. It really *had* been a coincidence that Mystery Witch, who had been stalking Caroline Chase all over town, was also staying at the same hotel as Ella Medeiros. Her being there had nothing to do with Ella at all . . . she was just staying in the same hotel as her brother. *When she lost track of me in New York, they thought I might have gone . . . gone back . . .* "You're going to France," Jane concluded dully. Her tongue felt thick and clumsy. "You thought—she might have gone there. Home."

André shot her a strange look, and she thought she might be stupidly repeating what he had just said. But she couldn't help it; she couldn't make her ears or even her eyes focus right. Everything was swimming in front of her, even André's dangerous purr of a voice.

Lynne hired them, she thought frantically; almost hopefully. *Finding me was a condition of the merger.* But things were starting to make an even uglier kind of sense than that. If Lynne found Jane alive, she wouldn't really need the Dalcaşcus for anything. All the parties and shopping trips and negotiating sessions were moving things along between the Dorans and the Dalcaşcus, but the best way to seal the deal would be to make sure Jane didn't pop back up again.

My lover is coming to kill me, she realized sickly. She had thought that she was just flirting with danger, but it had been in her bed nearly every night for the past two weeks.

"Now. Tell me why you chose London," she heard André insist from what sounded like a great distance, and she shook her head in confusion. She tried to speak, but no sound came out. "What brought you here?" he asked again, and this time the threat in his voice was barely masked at all.

Jane reached for her water glass, watching the hand that brought it to her mouth in sudden fascination. *Is my skin getting paler?* she wondered wildly. She had a panicked urge to try to hold up her knife to check her reflection. "A friend," she blurted out randomly. "I got a tip."

André's stare grew darker. "And?"

And now I'm going to turn back into a pumpkin. Into Jane, I mean. She knew it was too early, but she couldn't shake the feeling that she should be hiding her face, that it was changing back by the minute. She could practically feel her hair growing. "And nothing," she gulped desperately. "It turned out to be nothing."

"Ella," André rumbled, "I've been more honest with you than that."

"I'm sorry," she told the sickly spinning air around where she thought his face should be. "I need a couple more days to . . . run down leads. From my friend. But I think this was all a mistake."

"Apparently," he replied archly, but his eyes were blackly furious. A waiter approached their table, but paused and then turned away quickly. *No help. Just me and my stalker, here.* André leaned closer, and Jane focused on the way his black hair scattered the light. "Ella, we both know that Jane and Malcolm went their separate ways weeks ago. And I don't know what you're doing here, but I don't believe this 'tip from a friend' nonsense, either. We could be helping each other look."

"Sure, if I tell you everything I know," Jane retorted. *I don't even know what I know.* "It's not like we can split the reward—the real one, I mean." Three million dollars would be easy enough to divide up, but not the advantage some lucky hunter could get from bringing Jane Boyle back to Lynne. And as it stood, the Dalcaşcus would gain even more from Jane's untimely death than from anything Lynne might offer them for her.

"Ella." André smiled confidently, and Jane shrank back in her chair. "We can work out all sorts of rewards." He slid his hand across the table and grasped her left one before she could pull it back. His olive-skinned fingers traced the plain silver ring on her middle finger; it felt as though he had slid his hand under her skirt right there in the middle of the restaurant. "With your . . . talents . . . I'm sure we could find a mutually acceptable agreement."

He knows we're using each other, Jane reminded herself, dedicating every muscle in her body to not jerking her hand away. *He's just wrong about why.* No wonder he had remained so attentive even after finding out she was a witch. He was just as interested in Malcolm and Jane's whereabouts as Lynne was; Jane's bluff to interest her mother-in-law must have been equally intriguing to the Dalcaşcus.

Jane stared at her hand under André's. It looked tiny and trapped, and most important, it kept looking like Jane's. *Didn't Misty say the disguise could . . . slip?* "I feel sick," she whispered in perfect honesty. "Thank you for dinner, but it seems to be disagreeing with me." She yanked her hand free of his, gave an impossibly bright smile to everyone and no one in particular, and all but ran from the restaurant.

I have to get to Annette, she heard herself thinking distantly as she reached the street and began to run. *I'm not safe without her. Until she's back home, I'm not safe anywhere . . . not as anyone.*

Chapter Twenty-Seven

THE CHEEKY DRAGON WAS CONSIDERABLY LESS CROWDED for lunch than it had been for dinner. But there were enough customers to keep Anne fairly busy when Jane first arrived. Jane thought she saw a faint glimmer of recognition on the waitress's face, but if she had made an impression on her last visit, it apparently wasn't favorable enough to warrant Anne slowing down to chat.

Jane made herself stop staring at the busy waitress, instead turning to the dusty window below its neon Guinness sign. She had been examining her reflection almost compulsively since she had left André at Hibiscus the night before, but she hadn't come to any definite conclusions. Her hair was still dark and shoulder-skimming, her cheekbones still wide, her breasts and hips still narrow. *There's something around the eyes, though,* she fretted, leaning closer to the window. She touched a couple of walnut fingertips to her eyebrows, pulling the skin gently first one way, then another.

A second face appeared behind Jane's in the murky reflection, and she whipped around. Anne refilled Jane's empty coffee cup, and then swept on before Jane could catch her eye. *If I hadn't been so busy staring at myself* . . . She bit her lip; Anne's wavy golden hair had been close enough to touch.

Jane sipped her coffee, and immediately regretted it. It was bitter and watery and oddly acidic, and the more refills she got the worse they tasted. *I should just tell her,* she thought as Anne passed by her again with a tray of empty pint glasses, so close that Jane could have grabbed her free hand. The small lunch crowd had thinned out to almost nothing; it was as good a time as any. *I could just* . . .

The neon sign in the pub's window flickered warningly, and Jane tried to suppress the magic she realized was starting to build up in her system. The difficulty was sobering: it made Jane remember her one very good reason for not startling Anne. Before Jane had known about her own powers, she had thought she simply had atrocious luck with electronics—especially when she was upset. Once she had found out her real family history, she had guessed that Gran's magic had manifested her uncontrolled emotions as weather. She had no idea what Annette's magic might do when the girl was agitated, but it would be safest for all concerned to keep the drama to a minimum. She pressed her hands flat on the scarred wood of the table, working to calm her power.

Or, she decided suddenly, *I just get two birds with one, you know, whatever.*

As Anne rushed by again, this time with a stack of dirty plates balanced on one arm and two glasses pinched in her other hand,

Jane lashed her magic out like a lasso. It caught Anne just above the ankle, and Jane watched in horrified happiness as the girl, the glasses, and the stack of plates wavered for a long moment and then crashed to the ground.

Jane bounced off her stool as Anne struggled to her feet, wiping broken glass from her clothes. "Are you okay?" she asked, trying to hide both the guilt and the glee in her voice. It had been a mean trick, but it had also been kind of spectacular.

"Fine," Anne snapped, flinching away. Then she glanced up at Jane, and another flicker of recognition crossed her face. Her whole posture relaxed, and Jane smiled automatically at the friendlier body language. "Sorry about this mess," Anne went on, swerving around the bar and then returning with a broom.

"It's so not your fault," Jane insisted as supportively as she could. "I think you caught a chair leg; the guys at that table shouldn't have left them pushed out like that."

Anne shook her head ruefully as she pushed the largest pieces of glass and china into the dustpan first. "No one has to leave chairs anywhere." She smiled to herself, as if she were enjoying some private joke. "I'm cursed."

"Me, too," Jane blurted out impulsively. *I thought I was cursed for most of my life, anyway.* She wondered frantically how Anne's magic manifested. If she didn't know what was happening, unintentional magic could easily seem like a string of insanely bad luck.

Anne looked at her curiously before returning to her dustpan. "I suppose plenty of people think so," she offered noncommittally, her waves of hair hiding most of her face.

"No, really," Jane insisted, inching forward on her bench. "Electronics hate me. One time I swear I blew up a whole espresso machine."

Anne glanced nervously at the little drip coffee maker behind the bar, then back at Jane. "Just the once, though," Jane checked herself, her full mouth set in a straight, serious line.

"Just once that was coffee-related," Jane assured her. "But I *am* cursed with electronics in general. We should start a support group—or at least go looking for a cure."

"You could just go live in the jungle or the desert somewhere," Anne pointed out mischievously, sweeping up the smaller pieces.

"Mine *is* an avoidable problem," Jane admitted, "or it would be if no electricity didn't also mean no ice cream."

Anne laughed, a golden, musical sound that reminded Jane intensely of Malcolm. "I don't think I could give up my telly, personally," she offered, and then blushed a little. Jane vividly remembered her vision of the girl's small, sad apartment with its old-fashioned television tuned to the BBC.

"I haven't owned one since my last one blew up a few years ago," Jane admitted, taking a sip of her lukewarm coffee. It tasted even more like bitter water than the last cup had, and she grimaced.

Anne's mouth bowed into a puzzled frown. "Are you *really* cursed, too, then?" Her dark eyes searched Jane's face eagerly.

Jane tore open the sugar packet on her saucer and grinned. "I really am," she confirmed brightly, "so the plates just now must have been my fault. Let me get you a coffee, to make it up?" "*A coffee*," *just like Elodie says it*, she thought proudly.

Anne hesitated, her eyes darting around the room. "Okay," she agreed in such a strange and noncommittal tone that at first Jane thought she had declined. "I'll grab one. And a refill, if you want."

I just asked a barmaid to get herself coffee, Jane told herself, mentally rolling her eyes. *I'm pretty much a social genius*. But Anne was back quickly, and seemed almost happy to be sliding into the booth across from Jane. *Lonely*, Jane remembered with a rush of compassion.

"Although," Anne continued a little more animatedly as she passed the second coffee across the table, "if we really are *both* cursed, it's probably tempting fate just to be in the same pub. But at one table? One of us should watch out for falling rocks."

Jane smiled tentatively. "I think we can risk it for a little while— maybe we'll even cancel each other out."

Anne turned out to be pleasant company, if a bit awkward. Jane sketched Ella's biography for her, enjoying the freedom of it. She had purposely made Ella's background ambiguous and confusing in case anyone decided to check it out, but Anne had no reason to do that. So Jane invented details with cheerful abandon, mixing her English title, Brazilian name, and hybrid accent into a seamless—if long—life story. As she worked to keep their conversation lively, Jane wondered again how much Anne even knew about her own early life. Although she seemed open enough about current things, she showed no inclination whatsoever to delve into her past.

Jane left longer and longer pauses after her own made-up stories, but she didn't risk pushing any more than that. *She feels weird talking about her history at work; who wouldn't?*

"Would you like to get tea sometime? While you're here, I mean," Anne asked abruptly, and Jane jumped slightly.

Witches, she thought exasperatedly, even though she knew there was no way Anne could literally have read her mind. "I'd love to," she hurried to reply. "Tomorrow, maybe?"

Anne nodded enthusiastically and dug around in her half-apron for a pen. When she found one, she reached shyly for Jane's hand, spelling out an address on it in cramped blue letters. Jane, thinking of Lynne's elegant ivory calling cards, suppressed a smile: Anne was in for some serious culture shock when she got to New York. "Come by around four," Anne suggested quietly, her voice turning up at the end to make it sound like a question.

"I'll be there," Jane told her emphatically. Anne was guarded, but Jane suspected that she probably didn't have a lot of friends. Guilt turned her stomach for a moment, but she quickly decided that it must be the coffee. *I'm giving her answers,* she told the guilt. *She deserves to know who she is, and that's why I'm here—it's perfect.*

Then her brain whispered viciously, *André would probably kill me over this alone,* and she felt the fine brown hairs stand up on her arms. He hadn't knocked on her adjoining suite's door since their disastrous dinner the night before, but it was impossible that he would leave her alone for long. *Her sake, my sake—I'm here for a lot of reasons. I have to get this right.*

Chapter Twenty-Eight

THE HALLWAY OF ANNE'S BUILDING HAD AN INDUSTRIAL QUAL-
ity to it that might at some point have passed for "design" but
now was just depressing. The hallway was unexpectedly wide,
forcing Jane to wonder how much space had been wasted there
that might have gone toward larger flats, and where its paint was
chipped, she could see at least six colors of other paint underneath. *And who puts fluorescent lights in a place people actually have to
live?* she wondered indignantly, turning away from the crackled
mirror beside the unnecessarily wide staircase. There was, naturally, no elevator.

The whole atmosphere reminded her intensely of the flat she
had seen in her first vision, but walking into that very same flat
was still eerie. Anne had cleaned up for her guest, but that just
made the general shabbiness of the room more apparent. The
walls were a boring, unadorned white, emphasized by the fact

that Anne hadn't hung anything on them. The floorboards had wide spaces between them, and they creaked ominously beneath Jane's black ankle boots. Anne's furniture all looked either flimsy or secondhand, and after a moment of indecision, Jane chose a scarred wicker armchair. It swayed a bit under her weight.

Anne busied herself in the rust-stained kitchenette for a few minutes, returning with a tray containing an impressive spread of tea and tea-related items. She had assembled a variety of small, crustless sandwiches, scones packed with fat brown raisins, and sugars in fanciful shapes and colors. Jane felt her eyes widen a little at the incongruity of a Wedgwood teapot in the sad little apartment.

"My best friend gave me that for my eighteenth birthday," Anne told Jane, following her gaze to the teapot. "She said it was to give me an alternative to some wild pub-crawl."

"I wouldn't have pegged you for the 'wild pub-crawl' type, anyway," Jane pointed out gently, accepting the mug Anne offered her.

Anne sat on her dusty floral couch and stared at the threadbare pink rug beneath her feet for a moment. "I'm not particularly wild," she replied softly, and Jane's fingers tightened around her mug so fiercely that the dusky skin under her nails blanched as white as the half-moons at their base.

"Well, that's usually a good thing," she suggested. "And you said you moved around a lot when you were younger. It makes sense you'd want to feel more . . . stable, after that." *I certainly felt a little wild after never going anywhere as a kid,* she admitted reasonably to herself. The opposite scenario seemed just as likely.

"I guess." Anne stared down into her mug.

Jane, worried about losing the fragile bond she felt they'd

forged, leaned forward. "I so don't mean to pry," she lied, "but you also mentioned a foster home. I don't know why you were there, and you don't have to tell me if you don't want to. I just mean that it's probably quite reasonable for you to want some stability now."

For a moment, she thought that her transition might have been too abrupt, but Anne just took a gulp of her lapsang souchong tea and nodded thoughtfully. "I don't remember a bit of that, though. Not a thing before I arrived at the orphanage. They said I looked five or six, and in good health, and that's all I'll ever know about . . . before."

Jane leaned a little farther forward, causing her wicker chair to creak unpleasantly. She plucked a piece of sugar shaped like a pair of hot-pink lips off its porcelain tray and dropped it into her tea. "You mean you didn't remember anything? That can't happen every day; surely the people at the orphanage must have investigated." *Not to mention the entire population of the continent you were* supposed *to be on.*

Anne shrugged, although some visible tension remained in her shoulders. "Of course. And especially this girl, Kathy, who volunteered there. Her parents have all kinds of connections, but even they couldn't find out where I came from. But eventually the government had to place me with a family, who were . . . lovely. Really."

Anne's dark eyes welled up with tears, but they didn't fall. Jane longed to tell her that it was all right; she didn't have to talk about this if she didn't want to. *I need to know what happened,* she reminded herself, closing her eyes just a bit longer than a blink. *Even if it's hard for her.* "You say that sadly," Jane encouraged gently, dropping her voice half an octave to sound more soothing.

"The last time I talked to them I was throwing a tantrum,"

Anne murmured. Her square jaw clenched tightly. "It was six months in, and they had bought me new shoes—those shiny Mary Jane kind—and wanted me to throw out the ones I'd been wearing. Which had holes in them by then, but Kathy had picked them for me, and I was in the middle of a complete fit when the smoke alarms started going off. They made me leave, but their girls—Lacey and Renee—were playing in the attic, so they had to go back in. The fire was everywhere by then, though, and . . ." Anne trailed off and spread her hands helplessly.

Jane's mind flashed to Malcolm's hands, and she dragged it violently back. "I'm so sorry," Jane told her sincerely. Losing two families in a year seemed too much for a young child . . . even if she only remembered one of them.

"It was awful, but it wouldn't have been so bad if there hadn't been a fire at my next foster place a month later," Anne continued matter-of-factly, although her hands were wrapped so tightly around her teacup that her knuckles were white.

"That's a *horrible* coincidence," Jane agreed softly. *That's an absolutely awful power,* she thought silently.

"That's what Kathy said," Anne nodded, but went on to explain that other prospective foster families hadn't seen things quite the same way. Little Anne had quickly developed a reputation as a possible arsonist, and even people devoted to taking in troubled kids didn't want to risk having her in their houses. Another fire in her group home when she was eleven had sealed things, even though an investigation hadn't turned up any kind of evidence of a crime.

Not that it would have, Jane thought sadly, feeling an entirely new kind of guilt. *Knocking the lights out doesn't seem so bad when you compare it to burning the house down.* She felt a wave of empathy for

Anne, who wouldn't have had any idea what was happening . . .
or that she could have stopped it if she'd known how. *Lynne was
obviously no picnic as a mother, but at least she could have helped her with
her magic. Whoever took Annette from her completely destroyed the poor
girl's life.*

"But Kathy and her family kept looking out for me," Anne went
on positively. "She's the one who gave me this tea set, actually.
They've been there for me my whole life, or the part that I remember. So it's a bit like family, when you think about it."

Her face lit up with the ghost of a real smile, and Jane automatically smiled back. *They didn't take you in, though,* she bit
back. *Or find your real parents, even with all their supposed pull.* And
it wasn't as if Annette's real parents had been subtle about
their search for their missing daughter. No wonder Anne came
across so lonely, if a nice teapot was all her "best friend" had
come up with.

Jane snagged a smoked-salmon finger sandwich and nibbled it,
hiding as much of her face as she could with the little rectangle.
She felt guilty all over again thinking of all her own friends had
been willing to sacrifice for her, and they hadn't known her for
nearly as long as this Kathy had known Anne. *No close friends, no
one to teach her about her magic . . . she really lost everything.* Jane crossed
her ankle boots and considered her own agenda in a whole new
way. *I might actually be helping her,* she realized. *Not just telling myself
that—this could be good for her.*

Lynne was no picnic, certainly, but Jane was betting everything that she would mellow once her daughter was home. And
then she would be the perfect person to teach Anne to control
her magic, and to introduce her to a world where people actually
considered her needs. The way most of New York fawned over

the Dorans was downright ludicrous, actually, but for someone as used to being pushed aside as Anne was, it could be just what the doctor ordered. Jane frowned into her mug. *It never occurred to me that she would be a real person.*

Jane checked her thin tank watch as discreetly as she could. She had promised to meet Elodie later that afternoon, and her time was running short. *I did that on purpose,* she reminded herself, *so that I wouldn't be able to unload everything on her right away.* She was more tempted than ever to just tell Anne the truth—but that didn't mean caution wasn't still the smarter play.

When she looked up again, Anne was watching her intently. Jane twisted her watch face down awkwardly, hoping she hadn't been too obvious. Anne leaned back on the floral couch and tucked her feet up underneath her. "I didn't ask how long you were in London for," she said lightly, stacking one coltish wrist on top of the other. "Or where you were going after, now that I think about it."

"Back to New York," Jane answered truthfully. *And the rest depends on what you say to going back there with me.* Anne's full lower lip pouted, and Jane realized that she really had succeeded in making a connection with the solitary girl. "But I do have a little more time here—just not today. Maybe we could get together again tomorrow? I'd really like to talk more."

Anne nodded even a little more enthusiastically than Jane had expected. "You could come by after my lunch shift," she suggested, "or I could come see you, of course, if it's more convenient."

Jane had a vivid vision of Anne and André coming face-to-face in the hallway of her hotel, and barely suppressed a shudder. "I'll be in the area," she lied. "I'd love to come back here."

Anne glanced around at the bare walls and unsteady furniture, and Jane felt she could almost read the girl's mind. She leaned forward impulsively, ignoring the wicker chair's protest, and laid one of her brown hands on top of Anne's golden-skinned one. "I'll come back tomorrow," she repeated, and Anne smiled shyly. *And I'll make things better for both of us.*

Chapter Twenty-Nine

"SO SHE'S A PYRO?" ELODIE ASKED SKEPTICALLY, tapping a croquet ball toward a wicket with one hand while sipping a mimosa from the other.

"No," Jane insisted, turning her own mallet over a few times in a futile attempt to find a version that felt correct. "It's not on purpose. Remember how my computer was constantly going down?"

"That cute IT guy thought you were into him," Elodie agreed. "So did I, actually. This isn't the best example of how this stuff isn't on purpose, now that I think about it."

"I wasn't into the IT guy!" Jane squeaked indignantly, wincing when some heads turned their way. She had come straight from Anne's little flat to meet Elodie, but Elodie had been in the middle of a mandatory garden party thrown by her parents. Jane had arrived to find the Dessaixes' spacious lawn full of well-dressed and slightly tipsy diplomats. The hosts had prudently invested in a heated tent for shelter, but to Jane's surprise, the sun had finally come out, and spring was well under way. *I guess it sneaks up on you when it rains nonstop for days,* she admitted wryly, watching a pair of yellow birds chase each other around a stand of purple irises.

In her gloomy, rainproof city wear, she had felt distinctly out of place, but fortunately Elodie's clothes fit Ella's body a lot better than they had ever fit Jane's. Jane did suspect that the skirt of her borrowed pastel sundress was meant to be knee-length, but overall she looked the part of an embassy wife with nothing more dangerous on her mind than thank-you notes. "Trust me, Anne has no idea that *she* did any of that stuff."

"So she could do it again," Elodie pointed out, hitting her ball once more and then hopping up and down in triumph for reasons Jane didn't fully follow. "Like, if you tell her some really upsetting, crazy, life-changing thing, she could barbecue you."

"Not like it would be better to just spring Lynne on her," Jane argued reasonably. "I have to tell her *something* first."

"So what do you tell her that will minimize the freaking out, both now and later?"

Jane poked at her croquet ball, but could tell from Elodie's face that she was probably pushing it in the wrong direction. It was a question that had certainly been on her mind, but she didn't have an answer. She could, of course, just knock Anne over the head and drag her back to New York, but Jane wouldn't have the advantage of André's private jet on the way back, and she suspected that they'd be stopped before they got out of Heathrow. *And I hear that, since September 11, people are a little more alert to stuff like unconscious women being shoved into the overhead compartments.*

Still, the idea of Anne's flat, or an airplane, or half of New York, catching fire with Jane in it was profoundly unappealing. "I could tell her she's won a free trip through some lottery she must have forgotten entering," she offered.

"And then, when she gets there, that part of the prize is a free family?" Elodie sent her ball sailing in a perfectly straight arc, but looked annoyed about it. Jane wondered where on earth she had been trying to hit it, but didn't want to ask after nearly half an hour of pretending she had the slightest clue what she was doing.

"Trust me, being in that family does *not* come for free," she countered, sipping at her Manhattan. It was a little early in the day, she had thought, but no one at this particular party seemed to care about things like that. Although Elodie swore it had been under way for only an hour, two very prim-looking women had removed their shoes and were mincing happily through the pool of a large, white-tiled fountain.

"I don't know," Elodie mused, but there was a twinkle in her espresso eyes. She had straightened her bouncy black curls for the occasion, and Jane noticed with surprise that the two of them—usually as different as night and day—looked remarkably alike at the moment. *She could be my sister . . . my sister with much better cheek-bones.* Jane smirked at the irony of being jealous of her own fake looks. "You got the wedding of the century, plus a whole second identity out of the deal."

Jane frowned. "I *still* get junk mail about that stupid wedding, you know. Apparently this month trailing-sweet-pea bouquets are half-off. They don't seem to get that I already used mine."

Elodie raised an eyebrow, casually knocking her croquet ball into a post set in the ground, without even looking at it. "I win. Now can we focus, please?"

"Was it close at all?" Jane asked stubbornly, gesturing at the finished game with her mallet. Elodie rolled her eyes, which Jane took for a No. "Gran told me the truth in a letter," she continued more seriously. "But what really made me believe it was just before, when I put her ring on and felt it for myself. And you needed to see me do . . . something . . . before you were convinced. Maybe she *needs* to start another fire, to really feel what's going on in her."

Elodie rolled her eyes again, which Jane took to mean "You're even worse at strategizing than you are at croquet."

"Or I guess I could just tell her," Jane concluded resolutely. "Some of it—most of it. Leaving out as much as I can about me, but telling her about her. And her family—or most of it. As much of the truth as I can to get her attention without scaring her away."

"And you think you know how much that is now?" Elodie looked unconvinced. "After meeting her all of three times?"

Jane knew her friend had a point—after all, Jane still had no idea what had happened to Annette in the first place. She didn't have answers to most of her questions, in fact, but she was increasingly conscious that the third week of her disguise was already half over, and that by the time she met Anne the next day, it would feel "nearly gone."

Even more important, she felt as if she at least knew *something* about Malcolm's missing sister now, even after just three short encounters. The girl had had an awful life because of her magic, and had no idea where she had come from, and underneath her stubbornly guarded front, she was also deeply lonely. It wasn't as much information as Jane had hoped for—and she hoped she could get a little more the following afternoon, before making her big revelation—but it was still something, and if it was all she could find out, it still might be enough. Jane needed Anne . . . but by now she felt fairly confident that Anne needed her right back.

She tossed her hair off her shoulders—it really seemed to be growing too quickly—and opened her mouth to tell Elodie what she had been thinking, but at that moment, Elodie had the same look on her face, so Jane decided to hear her out instead. "I didn't know where to find you, and then this has all been so wild I forgot," she began, and Jane blinked, trying to follow along. "A box of your grandmother's things came to the apartment a couple of weeks ago. The postmark was recent, but it looked like it had been through a tornado, so I think La Poste beat it senseless, lost it, and then put a new sticker on before they finally delivered it. Of course, then I didn't even know where to send it, so I guess they're not all to blame."

Jane felt an electric spark run all the way down her spine and then on to her toes. *Gran.* She had thought the hidden ring and letter had been Celine Boyle's final message to her—could there be more? Gran had never been the sentimental type, but her harsh exterior had hidden a fierce and abiding love for her grand-daughter. Jane felt her eyes sting at the possibility of finding one more tangible shard of that love. "What's in it?"

"I didn't open it, dummy—you were missing. There was a man-hunt and a reward. I wasn't thinking, *Oh, maybe she wants Gran's old sweaters, wherever she is with her murdering druggie of a new husband.*" Elodie's voice was a fierce whisper, but Jane still looked around furtively. The linen-suited men and large-hatted women around them, however, continued to ignore them thoroughly, and no one seemed to be in earshot at all.

"Good point," Jane whispered back. She dug around in her purse until she found one of Ella Medeiros's calling cards, printed with the number of her suite at the Lowell Hotel. "Can you forward it here? To Ella," she added for extra emphasis. *Not Caroline Chase . . . or Jane Boyle . . . or Amber Kowalsky from the Milwaukee passport, with her crazy facial piercings. No wonder I'm not sure who I see when I look in the mirror anymore.*

"Sounds good." Elodie pocketed the card and twirled her croquet mallet casually in the air, nearly knocking over a tray of drinks from a waiter who ventured a little too close. When the frightened-looking man was safely out of range again, she smiled conspiratorially at Jane. *She totally kills this spy stuff,* Jane thought enviously.

"Want to come back to New York with us?" she asked hopefully. She let herself imagine it for a moment: she and Elodie holed up at the Lowell, giggling over room service and plotting Jane's next move. But deep down she knew she had already taken up about as much of her friend's time as Elodie could afford to spare. Besides, Malcolm had met Elodie a few times, and who could guess how much Lynne had learned from him before Jane had rescued him? "Don't answer that," Jane said, impulsively leaning in to give her friend a long, close hug. "You've already done so much."

This close to her goal, Jane couldn't afford any kind of mistake . . . and she could carry out the last few steps on her own. She had to.

By the time she got back to her hotel room, Jane was feeling tentatively optimistic—almost confident. Her plan was hardly foolproof, but it felt right to tell Anne as much of the truth as she could without putting herself in certain danger. *We orphans have to stick together, after all,* she thought, sliding off her cork-heeled wedges and kicking them toward the closet.

She even felt optimistic about Anne's ultimate fate at the Doran mansion. True, Lynne was currently pretty evil. But it was hard to imagine her *staying* so evil once her prized daughter was safely back home. Surely she would be grateful for such an unexpected gift . . . or, at the very least, she wouldn't need to scheme so hard once her legacy was secured. According to Malcolm, the shock of losing Annette had driven his mother half mad with grief. In her desperation, she had risked a dangerous last-ditch pregnancy, helping it along with dark magic . . . which had backfired and damaged the brain of the child, who had turned out to only be a son, anyway. Fully deranged from this second loss, Lynne had hidden little Charles away in her attic and concocted ever-more-sinister plots to secure her family's legacy. It might be too late for Lynne to really change who she had become, but undoing that first loss might steady her a little, and give her back some of her lost peace, Jane reflected absently, flipping open a folded piece of paper on her nightstand.

"*Dearest Ella,*" she read in André's bold, sinuous, precise cursive. "*I'm sorry to tell you that I must leave for France rather sooner than I had hoped. Although I would love to continue to share London with you, I will be leaving tomorrow evening. Sadly, I cannot rely on seeing you before then, so I hope you will forgive my saying good-bye this way.*"

"Passive-aggressive," Jane muttered: although the note was superficially pleasant, clearly André had not forgiven her in the slightest for refusing to share her information with him. He would have to stick with his original plan of heading to France and turning Saint-Croix-sur-Amaury upside down looking for clues.

But so much the better, she decided. Everything that mattered to her was safely out of her tiny hometown—including the one last box she hadn't even known about. She could deal with André glowering at her from across the English Channel while she convinced Anne to come to New York with her. And once she did, André's tracking efforts wouldn't matter anymore. He and Katrin could search high and low for Jane Boyle: by the time she reappeared, she would be useless as a bargaining chip. Lynne wouldn't need her for anything—and so neither would the Dalcaşcus.

For now, she was safely hidden behind Ella's face. Ella was the one who would be hunted when everything was said and done. Ella would be the one who had snatched the merger out from under the Dalcaşcus' noses, and Ella would be the one who showed up in New York with the missing Doran girl in tow and a short list of demands. If anyone was out for payback of any kind, they'd be chasing a woman who didn't exist.

She let the note fall back onto the nightstand, then let herself fall backward onto the quilted bedspread. Her feet bounced happily into the air, and she felt like her eighteen-year-old self again on the train to Paris: all her troubles behind her, and an unimaginable new adventure ahead.

Chapter Thirty

JANE RAN UP THE STEPS TO ANNE'S FLAT, THIS TIME IGNORING the peeling paint in the shabby, industrial hallway. She rehearsed her speech over and over again in her head, trying to make sure she remembered it all in the correct order. She was so busy polishing her wording that she collided squarely with a blond, faux-hawked young man who had been heading the other way. A rainbow of old-fashioned vinyl records spilled across the slick tile of the floor, and Jane made a halfhearted attempt to help him scoop them up. *Courtesy is nice, but I have an appointment,* she fretted, shoving a couple of the records haphazardly into the man's black-fingernailed hands. She ran on before he could thank or berate her, breathlessly mouthing the beginning of what she planned to tell Anne when she arrived.

On the fifth floor, Jane stopped to smooth down her hair and straighten the twisting waistband of her skirt, glancing anxiously toward Anne's door. There were four on that level, all a dark, uneven-looking green color that had carelessly been spread over their built-in peepholes. Number 18 was down a short extension of the hallway, and Jane headed toward it so briskly that the heel of her shoe skidded out from under her on the worn tile of the floor.

"Damn it," she hissed, balancing precariously on the other leg and rubbing her ankle. Righting herself, she limped tentatively a couple of steps toward the door.

Around the moment she realized her ankle wasn't really hurt at all, she also realized something was actually wrong. She stopped again, holding perfectly still this time. The soft rise and fall of a voice wafted out into the hall, and Jane tried to quiet her own breathing, which was still a little rough from her rush up the stairs. She leaned back toward the main hallway, trying to figure out what had bothered her, but as she moved, the voice got even softer. She took a careful, silent step in the other direction, toward Anne's door, and the sound got clearer. It stopped and was replaced by the deeper rumble of a second voice.

Anne wasn't alone.

Crap. Had she misread Anne's apparent loneliness? It could be impossible to tell her the truth about her past if she had other people over. Jane bit her lip so hard that she drew blood. *Now what?*

She hesitated in the hallway, feeling suddenly, horribly exposed by the open, echoing space around her. Her next move depended, she decided, on what she found inside the flat. She was a little early, after all. Perhaps a friend had dropped by unexpectedly, or the exterminator was overstaying his welcome. Even if a lot of people were there, she might still be able to get Anne alone.

It could still work out, she told herself, turning Gran's silver ring

on her finger. It would certainly help to know what she was dealing with before she walked into the middle of it. She had never
tried to read someone's mind through a closed door, but this
seemed like a good time to start.

She leaned against a cold, painted cinderblock wall, closed her
eyes, and centered her mind directly behind her eyelids. Breathing slowly and deeply, she let the magic begin to talk to her, tingling in her extremities and swimming through her veins until
she could almost see each drifting, shining particle of it. She felt
the kind of powerful stillness that Dee always encouraged her to
try for, and she smiled a little to herself. *Everything will be just fine,*
her magic whispered, and she sent it through the door as easily as
if the hinges had been standing empty.

The first thing she encountered inside was a smooth, blank wall
that her magic couldn't find any purchase on. *Anne,* she decided
immediately. Her mind felt just like Katrin's had, back when Jane
had thought of her as "Mystery Witch." The sameness reassured
her, and she slid her mind away from the slick surface of Anne's.
Feeling her way instinctually, she moved back and forth in a slow
zigzag through the rest of the room. Although she couldn't see
the inside of the flat, she remembered the basic floor plan from
the day before. She suspected that Anne was on the dusty floral
couch, and felt pretty sure her mind was sweeping the rest of the
seating area in her tiny living room. After a long few moments,
she found another person in the room, closer to Anne than she
had initially expected to find anyone.

That person's mind was a perfectly protected blank, just like
Anne's.

Jane's magic recoiled so hard that her head made a dull crack-
ing noise against the wall behind her; her entire body felt bruised.

There was another witch in the room.

Had Lynne found Annette first somehow? Was it one of her twin cousins in the living room? Katrin was still in New York, trying to find Caroline Chase. There were surely other witches in the world that Jane didn't know about yet, but there weren't supposed to be very many. The odds that one of them would just happen to be in Anne's flat right as Jane was about to reintroduce her to her family seemed astronomically small.

With all her senses as alert as she could get them to be over the storm of adrenaline flooding her system, Jane took a couple of hesitant, tiptoeing steps toward the dark green door. A burst of laughter from the other side nearly sent her scurrying around the corner, but in the same moment, she realized who she was hearing. She stalked back to the door, forgetting to be cautious in her shock, and pressed her ear against the cold paint.

"Kathy was so sorry she couldn't come," André rumbled on the other side of the door. "She worries about you, you know."

Kathy, Kathy, Kathy . . . Jane's heart flipped. Kathy was Anne's so-called best friend. *Small world,* she thought grimly, trying to wedge her body a little more firmly against the door. Anne murmured something in an understanding tone, but her voice was too low for Jane to make out the words.

Surely André knew who Anne really was—he wasn't the type to befriend solitary orphans just for fun. And besides, his sister would have been able to tell immediately that Anne was a witch, and Harris had said there was no one in André's life who hadn't been vetted by Katrin.

"We're working on a huge deal in New York," André replied to a question Jane couldn't hear. "Kathy has taken over a lot of the family stuff from Mom the last few years, so she's running the show. But when this trip to Alsace came up, I figured it was a good chance to check up on you."

Jane's heart began to pound so hard she thought it must be audible through the door, and she pulled back a little.

"She's always been so clever," Anne answered sadly. "I'm sure they must need her just constantly."

"Mmhmm." André cleared his throat. "I'm lucky to have such a dedicated sister, or else I'd never get any time off, myself."

"You never seem to as it is," Anne murmured.

Jane's mind spun chaotically. *Katrin did vet this "friend" of André's. Katrin has known her since she showed up at the orphanage in London after going missing across the ocean. With amnesia. And invisible to Lynne's magic.*

"I'm just sorry you can't stay a little," Anne said wistfully. "It's been, what, nearly four years now? Of course, that visit was just Kathy. So I guess you guys trade off seeing me." She giggled a little, but it sounded both strangely controlled and a little hysterical.

"You look well," André replied absently, and Jane seethed. The Dalcaşcus, she was quite sure, were the "friends" who had taken an interest in little Anne from the beginning, the ones she referred to as "like family." The ones who had looked high and low for her real parents, and kept tabs on her in the years since her mysterious arrival. *She might see them as family, but to them she's something else entirely.* Jane glowered. *To them she's just the little girl they kidnapped over twenty years ago.*

She stepped away from the door, and for a moment she considered blowing it off its hinges to confront André. Her anger sent fiery shoots of magic through her throat and hands, and she let the fury build, seeing an electric red tide rise behind her eyes.

"You really can't stay?" Anne asked. Her words were a bit

clearer now. "I've got a friend coming in a few minutes; I'd love for you to meet her."

"That's nice," André muttered, and he sounded louder, as well. "But I've risked being late for my flight as it is."

"Of course," Anne answered quickly, and from her muffled tone Jane guessed that she had ducked her head. "It was really nice of you to come by at all."

Jane heard footsteps approaching the door, and her body reacted instinctively. She ran as quickly and quietly as she could back to the main hall, all thoughts of a confrontation forgotten. Anne would never trust Jane if she attacked the girl's "family" right at her threshold. And to keep him from warning Katrin that she was on to them, Jane felt sure she would have to kill André. She felt her body shaking with adrenaline by the time she reached the stairs, and hysterical tears replaced the sea of red in her vision. She could fight, but she couldn't really win.

Her feet flew down the stairs, but she could hear the door opening one flight up. She could hear their familiar voices more loudly now, and André would be able to hear her racing footfalls in another second, too. Her heart ready to explode, she risked a glance downward: the staircase was laid out in a fat, lazy spiral. The central opening was wide enough that she could clearly see the steps on the levels below. If he looked down once he reached the stairs, he would see her. She shook harder, nearly missing her footing on a slickly worn step. *He can't see me.*

She darted off the staircase at the next opportunity, but there was no door to close behind her. The one just to her left, however, had no number on it, and, sure that she could hear his shoes on the staircase, she shoved her now-wild magic into its lock and then wrenched back hard. The door swung open with a creak that sounded almost surprised, and Jane leaped into the tiny electrical closet it had been concealing, dragging it magically shut behind her.

It was dark inside, and she nearly screamed out loud when the bare bulb screwed into the ceiling glowed to life. But she could feel what was happening easily enough: she had too much magic and too much fear and too much anger in her system all at once, and that usually ended only one way.

André's footsteps were just passing her floor. She held her breath, but she heard a fuse pop into uselessness behind her back, and then another. Loud cursing came from somewhere farther down the hall, and André stopped on the stairs.

Please, just go, she wanted to scream. But as she thought it, her magic knocked out both the light above her head and the ones in the hallway outside. It was completely dark; no more light filtered in from under the door. And André wasn't moving.

She squeezed her eyes shut so hard that tears welled up, but she couldn't stop the chaos in her heart. She could feel the smooth wall of nothingness that was André just steps away from her, and she tried so hard to break through it that she thought she might accidentally push him down the stairs instead. She shuddered, killing another fuse with a sickening pop.

Just when she thought she might completely lose it and burn the place down, André began to move again, and Jane slumped first against the wall behind her, and then down to the ground. She stayed there for a long, long time after she was sure he must be gone.

Chapter Thirty-One

SO THEY'RE JUST PLAYING EVERY GAME THAT EXISTS, JANE thought somberly once she was finally back in her hotel room. She had to almost admire the Dalcaşcus. In spite of being less overtly powerful than Lynne and her clan, they had a kind of enterprising spirit that would have been impressive if it werent so terrifying. After all, they had brought down Lynne's dynasty with one stroke, and now were looking to cash in on that, twenty-two years later, by allying with her. That was the kind of strategy best handled by experts.

Jane wriggled out of the Karen Millen cape she had picked up to keep away the drizzle and flung it unceremoniously onto a tapestry-covered love seat. A damp puddle spread slowly from its black-and-tan folds, but Jane ignored it and stomped down the hall.

I can't believe I nearly told her.

Anne might have believed her about the Dorans—she might have even been willing to come to New York with her. But there was no way she would have taken such a major step in her life without alerting the people she obviously felt closest to in the world . . . André and Katrin. And considering that the Dalcaşcus had been keeping Anne away from Lynne for quite some time, there was no way they would let mother and daughter be reunited . . . especially not now, when they were so close to the "merger" they had been working on for months. They needed Lynne to stay just weak enough to need them. Their hunt for Jane herself was further proof of that.

She stopped at her little kitchenette and turned on the flame below a sleek silver kettle. The water seemed to take forever to boil, but Jane watched the kettle without moving a single muscle until clear steam began to curl out of its spout. She reached into the cupboard for a leaf-green mug, but nearly knocked it to the ground with her still-trembling hands. She finally got it upright on the granite counter, set a teabag inside, and filled it halfway with hot water. After a moment's careful staring at her hands, she dug a flight-size bottle of bourbon out of the minibar and emptied it into the mug. She continued down the hall to her bedroom, holding her drink in both hands and feeling the warmth of it seep into her flesh.

What would happen, she wondered, if the Dalcaşcus did find Jane Boyle? If they thought they could use her somehow—or that they might be able to sometime in the future—they might just erase her memory the way she knew now they had done with Annette's, and then stash her somewhere "just in case." *Or they might just kill me outright.*

Time was running out for her. There were only nine days left of the Forvrangdan orb's power at the most, and she wasn't sure that it would even last that long. She had narrowly avoided an open war with the Romanian clan by not confronting André, but that reprieve would expire as soon as her disguise did. There wasn't a manhunt on for Ella . . . but the one for Jane was already well under way.

She stopped in front of the full-length mirror that covered the closet door. Standing an arm's-length away at first, then with her nose just inches from the glass, she inspected her face. *Broad cheekbones. Pink bow of a mouth. Long black eyelashes.* She stared and stared, until she had to admit that she wasn't entirely sure anymore what she was looking for. Her new face and her old one felt equally unfamiliar, and at the same time equally normal. It was impossible to tell if her looks were changing, and she turned away from the mirror in disgust.

Her almond-shaped eyes filled with tears. She took a long drink of her amber-colored tea, but didn't taste it. Her plan had seemed like a wild-goose chase at first, but as more and more pieces had clicked into place, she had gotten more and more confident. *I thought I was making the impossible happen,* she sighed miserably, *but I was just getting lucky.* She sank down onto her bed, wishing that the squishy mattress would swallow her whole, and curled up into a little ball.

There was no way in with Anne, she knew: nothing foolproof to convince her to trust a stranger over the people she had trusted her entire life. No one would agree to that without at least *talking* to their surrogate family about the accusations, and certainly no one as emotionally dependent on them as Anne had seemed to be.

I wish I hadn't found her, she thought, burying her face in her starched pillowcase. She would have been better off taking the head start that Malcolm had tried to give her, resigning herself to a life on the run. After everything she had done, she was right back where she'd started. And it felt even worse than it had a month ago.

She propelled herself upward with her palms and rolled off the bed and onto her feet, taking another generous sip of her spiked tea for good measure. There was no point in staying in London anymore; there was nothing she could possibly accomplish there. She hauled her navy suitcase out of the closet and began throwing in clothes by the armload. "Even a fake baroness really doesn't need *this* many shoes," she muttered angrily as she tried unsuccessfully to stuff a knee-length black boot in next to its mate. Everything had fit just fine on the way from New York, but she had also been a lot less upset when she had packed the first time around. With a hiccupping sob of a sigh, she dumped everything out onto the carpet and began again, rolling and folding and angling each item as carefully as she could manage through the tears that were finally starting to fall.

So I go back. And then . . . and then . . . And then nothing that she could think of, she admitted with a regret that bordered on nausea. She had nine days left as Ella, and she would have to keep being Ella for all of them. And after that she would have to go back to being Jane—or, more realistically, Amber Kowalsky or one of the other names on the passports Malcolm had given her, until she could get some fresh ones of her own.

She felt even sicker when she thought of her daring plan of staying in New York—right under Lynne's nose, she had glee-fully thought at the time. It was certainly true, but now there was nothing gleeful about the idea. It was just plain reckless; it had been from the beginning. She had been reveling in risking her neck because of some far-fetched theory that she might some-how take down the formidable witch who held all the cards. Jane, an orphan just barely scratching the surface of her own power, wasn't some scrappy underdog who was about to shock the world by turning the tables. She was just an underdog. Sooner or later, Lynne would find her and put her down.

She surveyed the room; there was nothing left to do at all except book herself on the next flight back to New York. She was sure, though, that that wouldn't be until morning . . . and in the meantime she would just have to begin her useless waiting right where she was. She sat down heavily on the bed again, then reached over and dialed the front desk. She told the crisp British accent on the other end that she would be checking out in the morning. He assured her briskly that he understood and then clicked off, leaving her with a buzzing dial tone.

Chapter Thirty-Two

JANE STARED AROUND ELLA'S NOW-FAMILIAR SUITE AT THE Lowell Hotel. Everything was just where she had left it, although the sharp corners of the linens and total absence of dust confirmed that housekeeping had been busy while she was gone. A blank-faced bellhop arranged her navy suitcase on a stand in the bedroom, then ducked out again before Jane had the time to remember that Americans usually tipped for things like that.

She sighed and flipped her gold Vertu open, pressing the ceramic power button lightly. To her surprise, when the screen glowed to life, it informed her that she had three messages waiting, the first one more than two days old. After staring at the date for a moment, Jane realized that she must not have bothered to get any kind of international plan with her fancy new phone. She rolled her eyes and tapped the keys to play back the messages, hoping she hadn't missed anything urgent. The middle one was from Elodie (who obviously did have international roaming), but the other two were from Dee.

I should just go back to the apartment, Jane thought fretfully as she listened to the first one. In it, Dee wondered where Jane was, told a funny-but-you-had-to-be-there story involving Kate and a piping bag, wondered where Jane was, again, and hung up. *I can't believe we've gotten so far apart . . . I didn't even think to tell her I was leaving town.*

It was true: she had been so worn out after the second spell she had done to find Anne, then so preoccupied with André the next morning, that it hadn't occurred to her to check in with her friend. She almost hung up immediately and called Dee back, but then she remembered the third message on her phone, and decided to finish them all first.

"Hey, Ella," Dee's throaty voice began, as careful as it always was now that Jane was in disguise. "I'm not sure where you are—hopefully somewhere good—but I wanted to let you know I won't be around this weekend. Harris's folks invited us out to their place in the Hamptons. Can you believe I've lived in New York so long and never been? Anyway, back on Tuesday, and if I don't hear from you by then I'm breaking into your hotel to look for clues. So call me, okay?"

Jane ended the call and sat looking at her phone for a few silent minutes. In the hours since her frantic packing in London, her misery had faded into a sort of fragile numbness, and she found that she had no particular desire to call Dee, or not call Dee, or do anything at all, really. She had accepted that her instincts were only as good as her luck, and it felt like there was really no point in even making decisions anymore.

I'm not going to call, she concluded eventually, closing her phone. It sounded like Dee was having a great time, and Jane didn't think she could bear to bring her friend down . . . or, if she was being honest with herself, to hear about how wonderfully everything was going for her.

"So now what?" she asked the empty room. Her voice sounded strange and hollow. Jane had never been one to just calmly accept her fate, and somewhere deep inside her something was screaming at the useless fatigue that had taken her over. She couldn't do anything to fix her messed-up situation; that much was clear. But in her heart, she also knew she couldn't sit in her room waiting to gather dust, either. If her original plan hadn't worked out and she couldn't think of another one, she would just have to push herself to do something—anything.

As she reached to push her phone into her purse, something about her hand caught her attention. *Didn't I notice Ella's nail beds at first?* she wondered. She had, she decided: she could vividly picture the white half-moons glowing against the tawny skin that was just two shades lighter than the walnut of the rest of her hand. Now, though, the white semicircles were floating against a background that looked much more like the unremarkable pink Jane had known her entire life.

I'll go see Misty, she decided. *She'll be able to tell if it's wearing off, or if I'm just getting too used to this body to tell it apart.*

She held her breath for a moment, waiting to feel a renewed sense of purpose once her decision was made. It didn't come, but she made her legs move toward the bathroom anyway. After her long, dull flight, the needling hot water of the shower felt like heaven, and Jane let it run over her hair and body for considerably longer than she really needed to. Finally, though, she reached for the restocked Bulgari shampoo and conditioner and got serious about starting her day.

She made it out of the hotel and into a cab without bursting into tears at the thought of her recent failure, and decided that pushing herself into action—any action—had been a very good idea. She paid and hopped out of the car when she saw the familiar black awning of Book and Bell, and almost smiled when she spotted Misty's wild, bleached curls through the window.

Five minutes later, Jane was installed in the back room with a paper cup of (bourbon-less) jasmine tea and Misty making sympathetic noises as she poured out everything that had happened in the week and a half since Jane had last been in the store. *It felt more like a year.*

By the time she finished, Misty's repertoire of noises had expanded to shocked, angry, and frightened, in addition to the sympathetic ones. She plucked Jane's empty cup out of her hand and crossed the room to refill it while Jane sat, feeling inexplicably as if she were waiting for a judge's verdict.

"Well," Misty said finally, and Jane straightened a little in her uncomfortable wooden chair. "I have a few things to say." She folded her permanently tanned hands in her lap and looked expectantly at Jane, who took a gulp of her tea and nodded. "First—and I know you didn't ask—but I think you're jumping to conclusions about Dee."

Jane raised an eyebrow; whatever she had expected to hear, this wasn't it. Then she remembered that it was Lynne Doran's favorite facial expression, and forced the second eyebrow up to match it. Then she felt silly, relaxed her face, and said, "Please go on."

"Things are going well for her—amazingly well, under the circumstances," Misty began, and Jane frowned a little; this, she knew. "But it's the 'under the circumstances' part that she's trying to get you to ignore when she tells you how great everything is.

She knows you feel responsible for what happened back in March, and she's afraid you'll feel guilty, or get distracted by worrying about her. She's not trying to throw anything in your face, Jane; she's trying to show you there's no reason for you to cut her out of your life . . . again."

"I didn't—" Jane began, but that wasn't true: she had. For three weeks after her disastrous wedding day, she had avoided Dee completely, and in the back of her mind, she had been gearing up to do it again now that her master plan had fallen through. "I put her in danger. I keep doing it," she mumbled, and Misty shrugged.

"She's a big girl, my dear. She's not going to run headfirst into a war zone, but she's also not going to give you a reason to get all protective and drop her. Like you did with Maeve, and then with Harris."

Jane shook her head, but those were even more impossible accusations to deny. "Dee hasn't told him about me, has she?"

"Of course not." Misty looked so shocked that Jane immediately felt guilty for even thinking it. "She's doing the best she can—he's still completely broken up over your disappearing act, you know. They came together because they didn't know what to do after you left, and now one of them knows you're back but has to pretend; can you imagine?"

Jane couldn't, and thousands of questions flooded her brain, but she bit them back. This was hardly the time for high-school-style crush drama, and Misty had already given her plenty to think about along those lines as it was. "Okay."

"Good. Now, thing two: you mentioned an e-mail about your wedding bouquet at some point during all that mess you just told me. Can you back up to that, please?"

Jane shrugged. "I get a lot of junk," she explained; she hadn't even realized that she had mentioned that completely extraneous detail. She wondered how long she had babbled on for, altogether. But Misty waved her hand in a circle, encouraging her to go on, so she sighed. "It's all just part of having the wedding of the century, apparently. Theknot.com has been sending me e-mails—one a week at least—with all these discounts and copies of the stuff Lynne had at mine and Malcolm's. You know: 'where to find the hottest dresses' and all of them look just like mine, or half-off on the same kind of bouquet I had. I can't decide whether Lynne would be proud she's set all these trends, or irritated that people are stealing her 'exquisite' taste. Probably both."

"That's a membership site," Misty said, as if it were somehow significant, and Jane frowned as she shrugged again. "They make you put in your wedding date when you sign up," the older woman added, still staring searchingly at Jane. "And yours has passed."

"You're just going to have to tell me what you're getting at," Jane told her helplessly.

"They should be sending you ads for thank-you notes, not dresses. Are you sure those e-mails are really coming from that site?"

"Who else—" Jane's jaw dropped open, and she sprang out of her chair.

"Back here," Misty told her tersely, pointing to an alcove beside the curtain that divided the two parts of the store.

Jane didn't remember if she had ever noticed the older-model Dell sitting on a shelf inside it, but she certainly noticed it now. Her fingers flew over the keyboard, even tapping frantically on the sides of it while the slow machine strained to obey all her commands at once. After what felt like much longer than it probably was, she had rescued the last four e-mails from her trash and had them side by side in narrowed windows on the screen. "They look legit," she murmured doubtfully, clicking on first one, then another, and scrolling around to see every part of them.

"Sure, except that no major Web site just gives out customer service info like that anymore," Misty scoffed, pointing to two numbers at the bottom of one of the messages.

Jane smiled and started to agree, but then she actually looked at the numbers. The first one was a normal American toll-free number. The second one, labeled "International Callers," had an international country code in front of it. "I've shopped on U.S. sites from France," she told Misty slowly. "That's not how they do it. International callers can't always use toll-free numbers, so they just give a different local one. They don't just pick a random country and tell the whole world to call that." She clicked on the next window, and then yelped in triumph: the toll-free number was the same, but the "International Callers" number was completely different. She opened a fifth window, making it tiny so as not to cover the others, and searched for a directory of country codes. "Brazil," she declared, closing the first e-mail with a flourish. "Then Chile." She clicked the second one off the screen. "Ecuador." Click. "And then . . . um . . . Laos." Her face was flushed as she stared at Misty. "Malcolm is in Laos."

Misty grinned, and Jane felt her own smile widening. The muscles of her face felt a little creaky after the drama of the last twenty-four hours, but there was no mistaking it: she was coming back to herself. "Not South America anymore," Misty pointed out helpfully, and Jane practically giggled; Lynne may actually have been on Malcolm's trail, but then he had jumped clear to the other side of the globe. He was still safe, as far as she knew, and now she might even be able to get in touch with him. *In an emergency,* she told herself steadily, *or when I have good news.*

"And I've got one last piece of good news," Misty told her seriously, and Jane's attention snapped to her tanned face. "Jane, Anne's still in London."

Jane recoiled physically. "Is that supposed to be a joke?" she asked, genuinely stung. If it was, it seemed uncharacteristically unkind.

"You know where she is, you twit," Misty clarified, rolling her eyes. "You didn't brawl with André and scare her away, or tell her the truth and freak her out. She's exactly where you left her, and no one knows you know but *you.*"

Jane frowned. "But I can't get anywhere near her."

"You don't need to," Misty nearly exploded. "You think Lynne can't afford a ticket to Heathrow?"

"She'd give me anything for that information," Jane realized slowly. Fragments of thoughts began to coalesce in her mind: the deal she had been thinking of striking with Lynne back before everything had gone to hell. "Okay. Now I need to run some ideas by you."

It's not perfect, she warned herself, but she could feel the telltale energy returning to her limbs. She felt hopeful, almost giddy, and she knew what it meant. Jane was, once again, on the verge of a daring, dangerous, and brilliant plan.

Chapter Thirty-Three

JANE HURRIED ALONG ONE OF THE PAVED PATHS THAT CURVED downtown through Central Park. She felt almost foolish, thanks to the stares she kept getting from other park-goers; upon reflection, the trench-coat-and-giant-sunglasses uniform that she had taken out of retirement for this occasion seemed to be attracting more attention than it was deflecting. *Apparently, it's more conspicuous in the park on a nice day than around the Port Authority in March.*

But it was too late to change, and she enjoyed the safe, cocooned feeling the outfit gave her. She needed every ounce of advantage she could get, anyway: she was on a particularly nerve-racking errand. Just the thought made her want to pull the collar of her coat a little more tightly closed, but she reminded herself sternly that, for the first time in a while, she was walking into an unpleasant confrontation while holding all the cards.

It was harder to hold on to that thought when she came around a bend and found Lynne, tall and stern and immaculately groomed as ever, standing in a small clearing under a chestnut tree. Waiting. Jane gulped down the lump in her throat and stepped off the path, feeling her red-painted Louboutin stilettos sink into the grass. Lynne's eyes raked slowly from Jane's vertiginous platform heels to the top edge of her oversize sunglasses, and Jane suspected that her mother-in-law once again disapproved of her wardrobe. *Mine . . . Ella's . . . until I start wearing nothing but Chanel, that'll never change,* she thought ruefully, and was gratified to see Lynne's eyebrows pull together at her obviously unexpected smile.

She respects confidence, Jane reminded herself, fixing the smile in place as if with glue. In Book and Bell the day before, this had all seemed fairly straightforward, but now, face-to-face with the woman who had ruined her life in an impressively thorough way, it was harder than she had expected to remember that she had the upper hand.

Lynne spoke first. "I believe you said you have some information for me," she snipped impatiently, and Jane felt stronger by the moment as she registered the tension in the other woman's voice. "I assume it has something to do with my son."

"It doesn't," Jane croaked, and cleared her throat hurriedly. "It's about your daughter."

Lynne's face was so immobile that it looked entirely different. "Jane Boyle? You mean my daughter-in-law. Although, of course, I love her like my own," she finished with a cruel smirk that made Jane shudder in spite of herself.

"She sent me here," Jane went on, visualizing the words she had practiced with Misty just before she said them. "But I meant your actual daughter. Malcolm Doran hired me to find Annette."

Lynne's expression turned thunderous, and Jane braced herself: when witches got that angry, bystanders weren't always safe. But Lynne was, of course, an expert in her craft, and nothing changed except for the air between them. "Annette is dead," Lynne finally said in a voice like a snake's hiss. "You of all people should know I couldn't be tricked into believing such an obvious lie."

Jane felt magic building in the older witch like a battery charging. She realized that she had to get the truth out quickly before Lynne lost her patience and attacked, and she braced herself just in case her time was running out too fast. "Stand down," she snapped, surprising both of them. But Lynne was still listening, so she decided to go with it. "I have proof." As slowly as she dared so as not to spook Lynne more, she reached into her handbag and pulled out her phone. She had already primed the photo of herself and Anne that Elodie had obligingly sent that morning (without so much as an "I told you so," Jane noticed appreciatively). She tossed the phone gently to Lynne, who caught it deftly.

Bitch just had to be coordinated, too, floated across Jane's mind. Most of her attention, though, was occupied watching every one of her enemy's muscles for sudden movements. The chestnut trees around them waved gently in the breeze, and where the late-April sun dappled Lynne's face, Jane could see that her skin looked unusually thin and tired. Lynne didn't speak or move, but she almost seemed to shrink into herself as she took in the photo.

"I don't know how it happened," Jane told her eventually, "but you were lied to." It wasn't the full truth: she didn't know the exact mechanics and she hadn't gotten confessions from any of the perpetrators. But she had already decided that she wasn't going to sell out the Dalcaşcus just yet. There was no real need to, since they would lose so much from Annette's return already—and probably have to run for the hills anyway, lest Anne recognize them and spill the beans. Besides, implicating them might make Jane seem petty or vengeful, and she needed Lynne to believe and respect her in order for her plan to work.

Lynne stared at the screen for several long minutes. Sparrows sang in the bushes, and a red-tailed hawk wheeled overhead. Jane could hear children's laughter somewhere nearby, although no one passed their little clearing close enough to be seen. She wondered if the magnetic charge of their magic helped keep passersby away; she certainly would have avoided their current spot if she hadn't had to be there.

When Lynne's voice sounded again, Jane jumped a little. It was hoarse and broken and nothing like her usual controlled purr. "Where?" she gasped. Her dark eyes swept up to meet Jane's, and Jane was stunned by the change in them. Lynne had always been cool, commanding, thoroughly in charge. Now, with her widened eyes and softened, uncertain mouth, she looked like a supplicant.

"I can tell you exactly how to find her," Jane went on. She said the words just as she had practiced them, but inside she felt shaken by the rawness of Lynne's need. *That was the whole point,* she tried to tell herself. It was harder than she had ever imagined, to bargain when Lynne looked more like a distraught mother than an arch-nemesis. Jane shivered a little in the warm spring sunlight and reminded herself that she had to be as careful as possible, just in case. "But I'm going to have to insist on some terms, of course."

Lynne nodded absently, glancing at the picture every few seconds as if she were afraid it might disappear. "Name them."

Jane cleared her throat again, still feeling unpleasantly guilty. "First, my employer insists that you immediately call off the search for him and his wife," she delivered quite smoothly, all things considered. "The police, the reward . . . it all needs to go away. Everyone must stop looking for Malcolm Doran and Jane Boyle, including you."

"Of course." Lynne frowned, and Jane reminded herself that she was only useful to Lynne in the absence of Annette, anyway. That condition had been, by far, the easier of the two.

"And then there's my fee. I took this job on commission, so to speak. I will need you to turn over your magic to me right now in exchange for Annette's current name and address."

Jane held her breath; she had no idea what kind of reaction to expect, but fireworks didn't seem unlikely. Rendering Lynne powerless was the only safe way to reunite her with Annette. For one thing, it made it that much less likely that she could ever change her mind and come after Jane. For another, it made it much less likely that she would make Annette miserable. Lynne could be a good mother, Jane had eventually decided, if she had to give up being the perfect witch. *Besides, if she picks Anne over her power, I won't feel so guilty about turning Anne over to her,* she thought anxiously.

Lynne reached into her handbag.

"What are you doing?" Jane demanded anxiously, rallying her own magic into something like a shield, but Lynne just smiled dismissively.

When the older woman removed her hand from her purse, Jane recognized the object she was holding as a silver athame. "Tell . . . Malcolm . . . that those terms are more than acceptable," Lynne announced placidly, and held the slim dagger up to her lips. She closed her eyes, and the earth spun sickeningly under Jane's feet. Lynne inhaled and Jane felt as though she were being smothered, and then Lynne exhaled onto the athame. Even in the relatively warm air, Jane could see her breath fog up the mirrored surface briefly, and then it disappeared as if the blade had absorbed it. And then there was nothing at all in the small clearing except for Jane, Lynne, and the small silver object Lynne was tossing gently back across the grass to her.

She didn't even hesitate, Jane marveled, fumbling to catch the athame. There was no question of a trick; she could feel Lynne's magic in the object. It coiled against her fingers below the surface of the silver, and Jane shuddered involuntarily as she shoved it into her own purse. She had believed that Lynne would trade anything for Anne—had been counting on it, in fact. But somehow the speed and ease of Lynne's capitulation had caught her completely off guard. *She truly does love her daughter,* Jane decided, feeling almost awed. For the first time since she had come up with the whole idea, she actually felt good about bringing the mother and daughter back together. Against all the odds, she suddenly felt sure she was doing the right thing, rather than just the right thing for *her.*

"Her name is Anne Locksley now," she told Lynne softly, and then went on to tell her every detail about her daughter's second life that she could think of. The only thing she left out was the involvement of the Dalcaşcus in Annette's disappearance. There was a decent chance Lynne would eventually figure out that part of the story on her own, but the woman's easy sacrifice had given Jane a happy glow she didn't want to risk having tarnished just yet. She liked this side of Lynne . . . and would be just as happy to be far away if the old, vengeful side ever came back out again. "I assume that this concludes our business," Lynne said finally. Jane scanned Lynne's face for any hint that this was all an unfathomably elaborate hoax, but Lynne's peach-lipsticked mouth remained soft and vulnerable.

"Please give your employers my best," Lynne told her briskly, tossing Jane's gold Vertu back as an afterthought. She hesitated for a moment, her eyes boring into Jane's, and Jane was unaccountably surprised to see that her onetime nemesis's eyes still had the strange, contact-lens-like layer of darkness over their irises. *Somehow I always assumed that that was a result of her magic,* Jane realized. *I guess it's just the way she looks.* It made sense, of course: both Malcolm and Anne had quite dark eyes. But something about Lynne's had always looked unnatural to Jane, tacked on somehow over her real eyes.

"I will," she replied hesitantly, and then forced her voice to steady. "I'm sure they would want me to wish you the same."

Lynne smiled an absolutely unfathomable smile, and for a second Jane didn't know if she wanted to hug the woman or run for her life. She did neither, though, because Lynne followed the strange expression up with even stranger words. "I always did see some of myself in you . . . Ella."

By the time Jane had fully processed that parting shot, Lynne was halfway down the path. *But she said that to me,* Jane suddenly remembered, *not to Ella. She had told me I reminded her of herself on my wedding day.*

Jane took a few steps back to the paved path and sank down onto a nearby bench, fighting the urge to laugh out loud. Lynne had seen through her disguise. There was no way of knowing how or even when the older woman had figured it out, but it didn't really matter. Lynne had willingly—eagerly—accepted Jane's terms, and all her magic was now safely stowed in the athame in Jane's purse.

I took her magic, and she knows who I am, and all she could think about was getting to Anne, Jane marveled, and slowly a weight she hadn't even realized she'd been carrying began to lift from her shoulders.

I did it.

She practically skipped out of the park. She couldn't wait to tell Dee . . . and Malcolm.

Chapter Thirty-four

THE NEXT MORNING, JANE FOUND HERSELF SITTING ON HER hotel bed, staring at Lynne's athame. It was more or less the same position she had spent the entire previous afternoon and evening in, but it didn't feel old yet. The thin, double-edged blade was as long as Jane's hand, and its mirrorlike surface seemed to almost absorb the earth tones of the bedroom. The handle of the athame was made of silver, as well, but the similarities ended there. Every inch of the hilt was deeply scarred with strange symbols and letters, and it was so tarnished that only a few gleams of the metal were still visible underneath the black crust. It was beautiful, really. The only problem now was deciding what to do with it.

The most obvious choice, of course, was to take its power for herself. She remembered the way she had picked up the silver ring Gran had left for her; she remembered her immediate conviction that it was *hers*. She felt sure she could do this again with the athame, and let its magic flow into her the way Celine Boyle's once had.

It was an attractive option in a lot of ways. She would be at least twice as powerful as she already was—more than powerful enough to keep any remaining enemies at bay. She would be unstoppable . . . or she would feel unstoppable, at least, and therein lay the problem with that plan. The magic in the blade was Lynne's, and Lynne was—or had been, at least—pretty impressively evil and power-hungry. Jane had never heard or read anything to make her think there was such a thing as good magic or bad magic, but there certainly were bad witches out there, and she was reluctant to inject their current into her own veins.

I didn't have to choose with Gran's ring, she reminded herself. She had *known* it belonged to her. This magic, on the other hand, was something she would have to consciously choose to take on, and she had no idea what consequences such a choice might bring. It might mean nothing more than that she was the most powerful witch around . . . or it might mean that the power in the athame shouldn't be hers but was anyway. It could change her somehow, and she might lose the ability—or the will—to get rid of it once it did.

And none of that even addressed what might go wrong *outside* of her if she took Lynne's magic. In addition to the power Jane had been born with, she had already received a huge dose of magic from Gran—more than she even knew how to effectively use yet. Adding the contents of the athame to her own potent magic would almost certainly attract the attention of the other witches who were still active in the world, most of whom had probably already heard the name "Jane Boyle" by now. The extra magic would make her even more of a target than Lynne's maliciousness had.

André and Katrin would be the first ones after her once they figured out what had happened, she knew, and the thought of the vicious Romanians stalking her around the globe made her shudder. And while it had been her plan to let Lynne think Ella had disappeared into thin air, taking the Doran magic with her, the fact that Lynne apparently had connected Ella with Jane made it even more dangerous to create new enemies for her fading alter ego.

Jane's fingers convulsed on the handle of the athame. The power in it was tempting, no question, but there was also something repellent about the feel of it against her skin, and she let the dagger go quickly.

If she couldn't take Lynne's magic herself, then what could she do with it? Part of her was tempted to just throw the thing into a Dumpster somewhere, but the idea made the hairs on the back of her neck stand up on their own. If it was a bad idea to use the magic, it was a worse one to let it out of her control.

So am I just supposed to carry it around in my purse like a toy Chihuahua? A cursed toy Chihuahua?

That hardly seemed like an ideal strategy. Most of the magical community would probably assume that she was using the magic; carrying it around would make her no less a target, yet with no more ability to defend herself. And if any witch worth her salt got within twenty yards of the little silver knife, she would absolutely know what it was Jane was carrying. Jane could feel it through the leather of her purse, across half her bedspread, pressing in on her dreams while she had slept.

I know where to keep something valuable, she realized with a sudden flash of hope. *I know where to put something secret.*

It was a Sunday morning, and banks must be closed, but she had James McDeary's card somewhere among her things with his private, emergency number on it. If anyone could get her where she needed to go, it was him. "First Trust Bank of New York," she muttered, digging through her enameled card case. "Corner of Rector and Trinity."

She left the bank an hour later, feeling about twenty pounds lighter. Just as she had suspected, the bank manager had been eager to help the baroness . . . even if he'd had no idea who she was. It was actually better that way, she decided: this time, he had done nothing but fawn all over her, while the first time they had met, when she had been posing as Malcolm's sister, he had suspected something. *Because I took the unicorn,* she realized, a small piece clicking into place in her mind. At some point, Malcolm must have mentioned that the "personal item" in his safe had belonged to his late sister, and then a very-much-alive sister had showed up to claim it. *No wonder he looked so freaked out.* Jane giggled to herself.

She had been walking uptown ever since she had left the bank, allowing the soothing buzz of the streets of Manhattan to drain the extra energy from her nerves. But when she reached Houston Street, she stopped cold.

She had come face-to-face with an electronics store's display window full of (THIS WEEK ONLY!) discounted televisions, all showing Lynne Doran's face. Jane stopped walking as the camera zoomed out, and a photo of Anne Locksley that looked like a passport picture—or maybe a mug shot—appeared beside Lynne's. TWENTY-YEAR-OLD MYSTERY SOLVED, the banner read. HEIRESS RETURNS TO OVERJOYED FAMILY.

There were plenty of similarly terse and sensationalistic headlines below various family photos: apparently, Anne's reappearance was big news. *Bigger than her brother's disappearance,* Jane thought with something that felt almost like jealousy, and then she laughed at herself a little. Wasn't that the point, after all? Besides, it really was a pretty spectacular story. Half the televisions were showing old photos of Annette as a little girl. At first, Jane guessed that they were Lynne's pictures, but there were at least a couple that had to be from later, after Anne became a British foster child. The other screens were promising interviews with the family; there was even a brief clip of Lynne's husband with a glass of whiskey in his hand and tears in his eyes.

Damn, that woman moves fast. Jane blinked, trying to count flight hours against the time change between New York and London. *I slept,* she decided eventually; obviously, Lynne hadn't bothered with such trivia. The full-on media blitz that her onetime nemesis had literally pulled off overnight was impressive, even for a Doran. As Jane continued on, she realized that news of Anne's triumphant return to the bosom of her loving family was everywhere: televisions, news tickers, even printed papers had all managed to pick up the story in a hurry. *It's like magic,* she thought smugly, and smiled as she hailed a cab.

The little screen facing the backseat had a promo clip of an interview with Laura and Blake Helding, who surprised Jane by managing to sit beside each other without clawing each other's eyes out. They presented a relatively united front, unwaveringly telling the story of Annette's supposed death in carefully edited bursts, interspersed with information about the amazing discovery that she was alive, after all. Ella's name, naturally, never came close to being mentioned. Somewhere in all the drama, Jane registered the news that Malcolm was in rehab somewhere in Austria, and his wife was home with her family, waiting for the annulment papers that would put a period at the end of her (totally un-newsworthy) ordeal. Laura elegantly implied that anyone who didn't respect poor Jane Boyle's privacy during this difficult time deserved to be drawn and quartered, while simultaneously exploiting Anne's tragic childhood for all it was worth. Jane was frankly impressed by her friend's media savvy, and even went so far as to wonder if it would be possible for them to stay in touch once the circus had calmed down.

Or maybe we don't have to wait that long, she realized once she got back to her room. A silver tray was waiting conspicuously on the little table just inside her door, and resting on top of it was a thick, creamy envelope. She didn't even need to look at the handwriting of Ella's name to know who it was from—she felt sure she would recognize that stationery for the rest of her life—and she slid it open curiously. Instead of the personalized note she had expected, what she pulled out of the envelope was a formal, engraved message . . . an invitation, she realized after a confused moment.

The Dorans, it seemed, would welcome her presence at an intimate gathering of friends and select members of the press intended to welcome Miss Annette Doran back to her rightful place in Manhattan society.

The soiree was set for the following Saturday night. It would be the last day of her disguise, Jane realized, and instinctively turned toward her full-length mirror to check her appearance. Almond-shaped black eyes stared back at her from Ella's mahogany face. In spite of her fears during the incredibly stressful previous week, the orb's spell seemed to be going strong. *Based on when I woke up as Ella, I'd have until midnight,* she reminded herself. She pulled the closet door open, banishing her reflection and replacing it with her impressive collection of party dresses.

Am I seriously considering this? I wonder what Anne will think, seeing me there, Jane thought with a little restless agitation, closing the closet door again firmly. But, of course, Lynne must have told Anne about her part in their reunion already. And if Lynne was willing to forgive and forget the steep bargain Ella had driven, why should Anne hold a grudge of any kind against her? She had been a little deceptive, sure, but obviously everything was working out for the best for everyone. *And in record time,* Jane mused: getting as many invitations as she felt sure had been sent out engraved on such short notice was nearly as impressive as the media blitz Lynne had arranged to coincide with her party-planning.

She turned the invitation over and over in her hands. It meant something to her that Lynne was willing to bury the hatchet to this extent, but it still felt wrong somehow to go and toast Anne's arrival in New York. *I did my part,* she decided. *They can take it from here without me.*

Chapter Thirty-Five

BY WEDNESDAY, JANE WAS THOROUGHLY BORED WITH BEING Ella. She hadn't been able to exchange more than a few quick text messages with Dee, who had apparently gone straight to work following her long weekend, and it wouldn't have been smart to risk being seen with her right now, anyway. Jane felt she had imposed enough on Misty's hospitality for the time being, and she certainly didn't want to see André, who had started sending aggressively flirtatious notes the moment he had returned, empty-handed and presumably furious, from Alsace. So Jane spent a good deal of her time in her hotel room, alternately reading *The Girl with the Dragon Tattoo* and tabloids. The discovery of the missing Doran was still big news, of course, fueled in part by speculation about what was sure to be the most elaborate coming-out party New York had ever seen.

By the time the front desk called to let her know that a package had arrived for her, her cabin fever had gotten so irritating that she nearly ran down the stairs to collect the delivery herself. She remembered just in time that royalty didn't do that sort of thing, and literally sat on her hands to avoid calling back every few seconds to ask why the bellhop hadn't reached her door *yet*.

Her excitement only grew as she took the package—a wide, flattish box covered in brown paper—and recognized Elodie's cheerful handwriting. The box looked fairly intact, and Jane guessed that her friend had thoughtfully repackaged the mangled box that had originally arrived from Gran's farmhouse. It didn't stay intact for long, though: she began by trying to pull off the paper and then, in her eagerness, wound up ripping straight through the cardboard beneath. Crisscrosses of tape held it together in unexpected and sometimes inconvenient ways, but she was determined, and in a few seconds she was looking directly at the last remnants of her inheritance.

It didn't look like much, she had to admit, but it didn't really matter: everything in the box had belonged to Gran, and that made it special to her. There were a few books in English, more in French, and a floral fabric–covered one that she set aside, noting that it looked like a diary of some kind. There was a pair of reading glasses with gray plastic frames in a soft leather pouch, two glass paperweights with flowers suspended inside, an ancient-looking Polaroid camera with no film in it, a little box that held a few seashells, and a collection of broken and dried-out pens. Jane lifted each item carefully out of the wreckage of the cardboard box, lining them up on the floor in front of her. The resulting display made her feel as though Gran were in the room with her, and she closed her eyes in a moment of pain. She reached out blindly until her hand encountered the cold surface of one of the paperweights, and let her mind slide back to the old farmhouse at the foot of the mountain.

She remembered the way that the dusty sunlight had fallen sideways through the small windows, illuminating the pink anemone in one glass bubble, the yellow rose in the other. She had held them up, turning them to catch the light, transfixed by the way they seemed to glow from within. Gran would be in the kitchen, filling the entire house with the smell of cabbage and boiled ham, or she would be in the living room, nestled in one of her overstuffed armchairs, the gray reading glasses perched on her nose. Jane's hands balled into fists as she opened her eyes. No matter how well things had turned out, she had already lost so much to this conflict. She was free to start over now, but with no family to return to, starting over was her only real choice.

She picked up the diary and flipped it over in her hands. The fabric was faded, but still cheerful, with white, red, and pink flowers overlapping one another on a periwinkle-blue background. Jane felt a little more apprehensive than she had expected: Gran had always presented such an intimidating, closed-off façade that Jane was almost afraid to find out what had been underneath. Even now that she knew what Gran had been hiding, and what she had been hiding Jane from, it was still hard to shake the feeling that she might regret invading her guardian's privacy. She took a deep breath and opened the front cover.

An empty white page stared back at her.

She flipped slowly through the blank pages, deflated. She felt sure, just as she opened each, that there was writing on it, but there wasn't. She closed her eyes, feeling a little foolish for getting her hopes up. But once she wasn't looking at it, the book seemed to thrum and almost tremble in her hands. *Something is here,* she insisted to herself.

She wondered wildly what would happen if she tried the same location spell with this book that she had performed on Anne's glass unicorn and then with her stuffed rabbit. Would she see through the eyes of Gran's body, buried in the little cemetery of Saint-Croix, or would she see something different, something about what had become of her grandmother's soul? She felt a chill at the thought, but she felt her magic begin to form a circuit, passing faster and faster between her heart and the book.

I don't want to see the present, though, she thought almost pleadingly. *I just want to understand the past a little better.*

It came to her in a flash: she had done exactly that once, without even meaning to. The force of her magic had shattered Anne's unicorn into countless shards, but before it had exploded, she had seen the girl the object had once belonged to. Without giving herself time to think, Jane gripped the diary, making sure to press Gran's silver ring against it as hard as she could. Then she poured herself into the diary, shoving her mind into the grain of the paper, flattening herself into its lengthwise plane.

Images rushed past too fast for her to see them, although she craned to look. But she was being pulled deeper, somewhere more still, and when she finally landed on what felt like solid ground, there was only one other image in front of her. "Gran," she whispered, nearly choking on the word. Celine Boyle nodded back at her.

Jane risked a glance downward, but whatever was beneath her feet was invisible. There was nothing but darkness on all sides of her, except that Gran stood in the same darkness, looking back at Jane expectantly.

"I'm not real," Gran cautioned her when Jane started forward, holding up a warning hand. Jane stopped obediently; she could tell now that there was something insubstantial about her grandmother, and also somehow ageless. She didn't look real.

"But you're here," Jane told her stubbornly, and then felt exasperated with herself; even in the magical non-presence of her deceased grandmother her instinct was to act like a child.

"I'm a memory," Gran replied simply. "I'm Celine Boyle's diary. You are Jane Boyle, and you have the power to read this, but I have no recollection of you gaining the knowledge."

Jane thought about that for a moment. She had no idea when Gran had made this remarkable spell, but Gran had died before Jane had learned about magic. So, of course, the version of her in the book wouldn't expect to encounter Jane, although she didn't seem especially upset about it. Jane's initial impulse to throw her arms around Gran had faded down to nothing almost immediately; whatever was standing in front of her, it wasn't the difficult, overprotective woman she had loved. *But she could show her to me,* Jane realized, *or . . .*

"Can you tell me about my mother's death?" she asked plaintively, and Celine Boyle nodded curtly.

With a sickening spin, Jane felt herself disappear into one of the strains of memory around her, which immediately became sharper, slower, more visible. "I wasn't there, of course," Gran's voice came from somewhere around her, although the image of her hadn't joined Jane wherever she was now. A younger Gran was picking up a phone, and Jane realized that they were in the kitchen of their old farmhouse in Alsace. Gran listened to the voice on the other end of the line, which was nothing but a faint buzz to Jane, and then her face began to crumble. Her grief was so raw that Jane couldn't help herself: she looked away, and the walls began to shift around her.

"I was told it was a car accident," the voice of Gran from the diary went on clinically, and a shifting collage of images showed Celine on a plane, talking to police, talking to neighbors, staring through an empty window, clutching ten-month-old Jane to her chest. "But I didn't believe it."

Jane frowned; she had wondered once if her mother's magical heritage might not have played a part in the flash flood that had swept her parents off the road one night. After all, Anne had accidentally killed her entire foster family because she didn't understand her magic and couldn't control it; might not Angeline Boyle have done something similar? It was the question she had wanted to ask in the first place, but hadn't quite been able to say out loud. She held her breath, simultaneously hoping Gran would go on—and that she wouldn't.

"I suspected a witch named Lynne Doran," Gran continued, and Jane's breath flew out of her.

"Lynne?"

"So I stayed in America to investigate."

Jane shook her head. "You brought me back to France the next day," she told the disembodied voice, but the images around her were telling a different story. Gran had stayed, and if the changes in little Jane were any indication, she had stayed for quite some time. "I don't remember this," Jane whispered. She knew she must have been too young to register where she was at first, but as her younger self passed three and headed toward four, she felt completely disoriented. At some point, they had obviously traveled to France; how could she have no memory of an international flight by then?

Meanwhile, the younger Gran was stalking a younger Lynne Doran, first in Manhattan, then in the Hamptons, then back again. Jane had the bizarre experience of watching Annette grow from a toddler to a young child, while Malcolm slid inevitably into his still-gorgeous version of an awkward preteen. Gran had allies in her hunt, Jane realized: a good-looking, dark-haired couple who were probably just over forty at the time. Something about the woman's eyes made Jane certain that she was a witch, and she watched Celine as avidly as they both watched Lynne. Sometimes Gran brought Jane along as she followed the Dorans, although more often she left her with a string of interchangeable-looking babysitters. Sometimes she would sit in their minuscule studio apartment, reading obsessively and making notes in the margins of old books that Jane couldn't quite see.

Finally, during one of those evenings at home, Gran's face turned ashen as she looked up from a page. "I didn't find the information I was looking for," her voice told Jane almost sadly. "I found something worse."

The images began to speed up again, and Jane was glad she had Gran's voice to make some sense of them. Gran had begun investigating the Dorans at the real beginning: she had researched Hasina. Jane didn't understand what Lynne's ancestress could possibly have to do with her own parents' deaths, but her guide to the diary seemed intent on showing Jane everything her grandmother had learned, so Jane paid attention.

Hasina had been one of the seven daughters of Ambika, the very first witch, who had split her magic among her daughters after her death. All seven had gained notoriety among their suspicious contemporaries, who had often tacked their reputations onto their names. Hasina, as Jane remembered from her own reading, had been called "the Undying." Jane had wondered why . . . but Gran had found out. As Hasina had felt her body begin to fail, she had dug deeper into dark magic than any of her six sisters ever had, and had found a way to live on well past her body's natural time: she had taken her daughter's.

"Wait," Jane whispered, but there was no stopping the narrated flood of images now. Hasina possessed generation after generation of her descendants, leaving each body when one of her daughters was grown and strong enough to hold her. It had taken her years to learn the spell, which took a full month to cast, but once it was done, the soul couldn't be shaken loose from its new home by anything but the next repetition of the spell.

Of course, that meant that Hasina could never be without a prospective host—or hostess, rather. A daughter was ideal, but not always possible. In a pinch, she eventually learned, a niece would do: as long as the new body was a witch's, and as long as there was a blood link between her and the last host, Hasina could make the switch. The witch she left, Jane noticed, tended not to live long afterward, and her horror at Hasina's atrocious betrayal of her own family—over and over—was tinged with profound sadness for them.

In the diary's memory, Gran followed the ancient witch's trail from book to book, from portrait to photo, and then, finally, inescapably, to Lynne Doran. Jane saw Lynne, protected from the summer sun by a long-sleeved shirt and floppy straw hat, sitting on a beach. In spite of her large sunglasses, she shaded her eyes with one hand, watching a small group of children run toward, then away from, the waves. Celine watched her from behind some tall dunes, her hands and jaw clenched. "It was her," the diary's voice hissed. "I'm sure of it."

"Lynne," Jane whispered.

"Not anymore," the diary replied clinically.

The images spun again, and Celine argued with the dark-haired couple on a deserted stretch of windswept beach. Something lay on the sand between them, and Jane recoiled when she recognized unconscious six-year-old Annette Doran. A nasty-looking bruise was already beginning to form on her right temple. "We can stop the chain," the woman was telling Celine in an urgent voice. "She'll never be able to have another one, not at her age."

"I won't kill a child," Gran insisted in the steely voice Jane remembered so well.

The man looked downright murderous at that, but the woman placed a cautioning hand on his chest and he remained still. "Then we share the work," she declared, and Celine nodded.

The scenes spun and shifted again, but this time Jane could follow them on her own. Gran lit candles around a hastily taken Polaroid of Annette, whispering and working magic, and then she turned to the frightened-looking girl herself with regret in her eyes. She led a blank-looking Annette and a happy, sturdy four-year-old Jane through Heathrow.

"She and my André are close enough in age to be playmates," the dark-haired woman's voice said from somewhere, "and Katrin is old enough now to take some responsibility for the family's needs."

Jane could recognize Katrin easily enough in the wary-looking, sharp-faced girl of about sixteen, who greeted Celine and her two charges at what Jane knew had to be the London orphanage where Anne had first remembered living. "Mama said to remind you to top up both spells," the girl told Celine flatly. "Memory and protection. They'll have to last, or I'm to kill her."

Celine just nodded, and Jane felt a prickle of fear. *She would let them kill Annette?* But she wouldn't, of course, Jane realized a split second later. In order to keep that from happening, Gran would have used the same protection spell on Annette that she had later used on her own flesh and blood. It had kept Jane safe in Paris for six years. It was as close to unbreakable as a spell could be: it lasted for the rest of the life of the witch who cast it. That one loophole in the spell was how Lynne had managed to find Jane: by killing Gran.

But Lynne never knew there were two little girls under that protection, Jane thought wonderingly. *And then I got lucky.* Lynne might have searched high and low for her daughter, using all the magical and non-magical means at her disposal. But there was nothing for her to find as long as Celine Boyle was alive, powering her fierce protection spells. Then, finally, Malcolm was sent to kill Gran, because Lynne needed an heiress. The irony struck Jane like a blow to the chest: Lynne could have found Annette just like Jane did, but she only could have done it *after* her plot to replace her daughter was under way. And why would Lynne have bothered to try, twenty-two years later? She would have been sure she had exhausted all her options. And then Jane had waltzed in with uncanny timing and found exactly what Lynne had stopped looking for.

"I found her," Jane told the implacable image of her grandmother frantically. "After you died, I found Annette."

The diary's Gran clicked her tongue against the roof of her mouth. "That's all right," she said briskly. "I only meant to keep her from Hasina."

Jane fell backward out of the diary then and lay on the floor gasping for breath. Lynne had searched for Annette . . . but Hasina had been looking for a body. *Blood-related, and a witch. My daughter with one of her sons . . . or her own daughter, back from the dead.* She rolled to her side, her stomach heaving as if she might vomit. The diary lay on the floor, innocent and motionless. *That's why Lynne wanted her back so badly,* Jane moaned silently. *That's why she was willing to trade anything for her.*

The image of Lynne's serene face in the clearing filled Jane's mind. She watched her onetime enemy pour her magic into the silver dagger, tossing it away like a worthless trinket. What was some magic, compared with eternal life? Besides, Hasina's next body had more than enough magic of its own—enough to kill already, without even meaning to. Jane tried to sit up, but her muscles couldn't seem to hear her.

I have to, she pleaded with her unresponding body. *It's not over.*

Jane had to get to Anne while there was still time to warn her.

Chapter Thirty-Six

JANE DIDN'T BOTHER TO GREET GUNTHER, WHO SEEMED, AS always, to be napping, as she stalked into the Dorans' mahogany-paneled elevator. She had finally accepted that the best plan was to wait until Anne's welcome-home party to try to get the girl alone, but now that the big night was here, she didn't want to waste a minute. She stabbed the code at the bottom of her invitation into the elevator's keypad, and the doors closed, followed by the gold gate behind them. The number-eight button lit up automatically, and the elevator began to move. Jane spun the beading on her evening bag anxiously, willing the floors to go by faster.

She had been unconscious at the time, but as far as she could tell, she had turned from Jane into Ella almost exactly twenty-eight days before . . . minus just a couple of hours. *Hope this thing doesn't go all night,* she thought wryly as the elevator finally arrived. There was no doubt in her mind that the shape of her eyes had changed, and her electric-blue pumps felt looser on her feet than she remembered from when she had first tried them on. If she didn't get in and out of the mansion quickly, she could be facing a serious Cinderella-at-the-ball situation.

She stepped out of the elevator and scanned the crowded atrium. Anne was nowhere to be seen. *A grand entrance. Obviously.* Thousands of candles were suspended from the ceiling, and Lynne had filled the open space with twisting vines and delicately branched trees full of tiny lights. The entire place looked like the enchanted wood from some fairy tale . . . after the fairies had already gone to work, of course. And with a stellar-slash-sickening view of the city, Jane remembered belatedly when she stepped around a stand of birch trees and found herself directly in front of the wraparound floor-to-ceiling windows. She gulped down the lump in her throat and grabbed a glass of champagne off the tray of a passing waiter before making her way back to the safer center of the massive room.

A pair of dancing green eyes caught hers from across the room, and she nearly choked on her drink. *Harris. Everyone in New York really is here,* Jane thought, her body pulling toward Harris like a strong magnet. She felt a moment of giddy happiness at the sight of his coppery hair and wide, easy smile, and it only deepened when she realized that he was alone. Then the happiness turned to guilt as she realized why Dee hadn't come: although this was certainly a plus-one type of occasion, Dee would never have taken the risk of putting herself in a room full of mind-readers. She insisted that her mental defenses had come a long way in the last couple of months, but considering all that she knew, and considering how powerful Lynne and the twins were, coming to the party would have been suicide. *And gotten me killed, too, so thanks for sitting this one out.* Jane, fully abashed, tried to project the thought downtown, toward their apartment, even though she knew Dee wouldn't be able to read it.

Jane started toward Harris eagerly, but bumped almost immediately into something tall, dark, and extremely well-built. "How lovely to see you again, dear Ella," André smiled coldly, taking her arm in what was definitely not a casual manner. His black eyes burned into hers, and she could tell he was absolutely furious.

"How was France?" she asked as brightly as she could, shaking her arm violently out of his grip.

"You did this," he hissed, leaning in so that no one else could overhear them.

"Can you believe it?" she asked, keeping a desperate smile on her face and stepping back. "I just ran into her and recognized her. I'm surprised to see you here, though," she added pointedly. She bared her teeth in an approximation of a smile. *Tell me how the hell you could risk coming here now,* she thought violently at him. He couldn't read her mind, but she felt sure he would be able to read her face. Out of the corner of her eye, she saw Katrin, half-hidden behind one of the little trees, glaring in her direction. One of the twins was with her, and she didn't look much happier. From the other side of the room, Harris was watching the two witches, even moving a bit closer to them. Jane wished fervently that he would look her way again; she could use an ally.

"I don't know what you mean," André's Romanian accent snarled at her. "I'm here to support my dear Anne at this momentous occasion. She has always been like a sister to me, you know," he finished urbanely, and Jane began to understand that she was about to get the same story he had fed to Lynne. She knew better—and she was willing to bet that Lynne did, too—but apparently it suited both of them to pretend that André hadn't been actively hiding Anne from anyone.

"She did mention that she had some friends from the orphanage," Jane offered tentatively, and André smiled like a predator hypnotizing its prey.

"My family has always been involved in charity projects, volunteerism, and so on," he confirmed. "Katrin, there"—he waved to his sister, who practically snarled at Jane in response—"was working at the orphanage when Anne came in. If we had had any idea who she was then, of course, we could have ended this story happily decades ago."

"Amazing that you never heard about Annette," Jane murmured, and André's eyes blazed again.

"Once we did, of course, we came here to investigate her birth family. We disguised it as merger talks so as not to arouse suspicion, but we couldn't in good conscience let our dear little sister go back to just any kind of people. We felt quite protective. I'm sure you can imagine."

Jane glanced around for Harris again, but his attention was still riveted on Katrin. *Over here, damn it,* she thought as loudly as she could without actually speaking, but of course he didn't turn her way. "What a lovely thing for you to have done," she told André blandly. *Yeah, no. No way in hell Lynne bought that, either.* But, for whatever evil reason of her own, she had apparently pretended to, and now Jane was stuck with two people who wanted her dead at the same party where she was about to try to pull off her most daring rescue yet.

She turned away from André abruptly, weaving her way quickly through trees and people until she had almost made a full circuit of the hollow square of the atrium. Taking up a position behind a cluster of Valentino-clad PR reps, she spotted André's back near where she had left him. His head turned back and forth, searching the crowd, and Jane sidled closer to the chattering group she was using as cover in case it occurred to him to turn all the way around.

But now that he wasn't actively trying to use or control her, André was far from her biggest problem.

Getting Anne out from under her mother's nose will be a hundred times harder than getting Malcolm out of the basement, she thought nervously, and then felt a sudden pang of regret for having to leave Charles behind. Maybe somehow she would be able to come back and go three for three with saving Doran siblings, but right now it was hard to imagine. *Plus, where could I take him?* She was fairly sure he would agree to go with her ... but then she'd be stuck with him.

Harris's close-cropped coppery curls flashed in the glow of the candles, and she realized that he was much closer than he had been. He made his way closer, parting the crowd politely and quickly. Jane turned toward him hungrily, and their eyes met. She started forward, her lips parting expectantly, but although she saw recognition in his eyes, that was all that they registered. Following the briefest of hesitations, he looked away and continued on, and Jane realized that he had just been going to the elevator. *Leaving already?* she wondered sadly. *Before the grand entrance?* She was fairly sure Harris didn't smoke, and she couldn't think of another explanation. She twisted her beaded evening bag between her hands, feeling unaccountably abandoned.

She almost decided to follow him, but just then the lights flickered and everyone turned toward the double doors that led to the building's main staircase. *I'm here for Anne,* she reminded herself. Everything else could wait. A whisper ran through the well-dressed crowd, an anticipation that Jane could almost touch. The doors remained closed for a few long moments, seeming to vibrate slightly under the focus of the assembled guests. The murmuring subsided, and a perfect stillness came over the room. When Jane felt that the entire eighth floor might explode under the tension, the double doors swung open as if by magic, and Anne stepped tentatively into the room. Her wavy hair was tied up into soft twists, some falling artfully down and others held in place by star-shaped white flowers. Her dress was white, too: a Grecian-looking thing that draped over a cord at the waist, fell to the floor, and made Anne's golden skin glow as if it had been polished.

A gasp flew around the room, and the almost painful stillness ended abruptly in a wild crash of applause from every corner. Anne smiled tentatively, turning back briefly to look at Lynne, who had remained discreetly in the shadows behind her daughter. Then she turned to the room and smiled again, and the applause became deafening.

Although Anne seemed to want to hug the interior walls of the room, it still took Jane nearly an hour to get anywhere near her. André was apparently still looking for Ella in the wrong part of the room, but Belinda Helding proved harder to shake. Her angry pewter stare followed Jane from spot to spot, until Jane lost her by ducking behind an ivy-and-light-covered trellis. She peeked out to try to find a clear path to Anne, and found herself looking directly into the taut, olive-skinned face of Katrin. Jane backed into the trellis, attracting a dark, piercing stare from Lynne, all the way across the room. Katrin spun fearfully toward Lynne, and

Jane took advantage of the distraction to scurry toward the bathrooms as inconspicuously as she could.

The Dalcaşcus don't want Hasina to move into Anne any more than I do, Jane thought angrily, glaring at the mirror. She splashed some water on her face and halfheartedly checked her disguise, out of habit. *We could—we should—be working together.* But caution born of experience argued otherwise: she hadn't ever been entirely correct about the Romanians' agenda up until now, and it would be insane to imagine that she really understood how they would react to her information.

She stepped out of the bathroom and back into the softer light of the party, and resumed the infuriating task of counting witches.

At long last, she found herself standing beside Anne, not too far from the back stairs and with a little breathing room around them. "Anne," she whispered, and the girl's dark-gold head snapped toward her. Anne's dark eyes were unfathomable, and Jane had no idea at all how she felt about her new family or fabulous party. *Just as well she doesn't look thrilled to be here*, she decided, since "here" wasn't at all a safe place for Anne to be. "I need to talk to you—please come."

Anne's face remained impassive, so Jane beckoned encouragingly as she backed toward the door of the small service staircase. After a moment, to her immense relief, Anne followed her. Jane tripped quickly down one flight and then entered the seventh-floor hallway. The door of the billiard room was just a few yards away, and Jane ducked into it, closing the door behind Anne after she followed suit.

Halfway out of breath, Jane was so relieved to have gotten this far that she impulsively stepped forward to hug Anne. "I'm so glad I got to you," she whispered. Anne's body resisted the hug, and Jane stepped back awkwardly. Anne's face was completely immobile, and Jane reached for her hands instead. "Look, I know this is going to sound—"

"You bitch," Anne snarled, and then something hard struck the back of Jane's head. Her vision swam and she fell down and away from Anne, who advanced menacingly on her. "My mother told me everything."

I doubt it, Jane thought, but as she opened her mouth to speak, a pool cue lanced through the air toward her head. She rolled away and it struck her shoulder instead, tearing the seam of her dress and, she was sure, leaving a bruise that would show up the next day. *If I make it to then,* she thought desperately, magically deflecting a pool-ball-turned-missile that came dangerously close to breaking her ribs.

"It wasn't bad enough that your family kidnapped me; you decided you had to cash in, too?" Anne snarled, her entire face distorted with her fury.

"It's not like that," Jane gasped, dodging a lamp and backing away again. The image of Celine Boyle and her Romanian allies standing over Annette's limp body flashed briefly in her mind's eye. *Okay, it's kind of like that, but. . .*

"Shut up," Anne all but screamed. "Your grandmother ruined my life, and then you used me again to hurt my mother even more!" She turned toward one of the heavy marble busts that lined the billiard room's walls, trying to lift it with her hands before sending it flying with magic. Jane ducked, but the bust flew wide of her by several feet.

"We can talk about this," Jane pleaded, holding up her empty hands. Anne narrowed her eyes, and Jane felt a searing pain on her palms. Blood trickled down her forearms, and she stared at Anne in horror. A potted plant flew at her while she hesitated, the rim of the pot catching her directly on the temple.

"You've talked enough," Anne's voice snarled from somewhere, and Jane flinched back.

She was dazed from the blows to her head, but she felt almost sure that she smelled smoke. She shook her head violently, sending an explosion of stars across her vision. "Please," she choked, "Lynne's not—"

"She's the only one I can trust," Anne cut her off, magically overturning an entire billiard table.

Jane moved back again, but not quickly enough, and it caught her just above the ankle. She heard a dull snap, and blinding pain shot up her leg as she fell. *She's going to kill me,* she realized dully. There was a piercing ringing in her ears that made it hard to think at all. *Lynne set me up, and Anne's going to finish me off.*

The girl moved toward her again, a blur of white and gold that Jane couldn't hope to ward off. Jane watched Anne raise her arms. She could actually see the deadly magic gathered in them. Even without the massive table lying across her leg, there was no way Jane could escape it. She closed her eyes and tried to steel herself for the blow.

A crash came from somewhere across the room, and Anne's advance stopped abruptly. The girl spun away from Jane, her killing energy fracturing in every direction. The smell of smoke was much stronger, and Jane struggled up onto one elbow and tried to force her eyes to focus. But there was no sense in what she saw: a tall, dark-haired man framed by a strange red light flooding in from the hallway.

André Dalcașcu had just saved Jane's life.

Chapter Thirty-Seven

"HELP ME," JANE WHISPERED, BUT THE AIR WAS THICK AND ACRID and she wasn't sure she could be heard at all.

With a furious scream, Anne launched herself at André, clawing at his face with her fingernails. Her uncontrolled magic raged around the room, seeming to pick up momentum as it went. Pictures flew off the walls, and the green felt of the billiard table in the corner caught fire.

Jane tried to protect her head with her arms, but the storm was only getting more violent. Somewhere near the door, she heard a sickening thud, and André howled in pain. *He didn't expect her to attack him,* Jane thought, looking up in time to see Anne land a kick that doubled him over. "Run, Ella," he gasped.

Their eyes met for a moment, and she became sure it was true: he had followed them from the party, overheard the altercation, and had come to try to save her. Knowing as she now did how unlikely he was to ever actually care about anyone outside his own family, she felt deeply moved.

"I'm trapped," she tried to call to him. Her voice sounded a little louder this time, but only barely.

Something stung the skin of her free leg, and she tore her eyes away from André. The hem of her dress had turned black in places, and glowing sparks worked their way up the silk that covered her leg. She was trapped *and* on fire. She looked up again just in time to see Anne sink her teeth into André's forearm.

The hell with this. Jane drew herself up as straight as she could, locked her eyes on one of the marble busts along the walls, and magically launched it at Anne's back. It was too heavy to throw hard, but it hit her almost squarely in the neck, and the girl crumpled to the floor.

She turned her power to the overturned table that was pinning her down. With a mental heave, she was able to drag her leg free, although when she tried to stand, she realized that it was too painful to put her weight on it. André crossed the room in two long bounds, and she leaned gratefully on his shoulder as they made an awkward, three-legged progress to the stairs. She didn't look down as they passed Anne's limp form; she was afraid to be tempted to wish her dead.

As they climbed down as quickly as her already-swelling leg would allow, she realized that the shrill ringing she heard wasn't just in her ears: it was everywhere. "Smoke alarms," she told André tersely, and he nodded.

"The elevator won't work," he replied, and she was relieved that he seemed to understand her train of thought. "Most of them will take the front stairs, but we still have to hurry."

"Trying," Jane grunted, and his arm tightened around her. "'S okay. I escape from this place all the time."

One agonizing step at a time, they made it to the sixth floor, the fourth, the first. Gunther had deserted his post by the time they passed it, but, as far as they could tell, they were the first ones through the heavy stone arch that led to the street.

Park Avenue was eerily empty, but she knew there was no way the stillness could last. Sirens were approaching fast from uptown, and somewhere in the not-too-far distance, a church bell was chiming over and over. *Midnight,* she thought; it had to be, but it felt too early. *Time flies when you're in mortal peril.* André had gotten her as far as the median of Park Avenue, but even though she could faintly hear a babble of voices approaching the lobby of number 665 below the wail of the first fire truck that had come into view, she needed to stop.

"Just for a minute," she pleaded. Her leg was throbbing dangerously, and she felt as though she could barely breathe.

"Ella," André began, bending down to bring his face close to hers . . . and then he stopped. She stared at him in confusion, and he stared back at her in what she slowly began to recognize as horror.

"Midnight," she whispered, and he let her go and stepped back so quickly that she nearly lost her balance.

"You," he growled, and the air around them took on the thick charge of danger.

Jane held up her hands between them, and even in the flat light of the street lamps she could tell they were her own. The breeze lifted her hair, and a long, blond lock of it swayed back and forth tauntingly in front of them. She looked up at him; farther up than she had ever had to the entire time she had known him.

"It was you all along." The moment of something like tenderness between them was over, she knew: over and never coming back.

She felt frozen, rooted to the spot as he raised his hand to strike her, but for the second time that night she braced herself for a blow that never came. Instead, André turned to face a new threat that Jane hadn't even seen coming: a bright red Dodge Challenger with a racing stripe down the hood screeched to a halt just inches from them.

"Get in," Dee called to her, shoving the passenger door open from the backseat. Harris grinned at her from the driver's seat. André grabbed for her, but his hands found only empty air as Jane tumbled herself through the door and slammed it shut behind her.

Jane could feel the purr of the engine through her seat as the car accelerated. Harris piloted it expertly around a fire engine that was pulling to a stop in front of the Dorans' mansion. Jane flinched and nearly covered her eyes as they rocketed straight for two more, but Harris didn't hesitate. He took them through a space between the trucks so narrow that Jane could feel the pressure change in her ears. A crowd had gathered on the sidewalk, and she could see flames beginning to lick out of the windows of the seventh floor. Harris downshifted, and the engine growled, and the entire scene disappeared from view almost as soon as Jane had registered it.

"You're not even going to say hi?" a chirpy voice quipped from the backseat, and Jane whipped around.

"Mae?" There was no doubt; the elfin features, penny-colored eyes, and wild red curls belonged to Maeve Montague, Jane's very first friend in New York. *The friend Lynne nearly killed because of me,* she thought guiltily, but it was impossible to regret Maeve's presence no matter how much danger they might be in now.

"Back from physical therapy and better than ever," Maeve smiled, and Jane, too far away to hug her the way she wished she could, reached back and squeezed the girl's tiny hand instead.

"How did you guys know?" she asked finally, when they had crossed over to FDR Drive and were safely off the city streets.

"Our grandmother and aunt had been saying all kinds of dire things," Harris answered, his green eyes constantly flickering back and forth between the road and his mirrors. "Doom, gloom, all-out war. My cousins and I have all been trying to keep an ear to the ground, but they couldn't even tell us what we were listening for. So I went to the party tonight, and guess who I saw there?"

Jane blushed, and then blushed harder when she realized that she was back in her own pale skin that showed every change of shade. At least it was dark in the car, she decided. "I'm so sorry I didn't tell you—and please don't blame Dee. She wanted to, but I wouldn't let her."

"What the hell is she talking about?" Maeve piped up from the backseat.

"He didn't mean you, Jane." Dee chuckled hoarsely.

"No," Harris explained, frowning a little. "I saw Dee's boss."

Jane spun her torso around in her seat as far as it would go. "Come again?"

"Kate," Dee confirmed, and from her tone of voice Jane suspected that she was blushing now.

Freaking Kate again. "She was doing the catering?" Jane turned back to Harris, waiting for some kind of further explanation. "The canapés didn't suck," she admitted belatedly.

"She wasn't a caterer," Harris said grimly, and Jane finally caught up.

"Katrin. Kathy, Kate . . . Katrin Dalcaşcu." *How many nearly-the-same aliases can one woman have?*

Harris nodded, but it was Dee who spoke next. "Jane, she must have seen us together, before you went undercover. She was working me the whole time."

"She was already stretched pretty thin, protecting her awful brother's mind from being read," Maeve went on, "and she doesn't really have much magic of her own to start with. She's got two daughters, and the rumor is they're total duds. Plus she had to use some to make it seem like she actually knew how to cook. And then Dee had been working on blocking out mind-readers, anyway, so between all of it Katrin had to come at you some other way."

Jane turned around again, deeply impressed. No matter how many other ways Katrin's magic was being used, for Dee to have kept a determined witch out of her head when she hadn't even realized that she needed to was extraordinary. "Seriously?"

"So when I saw this 'Kate' schmoozing with Belinda Helding, I went straight to pick up Dee, and Mae, and get the hell out of the city," Harris continued, his eyes still ever-alert. "Grandma and Aunt Charlotte still couldn't decide what to do, or whose side we were on, or if anything was even really going on, but enough was enough."

"And he was headed upstate when I told him he didn't quite have everybody," Dee finished softly, and a warm feeling spread through Jane's belly.

"You came back for me," Jane whispered, leaning back against the headrest. Even the ache in her leg was beginning to feel just like another kind of heat, and she thought she could almost fall asleep.

"Of course," Maeve confirmed, sounding indignant. Jane smiled; she was sure Maeve would have a few things to say about being kept out of the loop for the last couple of months.

The thought sobered her, and she felt a stab of doubt. How long could their enthusiasm really last in the face of the stark reality ahead of them? "I really appreciate it," she told them sincerely. "But as soon as we're clear of the city, I'm going to need you to—"

"Split up?" Maeve asked sarcastically.

"Go somewhere safe," Dee drawled.

"Leave you to face the danger on your own," Harris finished, rolling his eyes and shifting lanes.

Jane bit her lip. "One witch," she sighed, "and a Wiccan, and two people who know more than most about magic. But one witch. War really is coming, and doom and gloom and everything you've heard. I can't keep you safe on my own, and I will *not*—"

"We're sticking together from now on," Harris interrupted grimly, sparing Jane an emerald glance that cut her to the bone. "End of discussion."

He smiled mysteriously, and Maeve cleared her throat significantly. Jane turned to her, and as she did, she felt a strange pressure building in the car, like the charge before a thunderstorm. Maeve was staring at a space in the air between them, and just when Jane opened her mouth to ask what she was doing, something floated up into that space. The headlights of the cars traveling in the opposite direction caught it over and over like a strobe light; it was a silver tube of Givenchy Tempting Coral.

The lipstick hovered in the air, trembling slightly, and with an effort Jane could feel almost physically, Maeve tore her eyes away from it to lock them with Jane's. She looked exhausted but fierce, like a warrior. The lipstick stayed in place even after Maeve had stopped looking at it. "Want to freshen up?" Maeve asked through a tensed jaw, and the silver tube moved even closer to Jane.

As she reached up and pulled the lipstick out of the air, her battered muscles aching from the effort, Jane ignored the pain and focused on only one thing: the feeling of hope rising in every inch of her.

Gabriella Pierce

GABRIELLA PIERCE is an American living in Paris with her two dogs. This is her second novel.

BOOKS BY GABRIELLA PIERCE

666 PARK AVENUE
A Novel

ISBN 978-0-06-143477-8 (paperback)

The beginning of the richly gothic
contemporary series about the
darkness lurking behind the gilded
halls of New York high society, and
the elite Upper East Side witches
who rule Park Avenue.

"Fast paced and rich in detail, it's
an enticing tale bound to attract
readers—whether piqued by sorcery
or not—and keep them hankering
for more."

—*Romantic Times*

THE DARK GLAMOUR
A 666 Park Avenue Novel

ISBN 978-0-06-143490-7 (paperback)

When Jane Boyle married her prince
charming, she didn't get the fairytale
ending she'd hoped for. After all, it's
hard to live happily ever after when
you discover your mother-in-law is a
witch.

"Both chilling and chic, frightening,
yet fashionable—pure evil has never
been this much fun!"

—Kerrelyn Sparks, *New York Times*
bestselling author